STRANGELY FUNNY VI

MYSTERY AND HORROR, LLC
CLEARWATER, FL

STRANGELY FUNNY IV
COPYRIGHT© 2019 MYSTERY AND HORROR, LLC
CLEARWATER, FL

EDITED BY SARAH E GLENN

All stories in this anthology have been printed with the permission of
the authors.

This is a work of fiction. Any resemblance to any actual person living
or dead, or to any known location is the coincidental invention of the
author's creative mind. This includes historical events and persons who
may have been recreated in a fictional work.

ISBN-13: 978-1-949281-05-7

STRANGELY
FUNNY VI

ACKNOWLEDGEMENTS

There are a number of people without whom this book would not have been possible. First and foremost, we want to thank the loyal readers who love and buy these stories. We could not have kept the series going without your support.

Sarah and I also want to thank all our authors. Some of you are regular contributors to the series. After seven volumes of Strangely Funny, you're old friends whose stories we look forward to seeing each year. Others are making their first appearance in these humorous tales of the paranormal. Welcome to the club. Whether a first-time visitor or a regular contributor, your stories are appreciated.

As always, a special thank you goes out to Kathy Glenn. Her love and support mean the world to us.

TABLE OF CONTENTS

ANGEL IN HELL'S KITCHEN

By Beverly Alice Black

Angelina paced among the clouds, slowly undulating her wings. Gabriel had promised a response by now, though the smirk on his face hadn't boded well. She'd been an angel since time began, and enough was enough. She wanted a promotion.

As she pondered her prospects, she heard a crackling and looked up to find a cherub gliding toward her. His double wings hid his face, but there was no mistaking the flaming sword he swung and his incandescent blue glow.

"Praise the Lord," the cherub said as he passed. "Your request will be denied. Praise the Lord."

Angelina bit her bottom lip, then turned to find Gabriel floating toward her. He basked in a whiteness that was completely unnecessary and a bit showy to boot. Angelina narrowed her eyes against the glare.

"The cherub already told me. They're never wrong."

"He doesn't feel you merit a promotion."

"But I've accepted every assignment. I have a ninety-nine percent convincement rate."

"I wouldn't brag about that. Angels are supposed to be perfect."

Drifting in from the sidelines came two burly blond angels who came to a halt, one on each side of Gabriel. Angelina peered up at them but carried on. "You can't convince a drunk he's seen an angel. At least, not once he sobers up. Half the time they forget they even met me."

"In addition," Gabriel said, "our records indicate you had

110,482 incidents involving instantaneous insanity inducement."

"It's not my fault I get the crazy ones. That's what happens when you make me tell a pregnant Luisa that she needs to find a new man because her beloved Manolo is banging her best friend, Leti."

"Language, Angelina! Language."

"My point is, you got Mary. I got Brandi from Fayetteville. C'mon! I've waited forever."

"Angelina, you know He thinks pride is the greatest sin."

"I'm not prideful! I'm bored. I want something interesting to do for a change."

"He's casting you out."

"Whoa! Hold it. I just wanted a little promotion."

"It's a temporary assignment."

Gabriel nodded to the bouncers, and Angelina felt herself lifted by her arms.

"But I'm not warring against God. What are you doing?"

The angels whisked her through the clouds so fast she saw nothing but a blur of white and blue. Suddenly she was falling, tumbling, somersaulting down, down, down.

Angelina awoke on a massive rock, its surface scratchy but dry and warm. She jumped to her feet at the sight of a grayish angel with droopy wings and sad eyes.

"Girl, I told you to leave well enough alone."

"Oh, Apollyon! Please tell me this is some kind of a joke."

The angel jangled his keys and leaned over to open the door to the abyss.

"Michael gave strict instructions that you be assigned to the kitchen."

"Hell's kitchen?

"'Fraid so."

"With Chef Damnsay?

"That's the one."

"But I've heard horror stories about him. I heard he once ordered a devil to cut off his own tail, chop it up and make shish kebobs. That's just not right."

"Look, Angelina. They need help down there. You'll see."

"But I can't cook! And Chef Damnsay ..."

"His bark is worse than his bite. If you do well, you'll probably get an early release."

Angelina fell into a very dark, very hot tunnel which grew hotter the farther she fell. The tunnel dead-ended at the entrance of the kitchen. The deafening roar of males laughing and swearing combined with pots dropping and pans banging scared Angelina. She shook in her slippers, but eventually stepped forward and peered into the cavern's entrance.

Ten red demons ran around on their cloven hooves, screaming and chasing each other. Two remained at their stations stirring and stewing, while one with a tuft of grisly gray hair growing from his chin threw pizza dough in the air over and over until it reached double its proper size. He then tossed it right on top of the demon at the next station—the littlest demon in the room—covering him from horn to hoof with white dough. Immediately, the room erupted into peals of laughter and nasty guffawing, but then, as fast as a man could spit, they saw her, standing in the entrance. Silence fell.

They stared at her, and she at them as her heart pounded. Where before she'd seen a room full of red devils, now she noticed each was distinct. Some had long horns and others had stubs. Some had beards and others had none. Their cooks' coats were covered in blood stains, chocolate, and chicken grease, but most unnerving was that every demon had a long tail with a point at the end and each of these tails swished slowly back and forth like rickety fans. Angelina felt like her feet had turned to wax and melted right there, sealing her to the floor.

"What in bloody hell is going on over here?" boomed a voice from the side of the kitchen. A fiery red devil with straight horns twelve inches long and an immaculate white chef's coat rushed in. "Who gave you permission to stop?"

Slowly, Chef Damnsay followed the gaze of the others. His mouth fell open. That's when the heat, the stress, and simple fear overwhelmed Angelina, and she fainted like a deflating souffle.

Angelina awakened on top of a desk in Chef Damnsay's cluttered office and found him stroking her alabaster hands. She pulled back, but his cloven hooves suctioned onto her like a goat grasping a mountainside.

"So perfect," he murmured.

Angelina stared at the chef, her heart pounding. His yellow eyes held strange pupils, large and rectangular. He smiled at her.

3

"I need you. My boys are good at mashing and pounding and a few have learned to slice and chop, but we are encumbered," he said, releasing her hands and brandishing a hoof, "by our anatomy." Grinning wider, he added, "And by our natures."

Angelina swallowed hard. "I don't really know how to cook, Chef."

"Not to worry. Today, I need you to bake. Lucifer has requested pizza. My crew can handle that. But he is also insistent on having a cake and breaking eggs is near impossible. Even I haven't mastered the technique."

Angelina relaxed a bit and offered a smile. "I might be able to whip up something."

"Great! But no Angel Food cake."

"What?"

"We had one of your lot down here four hundred years ago, created this white monstrosity and made the entire legion sick for days. Lucifer likes chocolate."

"I only know how to bake Angel Food."

"Think of something else," he said, nudging her off the top of the desk. "And don't let these idiots talk you into Devil's Food, either. Lucifer specifically told me he doesn't want another slice of that this entire millennium." The chef pushed open the rickety door and knocked over the entire cooking crew who'd been hovering next to it.

"Get back to work! Bloody hell."

A chorus of "Yes, Chef!" echoed off the cavern walls, and the devils hurried to their stations, but all eyes followed the angel.

"You work with Fron," Chef Damnsay said, nodding to a slender demon who was more pink than red. "He is one of our newer cooks." With that, the chef marched past her and out the way Angelina had come in.

Fron bowed. "This is a real honor, Miss Angel. What are we making?"

Angelina thought hard. It had to be something good. The better the cake, the faster she'd get out of here. Or should she make something really awful, so they kicked her out? But maybe the devils would like something awful.

"I once knew a woman from Arkansas who showed me how to make a mean Mud Pie. Do you have coconut?"

"Sure. It grows in warm climes."

4

Angelina peeked at the youngster to see if he was mocking her, but he seemed sincere.

"We'll need cocoa powder, sugar, some marshmallow cream, four eggs."

"Slow down."

A demon with a five-inch beard and a big grin clip-clopped over to her, carrying a canister. "You can use my sugar, Sugar," he said with a wink.

"Hey," yelled a big one from across the room. "Leave her alone. She's not interested in your kind, Furcid." The big one approached, his shoulders squared, chin high.

The sugar devil twisted around, his tail switching.

"And what kind would that be, Hito?"

The two lowered their heads as if to butt horns but, without thinking, Angelina stepped between them. "Stop acting like animals. We have a job to do."

Angelina watched them back down and realized she might have more pull here than she'd ever had in Heaven.

"Furcid, thank you for the sugar, and please go wash those pots and pans in the sink by your station."

The devil slunk away, smacking the closest cook for no reason.

"We all have to work together to fix this kitchen so when Chef comes back he'll be impressed. Hito, please pick up all those boxes and get that back area in order. Fron, grab a broom and sweep the kitchen. And you," she said pointing to the littlest demon still pulling pizza dough from his hair, "go clean up and get back here as soon as you can."

The little demon smiled and hurried out the back.

The crew made quick work of the messy kitchen and each demon seemed proud of its new condition. Angelina found clean coats for the workers, and they looked downright spiffy once they washed up.

Angelina still had to put up with some bickering and an occasional spud tossed at someone's head, but by the time she poured the batter into the cake pans, the place sparkled and so did the demons.

That evening Chef Damnsay pulled her back into his hole of an office. "Lucifer gushed over your dessert. He wants you to be Head Pastry Chef."

"But I don't know how to bake!"

"Not to worry," he said pulling down a very large, very dusty cookbook from his office shelf. "We have hundreds of recipes in here."

Though she protested, Angelina immediately became second in command. Every devil wanted to meet her because her beauty and brains were quickly becoming legend. Applications for cook positions tripled. And Angelina herself relaxed and settled into being a celebrity. The demons gave her her own room, filled with satin and silk and a luxurious king-sized bed. They jumped at her desires, hurrying off to do whatever she wished. But most importantly, Angelina became a top-notch pastry chef. Of course, she had no competition because few could whip egg whites or use the cake decorator, but she'd finally found her calling.

It was just at this time, when she had put the finishing touches on a Black Death pie, that she felt a tug on her sleeve. Looking around, she saw no one, but the pull was undeniable. Suddenly, she was drawn out of the cavern entrance and up the dark tunnel. She tried to call out, but it was as if some invisible hand had covered her mouth. She flew backwards and popped out of the entrance to Hades, zipping past Apollyon who waved weakly. In a flash, she stood in front of Gabriel.

"You weren't supposed to like it."
Angelina shook her groggy head. "That was bloody rude."
"Hey! Watch the language. I told you about that before."

"I finally find something I like to do, something I'm good at, and you ..."
"You're an angel, not a pastry chef. We don't even have kitchens up here."
"I liked it down there."
"I'm sure you did, but your time is up. We need you to go to Tegucigalpa."
"Ugh!"
Just then a cherub passed by, face covered, sword blazing. "Peace be with you. Praise the Lord."
Angelina jumped to attention. She had her solution. "I want his job!" she said, pointing to the back of God's messenger.
"You can't be a cherub."
"I want to be a cherub. Better yet, a seraph! Go ask Him. See what He says."
"I'm not asking Him something like that. You got rejected for

6

archangel. How do you expect to be one of the holiest beings, to sit in the presence of God?"

"Are you afraid to ask Him? Afraid He'll get mad at you?"

"No, I'm not afraid. It's just clearly banishment grounds for you. Oh," he said, wagging a finger at her. "I see what this is all about."

The cherub passed in front of them again. "The angel is corrupted. Praise the Lord."

Every once in a while, you have to take your future into your own hands, and that's what Angelina did that day. In a flash, Angelina shot out and grabbed the flaming sword from the cherub, who uncovered his eyes in shock and stared at her.

"Angelina!" Gabriel cried. "Have you lost your mind?"

"I can too be a cherub. Look!" Angelina covered her eyes with her wings and slunk about waving the sword in front of her. Laughing, she stopped. "See? It's easy!"

"This is an outrage," shouted Gabriel.

"It's blasphemy," cried the cherub.

By now a crowd had gathered, and the two blond bouncers reappeared. Gabriel pointed at Angelina, and the bouncers grabbed the sword from her and dragged her away.

Down she fell, faster this time but with no fear. When she tumbled into the kitchen doorway the devils let out a cheer so loud it was heard three levels up. Fron, Hito and Furcid helped her to her feet and danced a jig with her while Chef Damnsay stayed in the shadows, licking his lips. Angelina's wings were clipped that day, and her world would never be the same, but she didn't mind. After all, she, too was encumbered by her nature.

Beverly Alice Black is an immigration attorney in Philadelphia, Pennsylvania during the day and a fiction writer at night. Her short stories have been published by The Saturday Evening Post, Disturbed Digest, *and* Enchanted Conversation. *Follow her on Facebook at Attybeverlyblack and on Twitter @AuthorBevBlack*

GHOST HEIST

By Kate Franklin

Margaret stormed into the office, leaving my sputtering receptionist in her wake. I had avoided her for two weeks. I knew what she wanted, but I had no solution to the problem.

"Ben, you lied to me about the house I bought last week." She slapped a printed contract my desk.

"Yeah, the ghost." I shuffled papers across my desk, not looking up. "I mean, I can explain about that."

"Let's hear it, then."

I scratched my head as I looked at the listing. "The property was appraised as 'moderately haunted'."

"'Moderately haunted', my ass! That report is wrong," she insisted. "I haven't seen or heard anything the least bit ghostly."

"It says here there have been some reports of sightings over the years, especially in the garden."

"Not good enough. I want my guests to feel the chill." Margaret had planned an upscale B & B on the Golden Oaks property. "I want them to experience moans and rattles and come down to breakfast gushing about a ghost sitting at the foot of the bed when they woke up."

I told her the house was a fixer-upper, but it was a bargain. "Haunted houses are really losing their popularity."

"Exactly," she exclaimed. "With people giving up their ghosts, sometimes even having them exorcised or put to rest, there will be a strong market for haunted vacations." She insisted it was a great business opportunity, and I couldn't disagree.

Ghostcations were growing in popularity. Once the novelty wore off, people realized that keeping a spirit was too much work. You never knew what might wake you in the middle of the night. It was time-consuming to have to search for your car keys every morning. And while the bloodstains and offal smells might be fun for shocking guests, they were nasty to live with.

Margaret dropped a sheet of folded paper on my desk, pushing it toward me like a weapon. It was my own flyer. I knew what it said. "Ghost Guarantee." I hadn't seen that around for a while. I had hoped all of them had been collected and disposed of.

"This is an old flyer," I explained. "I was new in the business, and I thought it would be a good gimmick, something to help sell homes, you know."

She didn't know. "I don't care. It's here in writing. I want you to honor this flyer, or I'll destroy your reputation." The look she gave me said no matter how many successful deals we'd made in the past, she wasn't in the mood to bargain. "You'll never sell another house, haunted or not."

Pointing to the deed again, she snarled, "I want a verifiable haunting in this house."

Then, she turned her laptop to face me. "What do you think the authorities will have to say about *this*?"

I stared at the images on the screen as Margaret glared.

"You have one week." She folded the laptop, removing the CD, clearly marked "copy," and stormed out. As relieved as I was to see her go, I wasn't sure a week would be long enough.

I drove out to see what I might be able to do about Golden Oaks Manor. It looked haunted for sure. A large turn-of-the-century structure, 1899-1900 that is, the house looked desolate. Shutters hung off cracked windows, vines climbed over the exterior, and the wind made a moaning sound through the rooms. But it wasn't ghostly. Even without my electronics, I knew it wasn't haunted. What a waste of a dilapidated old structure. This house had been on my books for years. One of those in-between places—not remodeled enough to sell as is, but too poorly visited to qualify as a first-class haunted house. My client couldn't turn the property into a profitable B & B without a strong ghostly presence.

Haunting became part of the real estate world in the 2040's.

Ghost identifying became provable and profitable just after the turn of the century, 1999-2000, that is. Once the ectograph was invented, ghosts could be confined, and real estate companies jumped on it. Lots of other businesses sprouted up around then, too. There were ghost communicators, ghost genealogists, ghost fashion consultants. Ghost astrologers explained spirit personalities based on the day the person died. There were even ghost matchmakers. It was a crazy market for a while.

Then there were the ones who wanted to "free" the ghosts and send them into the light to Nirvana or Heaven or whatever. Next came the huge debate about whether ghosts should have rights. Finally, the Supreme Court ruled that once a death certificate was issued, a person's civil rights ended. It seemed reasonable to most people that ghosts should not be granted the rights of living people, but some politicians argued for the right of ghosts to vote, claiming it had been standard practice in Chicago throughout the twentieth century.

I examined the inside of the house, room by room. I brought in my portable ectograph, but I didn't need it. I could tell without any electronics that this house had been mislabeled. No wonder it had been sitting on the books for so long. I read the history as I walked. Reports of flashing lights had turned out to be the result of squirrels chewing wires in the attic. Tapping in the walls had been identified as a water leak in the bathroom pipes. It had some great features for a client looking for a home to remodel, but I couldn't feel a nonhuman current. After I had examined each room of the house, I carried the graph to the garden, the one spot where a presence, slight though it was, had been reported.

I sat on the rusty iron bench with the ectograph machine turned on at my feet. There was a barely audible hum, like a radio turned to the lowest level of volume. I looked around. Nothing but a completely natural breeze moved through the trees. "Okay," I said out loud. "If you're here, come on out, I'd like to chat with you."

As I expected, there was no response. I have never been much of a spirit communicator. They don't seem to want to talk to me. I packed up and headed for my office, to make an appointment with someone who *could* talk to ghosts.

Becky had been my ghost expert for years, going back when ghost hunting was a profitable activity for real estate agents and other business owners. Now she was less involved in the retail side of haunting, and more into academia. The sign on her door read "Rebecca Wilson, Director, Paranormal Research and Training."

"I'm really not into haunted houses so much anymore," she explained as I took a seat in the soft leather chair in front of her desk. Back in the day, when we first met, Becky was meeting clients in coffee shops. Ghost hunting had been very, very good to her.

"I know." I nodded. "But this is an important case. It isn't like the ones we used to have."

"You mean it doesn't involve illegally moving ghosts from one place to another?"

She exaggerated. We had worked just a speck outside the law. It is illegal to remove a ghost from one house and place it in another without a permit, and that takes weeks, months sometimes. They have to do research and investigate both locations to make sure the move will be beneficial and not cause harm to the spirits or humans. The experts will tell you how dangerous it is to interfere with a haunting for the ghost, and sometimes, for the living who attempt the move.

It seems that ghosts are pretty specific about who and what they haunt. They have a reason, and a strong one, to remain on Earth. Trying to change that can cause a surge in the ghost's power. Cases have been recorded where an inept ghost move resulted in explosions and implosions shooting haunted houses ten feet into the air, which then rained down on any unfortunate person who happened to be around. Ghosts who are forcibly moved from their favorite haunt become enraged and not too concerned about taking their anger out on innocent parties. But Becky was a real pro. Her persuasive skills on the paranormal level were equal to the proverbial salesman unloading ice to Eskimos. She could make a ghost *want* to move. I knew she could lure a decent haunting to the Golden Oaks Manor.

"I'm so over that," Becky insisted. "I have a whole new career. It's more interesting, safer and completely legal."

"I wouldn't ask you to do anything that isn't legal," I protested, but we both knew I was lying.

"Sure," she countered. "Just like the Mansfield ghost and the haunting at Cedarwood Mansion. C'mon, Ben, I know you."

"You used to know me, but I really did give up the illegal stuff. I haven't moved a ghost for more than five years. Besides," I explained, "selling houses that are already haunted is a booming business right now." This time, I was telling the truth, and Becky seemed to believe me.

"So why the relapse? What's making you so sure you have to move a ghost?"

I told her what my client had revealed that morning. "I know about the Cedarwood haunting. I have proof," Margaret sneered, "that you illegally moved a ghost from one place to another and that two people died."

I hinted to Becky that if I were brought up on charges, her name might come up. "Not that I'd bring you into it," I assured her. "I would never do that to you."

I could see her puzzling out how true that statement was. "Tell me about the property," she finally said.

I opened the laptop and clicked through the maps, the x-rays of the ground, and the ectographs.

"There's hardly anything here."

"I know, that's the problem, but look at this."

I switched videos and Becky jumped back as the screen flashed and crackled. "Summerville Drive," I said. "It looks like a very powerful ghost."

Becky shook her head. "That's some pretty strong energy. I'm not sure I want to work with something that dangerous."

"But, Becky, you did before. The Cedarwood ghost was much more powerful than this. You were the only one who could communicate with it."

"I know, but he almost killed us."

"Almost—Becky. But didn't you learn a lot about ghost communication? Isn't that where you got these skills that are so valuable now?"

I thought maybe I had convinced her. Becky was, after all, a reasonable woman. I could see that she was thinking it over.

"It has to be this ghost?"

"This one looks like the best we can find."

Becky breathed out, hard. "I don't know," she said. "It's really dangerous and illegal. We could both get in a lot of trouble."

"We're already in trouble, Becky." I pointed to the time-stamped video that clearly showed Becky, the ghost and me at Cedarwood Manor. "I really need you to help me. Besides, I can pay you well for this."

"How did your client get this video? There was no police investigation."

"Somehow she wormed it out of the owner of Cedarwood." I

shrugged. "She's probably blackmailing him, too."

She looked at the clock, frowning. "Let me think about it."

I left with an uneasy feeling. I hoped Becky wasn't planning to call the authorities. But she'd get herself in trouble if she did that. I'd just have to wait and hope she would help me.

Back when we did the ghost heist before, the circumstances were very different. It was for a house that *had* a ghost, just not a very active one. It was more than the rumbles of current I detected at the Golden Oaks property. It had been a full powered spirit, but a shy retiring ghost—until we moved another entity into the house. I had never realized how possessive some ghosts can be.

In this case, Ghost A, the one that came with the Cedarwood house, was pretty much a placid haunter. She blew wind through the house and wafted smells throughout, nice flowery smells. The ghost seemed like a sweet old grandmother.

The homeowner wanted a really powerful ghost to haunt his guests, and I think mostly his mother-in-law. He wanted the sounds and gusts and disgusting odors too. We found what he wanted, but the ghost was firmly planted in an abandoned estate that was barely holding together. Neighbors complained of screaming and huge gusts of wind that were sometimes not confined to the property. I offered to help the neighbors out by getting rid of the nuisance ghost. The way Becky and I saw it, we were doing several people a favor, and getting paid for it.

So, Becky started her campaign to lure ghost B out of the comfort of his accustomed surroundings. It was difficult work. We brought the ectocage—a great invention that we weren't supposed to have. E-cages are strictly limited to the law enforcement department that handles dangerous spirits. But as with anything else, if you have the money, you can get it.

Becky had done her homework. The ghost was large and powerful, a perfect haunt for Cedarwood. No one had lived in his house for decades. It was falling down. Probably the supernatural energy was all that was keeping it there. It was the perfect situation. The neighbors wanted the ghost gone and were willing to pay for it, and it was the ideal haunter for our property. What could be better?

Everything started out okay. Becky made contact. The ghost seemed very communicative. I could only hear Becky's side of the conversation.

14

"So, you lost your physical life here in this house?"

"In the garden? What happened?"

"Your own wife? Wow, that's terrible."

"Where is she now?"

"If she sold the house after you passed, why have you been haunting here ever since?"

Becky turned to me. "This is an old ghost, as we would say, but he doesn't have any concept of time."

We agreed that, judging from the condition of the property, this ghost had been drifting around the mansion and the adjoining property for several decades. Becky started her pitch. She told the ghost that he wasn't reaching people here. There hadn't been any people living in the house for a very long time.

"If you want to make a statement, create some noise about your situation, you'll need to move to a place where there are more people."

Becky shook her head and hmmed as she listened to the ghost's reply.

"He doesn't want to move. He still thinks his wife will come back. She murdered him, and he wants revenge. I have to convince him that she will never return here."

I'm not sure whether Becky actually lied to the ghost or if she just made suggestions. I had walked away from the interchange to answer the call of nature. It was, after all, pretty much a wilderness out there. When I returned, Becky had the ectocage open. It was a force field, you could hardly see, but if you put your hand in the way, you'd get a shock for sure. I kept my distance, but Becky steered the spirit into the field, then she pushed a button on a control. The air around the cage crackled and became thicker. I noticed a crisp breeze and an acrid smell.

"Let's go," Becky said. He's in here."

I took her word for that. Becky used the control to move the mass of pulsating energy to the back of the van I had rented for this move. It always amazed me how little space ghosts took up. Not even as much as the person would have when alive.

"It's a concentration of pure energy," Becky had explained. "There is no mass to take up space."

It was an uneventful drive to the property where we planned to relocate the ghost.

I was always nervous when we moved ghosts. Afraid the

15

authorities would stop us and ask for permits, worried that the spirit would escape. Concerned that it just wouldn't work out. Becky was always quick to reassure me. "Everything's fine," she'd insist. "Nothing can go wrong."

It certainly seemed that way. We got to the house and Becky began the process of getting the ghosts together. It was a lot like introducing cats. You didn't want to just throw them together and hope for the best. You had to introduce them slowly and carefully.

Ghost B was quiet in his cage, a good beginning. But we were soon to learn that these two were especially smart and experienced ghosts They were biding their time. The original ghost kind of sniffed around, not too sure what was going on. Becky had told me that Ghost A was so placid because she had lived a good life. She had no spiritual ax to grind. "I can't understand why this ghost is here," Becky said at the time. "This ghost should have moved off into the light long ago. She wasn't part of any violence here. According to what she communicated to me, it was a lovely peaceful life."

I shrugged. I couldn't explain it. I knew from working with Becky that the most powerful ghosts were those who had lost their lives through violence. Murder victims were the ones with the most motivation to haunt. They wanted justice, either through exposing their murderers to face legal action or to seek vengeance themselves. The ghost whisperers and mediums were not too successful at sending these entities on, but the vengeful ghosts were a goldmine for the haunted house business.

Becky unlocked the ectocage and said something I couldn't hear to a ghost I couldn't see. There was a swish of leaves, as something brushed through the trees. "Uh-oh." Becky jerked back from the opened ectocage. "I wasn't expecting that."

"What's up?" Despite Becky's assurances, I knew something was about to go wrong.

"The ghost that lives here is actually much more powerful than we thought. She wants peace and quiet, that's her goal. But if another ghost tries to haunt here, she drives it away."

"It can do that? The ghost can do that?"

"Yes."

I wasn't sure if Becky was answering me or replying to a question I hadn't heard. Then she turned and looked at me.

"Yes, the ghost can do that. She is extremely powerful because she doesn't just drive ghosts away. She absorbs their power."

"Then let's grab our ghost and get out of here." It seemed an obvious solution to me.

"It's not that simple. Our ghost is out of the cage and he's ready for a fight."

Just then a crew of workers arrived to do some work on the house. They piled out of their van as the sparks began to fly.

The wind picked up to gale force. There was crackling, moaning, and some of the worst smells I had ever experienced. The ghosts were at war. We were barely able to stand against the force of the wind. Then it started to hail: big bullets of ice, then baseball-sized hail, and after that, all hell broke loose. Jagged pieces of ice the size of watermelons flew through the air. We ran toward the house, ducking inside, but the two workers didn't make it. They were crushed by the force and size of the hail.

Then it stopped and there was an eerie silence. Becky ran out the door with her ectowand. Somehow, she managed to get our ghost back into the force field. We raced back to where we'd started and let the ghost loose on his home turf.

There was nothing we could do for the dead workers. There was no point in going back. The owner of Cedarwood Manor was far away when the crime happened. We didn't know until we watched Margaret's video that he had left a camera filming the grounds. Fortunately for us, neither did the police. With no witnesses, just a flood of melted ice, the authorities chalked it up to an unexplained weather phenomenon. We were never identified as the perpetrators of the mayhem. But it scared Becky. We'd never worked together after that.

"All right." Becky agreed when I called her the morning after my appeal. "I'll help you this one time, but only because I want to see that it's done right." But she didn't refuse the money I had promised her. I called Margaret and reassured her that she would soon have a strong ghostly presence for her B and B. She insisted on coming to the event. I insisted that she bring the blackmail proof. We had a deal.

It was a dreary morning, with an uncomfortable sense of déjà vu. I hadn't had a close encounter with a strong spirit since the debacle at Cedarwood. It felt much too similar. Becky brushed my concerns aside. "This is a different entity. It's not going to be crazy like before. I know exactly what I'm doing. Besides, the presence that's already at the mansion is tiny. It's not really a full-fledged ghost."

Just like before, it all started out smoothly. Becky got the ghost into the ectocage in record time. She had interviewed him and learned that this spirit was strong but reasonable.

"He's like a big bear," she told me. "Powerful and immense, but not as dangerous as I'd expected." Becky seemed to enjoy getting back into the field. "He doesn't care where he is. He likes haunting and making noise," she explained. "He's like a big kid who doesn't know his own strength."

I wasn't comforted that our spirit was an overgrown boy.

Becky explained what we wanted to do at Golden Oaks. She told the ghost that there was another spirit, in residence, but it was a minor presence, nothing for him to worry about. "I think you'll really like it there." The ghost did what would be a spirit version of a shrug. Becky was ready to go.

Again, it started out calm. The client arrived with a flash drive. She waved it at me. "We'll see what happens first, then you get this material."

I nodded. All was well.

What are you doing?" She challenged Becky. "Why aren't you using the ectowand?"

"There's no need. This is a very cooperative ghost."

"How can you be sure of that? I've seen videos of this procedure, and it requires a strong hand."

Becky glared at the woman. "Well, I've produced most of those videos, and I know what I'm doing. I suggest you get out of my way."

This was definitely not going the way I'd hoped. I tried to smooth things over. I stepped between Becky and Margaret, but suddenly the wind picked up. I was aware of an electrical charge and the smell of ozone. The ghost was there between us.

"So, let's get going," the client demanded. "Let's see what he can do."

"Trust me, ghosts don't want to be rushed." Becky retorted. "You have to let them settle in."

"Look, this is my ghost. I've paid for it, and it will do what I want." She tried to push Becky out of the way.

I could have told her that was never going to work. Becky had dealt with many strong spirits, and this human bully was not going to get to her. I was right. Becky turned on the woman, shoving in return. "Get out of my face, or I'll take the ghost back to where he was."

Margaret grabbed the wand from Becky and waved it wildly, pushing the dial to the maximum strength. "Go ahead, ghost, get mad, screech. I want a powerful ghost that will make people take notice."

"You're going to get us all killed," Becky screamed as the smell of ozone thickened and the wind picked up. The soft moaning deepened into a roar. "Give me that wand."

"Don't get in my way," Margaret shouted at Becky as she swept the garden with the ectowand at full power. "You'll be sorry if you do."

The wind swirled and shrieked around us as the women grappled for control of the instrument. Becky struggled against the wind as she tried to jerk it back, pointing it away from the ghost. As the two pushed and pulled, the energy volume on the wand crackled and popped. The ghost's howls became louder.

There was a sudden gust as the instrument glowed and vibrated. It flew back at Margaret, cutting through her forehead, and lodging itself in her brain. Blood trickled over the dial and the tool shut down. My former client slumped to the ground. She took one last breath, and her eyes blazed as she said, "You'll be sorry. I'll make you regret this." Then she was a lifeless heap.

"Quick," Becky said. "We've got to get out of here."

She lured the ghost back toward the ectocage as I bent over the corpse to retrieve the blackmail material that had fallen from her grasp.

"Her ghost will come out any time now, and it won't be a happy camper. Let's go, Ben."

"She said I'd be sorry. Do you think she means to haunt here at Golden Oaks Mansion?"

"I'm sure of it." Becky nodded. "She died there, and she is really pissed. There's no way this spirit is going into the light anytime soon."

I followed Becky to the van, smiling as I looked over my shoulder at the wreckage left in our wake. "Look at the bright side, Becky. Now, we have a strongly haunted B & B that will sell for a fortune."

Kate Franklin lives in Sarasota, Florida, where she teaches college English and Creative Writing. Kate enjoys reading, writing, gardening and driving her Subaru Cross Trek to the beach in her spare time. She loves to travel. Kate's travel adventures have included Europe, Argentina and Antarctica. Kate's mystery and science fiction short stories have been published on-line and in print anthologies. Her story, "Coin Karma," was a featured podcast from the Liars' League in London.

The Tattooed Mermaid, *her first novel, won a silver medal from the Florida Authors and Publishers Association. She is working on the sequel,* Mermaid Park. *Kate is a member of the writing groups Sisters in Crime and Saturday Sleuths.*

THE CREEPING CRUST

By R.C. Mulhare

A slow weeknight in the Arkham Haunted House of Pizza—yeah, I know, a pizza parlor in Spooksville, Massachusetts. It had a name cashing in on the spooky tourism, but not a lick of supernatural activity to back it up, to the dismay of the tourists who come expecting to see the chairs dancing or pizza crusts floating around the kitchen. My cousin Shay and I were bored out of our minds. I had the phone and delivery, while Shay manned the ovens and made the pizzas. Good thing we had Shay cooking: I would have made up a bunch of basic pizzas and reheated them in the oven, which would bring down our boss', Marty Rosetti's, Italian wrath on our heads.

I pulled my gaze away from the old-school rotary phone on the wall next to the front counter. "Remember how Grandma used to say a watched pot never boils? I guess the same works for phones."

Shay looked up from chopping green and red peppers for tomorrow's salads and subs. "Thought you had readings for class tomorrow?"

I looked to my books under the counter. "Already read them."

"Speed reader," Shay said, impressed, then went back to chopping peppers.

"Slow night in a pizza place in a spooky New England town. Sounds like a set up for a creepypasta."

Shay snerked. "Creepypasta. Someone's going to call for pasta because you said that."

As if on cue and to continue the story, the phone rang. I grabbed the receiver. "Arkham Haunted House of Pizza, can I take your order?"

"Yes, do you make deliveries?" a soft, high-pitched voice asked.

I pulled an order pad toward me across the counter. "Yes, we do, as long as you're ordering from Arkham or one of the surrounding towns."

"Ah, we're in Danvers."

"We can do that. Now what would you like?"

"May we have two pizzas, one with every kind of meat you have, and the other with every kind of vegetable you have?"

With that second pizza, I half expected her to ask for soy cheese, something we'd recently started carrying. "Anything else?"

"Could we have a bottle of Sprite?"

I added that to the order. "Sure thing." The caller gave the address, on the far side of Danvers, nothing I couldn't manage if I pushed the speed limit. "Okay, it'll be twenty minutes for the pizza and it'll likely be another fifteen minutes for delivery. If it takes longer than that, you get half off the order."

"Oh, thank you! And may you have a blessed evening."

I hung up and handed the order slip to Shay. "Have a blessed evening? Who asks that?"

"Probably a modern witch. They're all over the place, that neck of the woods, not just in Arkham." Shay took the slip and, grabbing a pizza pan, quickly laid out a freshly stretched crust.

"Wannablessedbe? Blessed Wannabe?" I asked, as Shay passed me the crust and prepped a second while I ladled sauce out of the pot on the stove next to the prep area.

Twenty minutes later, with the store dome attached to the roof of my mini-wagon, I tucked two insulated carrier bags and another bag with the soda into the shotgun seat. I punched the address into the aftermarket GPS on my dashboard. The map confirmed my earlier concern: the order would take me into the boonies. No time to hesitate. I pulled out and followed the directions to Route 114, taking a right onto one of the lower roads.

True to the horror story, the houses thinned out to a few old farm houses before the directions led me down a private drive leading into the woods, the gnarled trees reaching up to the darkening April sky, the lights in the windows glowing in the shadows.

The calm voice of the GPS led me down another narrow side road, the trees and bushes on either side reaching out toward my car. *You've read too many scary stories on Reddit and listened to too many videos on*

YouTube, I told myself.

The road opened on a compound, one of those rambling affairs found in the countryside, away from the urban areas with their mingling of chain stories and family-run places. No Dunkin' Donuts signs glowing through the trees here. A barn with a weather vane and a row of lightning rods passed on my left, a carriage house passed on the left. Ahead, with a circular drive before it, a three-story Colonial, like two houses pushed together, loomed up. A light shone in the attic, but no other signs of life showed. I'm walking right into a cliché-fest, I thought. Better leave the pizza on the stoop and get the hell back to Arkham.

I scooped up the pizza and the soda and got out. As I approached the front steps, the light over the front door switched on, and the door opened. A short, plump woman in a black, witch-like dress looked out and waved to me. Rain fell from clouds overhead that hadn't moved in when I went out. I ran for the door; the woman stepped aside. "Get inside! You'll catch your death," she cried. I didn't have to be told otherwise. She shut the door against the wind that rose, blowing the rain in after me.

"Yipes!" I said. "I know the weather changes suddenly around here, but this is ridiculous."

"I hope I didn't scare you. I didn't want you getting soaked and catching cold," she said.

"Thanks," I said, surprised. One part of me wondered if I'd judged this place too rashly, while another part warned me to keep my feelers out.

Chanting of some kind rose from the depths of the house, guttural and in a weird key compared to Gregorian chant or the kind I heard at the Arkham Witches' events on the town green.

She rummaged in her pockets. "Oh dear, I left my wallet in the other room. Do you mind waiting while I get it?"

"Not at all," I said, intending to blow the joint on the first chance I got. She beckoned me to follow her down a short hallway. Something had shorted out my self-preservation centers, and I let her lead me into a kitchen. The table top was set with a small buffet. It included an array of snacks and hors d'oeuvres, plus stacks of paper plates and cups with a stylized spring tree design, but there was no place for the pizza.

"Hey, should I put this here on the kitchen table?" I called out, looking to the kitchen counters, cluttered with more than the usual spice containers and several glass jars containing what looked like dried leaves and twigs.

The chanting stopped, the chubby woman came back with her wallet, digging out two twenties, putting them into my hand. I slipped them into the money pouch strapped to my waist. The woman held out a ten. I hesitated. "Oh, don't looked stunned. You earned it, coming out this far in weather like this."

I tucked the bill into my pocket. "Huh. Thanks!"

A rumble of thunder echoed overhead and as if on cue, the rain lashed even harder against the kitchen windows. "Oh dear," the chubby woman said.

"I really should run. They're gonna need me back at the store." I slid the pizzas out of the warming bags, about to hand them to her.

"I hope they'd understand if you stayed to wait out the storm," she said.

Warning bells clanged in my head, but I said, "Well, okay."

A door opened in the wall behind us, and three middle-aged people in black robes with violet embroidered trim emerged. "Any luck opening the portal?" the chubby woman asked them.

"Nope, sorry," a biker-looking guy with heavy silver rings in his ears replied.

A reedy-looking woman eyed the pizza boxes. "I think we need something bigger."

The wind and rain rose outside. The group of cultists looked to the window, now drenched by the storm. "He comes," said the third guy, a hollow-cheeked guy with a shaven head.

"Maybe we should get to the basement before this gets any worse," the chubby woman said.

The reedy woman looked at me. "Is it wise to admit her to our sacred space?"

"Morgon, there's a door between the ritual space and the rest of the cellar, I'm sure Clarisse closed it," the biker guy said.

"But if he should come through ..." the reedy woman said.

My phone pinged. I took it out, finding a weather alert. Biker Guy had his phone out as well.

"Strong Weather Warning: Essex County" The rest detailed a report of strong winds and rain, with "falling trees" and "area flooding". And then "Funnel cloud detected: Danvers."

"Chaos, we'd better get below, the duffer too," Biker Guy said.

"If you insist," the reedy woman said.

24

"Come with us, child, there is nothing to fear," the hollow-cheeked man said, not that it reassured me.

"Dude, you know how many horror movie creepers say some variation of that to their victims?" I said.

"Albert's harmless," the chubby woman said. "That tornado, however, isn't."

"All right." I followed them through the cellar door and down the stairs ...

... and into a very ordinary basement rec room: ping pong table, worn but clean couch, bookshelf of board games, card table, old easy chairs. The scent of incense hovered in the air, wafting from under the faded purple brocade curtains that half-covered an open doorway at the far end of the room, where you'd expect to find the entry to a utility room or a closet for the water heater. Part of me reasoned they could have used the incense to cover a bad smell, maybe from a leaking pipe. The muttering chant had stopped, but I *felt* rather than heard a deep note, almost like weird old machinery. Weirdest sump pump I ever heard, I thought, the horror movie watcher in me having none of this.

The chubby woman and the reedy looking woman, meanwhile, took the pizzas from me and laid them out on the card table. "Can't let this go to waste, if he doesn't come," the biker guy said, lifting the lid over the meat pizza and helping himself to a slice.

"It might be going to waste in a different way," the chubby woman said, looking him up and down with a little smirk.

"Ha. Ha. Ha," Biker Guy replied, shoving the corner of the slice into his mouth.

"Living dangerously?" I chuckled nervously. They hadn't tried to kill me. They'd even worried for my well-being. Probably to lull me into a sense of false security.

"Clarisse is taking a break," the reedy-looking woman said, looking to the curtains.

"Probably she needs some food," the chubby woman said. Man, they sounded almost like the people in my aunt's Bible study group, the one time I tagged along. Not the using Bible quotes every other sentence, unless these folks started quoting their Books of Shadow, or some Creepy Book of Creepy Magick, but the way they talked so casually about their practices.

"I should get going," I said, in case they got even more casual with me. As if in reply, the wind raged even louder, and the house creaked like a tree in the storm. A crack of thunder roared somewhere nearby.

Biker Guy, still munching on his slice, stopped in mid-chew to look at the ceiling. "Think that's a no."

The hollow-cheeked guy also looked up. "That was close."

As if in response, the weird hum grew more intense. The cultists seemed indifferent to it. "Can you guys feel that?" I asked.

Hollow-Cheeked Guy looked to the concealed doorway. "He calls."

"Sounds hungry," Biker Guy said, reaching for another slice. Reedy-looking woman whapped his hand with hers.

"I'm serious, I really should get going," I said, with a nervous laugh.

"You've been reading too many silly horror stories, kid," Biker Guy said. "We don't offer him stuff with a nervous system, broadly defined."

"Any time that we have, we prepare it properly, and we certainly don't offer him humans," Hollow-cheeked Guy said.

The hum intensified till I swore my ears would bleed. Even the cultists looked uncomfortable. Hollow-cheeked Guy looked toward the curtains. Someone beyond it screamed; the cry cut off abruptly.

Something lunged from under the curtains. I expected a person, running for safety. Instead, something like an elephant's trunk emerged, paler than a dead fish, flopped out, reached about the floor. The end reared up, reaching in the air. Suckers like round mouths ringed with teeth covered the underside. The cultists moved aside as if something nonthreatening had entered the room.

"What the feck is that?" I said.

"He beckons," Hollow-cheeked Guy said, voice hushed in the first hint of any cultist-like reverence I'd seen from these people. I'm not sure what I expected: bowing and murmuring supplications like those caricatured natives in some 1940s jungle movie, or standing in a joyous awe like the people of Summerisle.

The tendril, or tentacle, or whatever it was from beyond reached to the table, snatching up the pizza box. The sucker-like mouth on the tip dilated and engulfed the pizza, box and all. It pulled it in whole, like a snake swallowing a rat, the sides of the tendril rippling.

Biker Guy started setting down the second slice he'd picked up and pushed the box toward the thing. The tendril whipped toward him, first grabbing up the pizza box and engulfing it. I expected—maybe hoped—the thing would retreat. Maybe this tendril monster-god would be happy with some pizza. Instead, it whipped up and grabbed Biker Guy by the head.

The tendril closed its mouth over him. He threw up his hands, the only sign of shock or fear he'd displayed. The tendril engulfed him, drawing him inside: clothing, boots, and all.

I staggered back and ran for the stairs. The surviving cultists didn't try to stop me. If anything, they were more occupied in reacting to their fellow's encounter with their tentacle god: gasps of dismay, and then a yawp from Hollow-cheeked Guy.

"Y'golnlach, put him down!" the chubby woman yelled.

As I burst into the kitchen, the rational part of me wanted to run to the phone or whip out my own, call the police and report this, but what could I tell them? Some middle class, middle-aged people in an old house in the woods, which had probably belonged to the family of one of them since the Mayflower, had called a hungry tentacle god into the basement? Yeah, and get my sorry self sent off wherever they sent people since Danvers State Hospital got turned into condos. I ran out the front door, into the lashing rain driven by the wind.

True to the cliché, a tree branch had fallen across my car. I would not get stuck there, or find out if the thing could extend its tendril to the front yard. I ran down the driveway, dodging fallen branches and ankle-deep puddles. The bushes whipped at me, twigs catching at my hair and clothes.

A falling branch clipped the side of my head, and everything went dark.

I came to again in what felt like hours or days later. The rain had subsided, and I lay on a gurney by the side of the road, blue and red lights flashing around me. Two EMTs worked on me, one shining a light in my eyes. A female police officer knelt over me. "Miss? Miss, can you hear me?"

I winced at the light. "Mmmf. Yeah, I can ..." I was too sore to get up, and I welcomed the second EMT laying a blanket over me. "How'd ... you know ... to find me?"

"You've got a good coworker," the cop said. "You were gone well over an hour, so they called it in.

"So, what happened here? Did the storm scare you? Strange people in the house?" the cop asked, as the EMTs hoisted the gurney and carried me to the waiting ambulance.

I wanted to tell them the whole thing, but instead, I replied,

27

"Went down all right. People let me stay inside. I just … branch hit my car. Tried to run for it."

"Anyone would, in a storm like this. You run into a tree branch?" she asked.

"Branch ran into me," I said.

Mr. Rossetti covered my hospital bill and gave me a week off after that bad call. But after three days, I insisted on going in. I'd had a bit of a concussion, but not enough to knock me on my back for a while. I wanted to make up for the insulated bags I'd left in my hurry, and I had to find a new car. "If I stay home and rest any longer, I'll start climbing the walls," I said.

I kept busy in the kitchen, applying myself to kneading pizza dough like never before. Shay manned the phone between helping me out and running deliveries. "You sure you can handle being here?"

I laid a wad of dough out in one pan. "You've asked me that question, in one form or another, ten times since I got here. I'm wondering if you can handle delivery, with your lack of a sense of direction."

"That's why I got the GPS thing on my dashboard."

At that moment, the phone rang, saving me from continuing this awkward conversation. Shay grabbed the pad on the counter while picking up the handset. "Arkham Haunted House of Pizza; may I take your order? Yep!" Shay scribbled on the pad. "Yep, we can do that. Now is this a pick up or shall we deliver it? Got it. That'll be ready in twenty minutes. We'll see you then." Shay hung up the phone, tore the slip off the pad and, coming back to the kitchen, hung the slip on a peg over one of the prep tables. I scanned the order: two raviolis with sauce, one spaghetti and meatballs with sauce and cheese.

I panned up the raviolis, sliding them into the oven to heat. I reached to the cauldron of spaghetti on the back burner and, with a pair of tongs, set to work.

The minute I hoisted out a hank of noodles, a jolt of fear stabbed down my spine. I dropped the noodles back into the pot and stepped back, breathing hard.

"You okay there?"

"I'm fine, just … the other night."

"You want to talk about the other night?"

"You got a shrink license?"

Shay stepped into my sight line and looked me in the eyes.

"Something else happened, besides you getting spooked by the storm. You can talk to me about it."

The bells on the front door jingled as someone entered. We looked out, spying a tall, burly guy dressed in a black leather vest over ripped jeans, patches that looked like bike club insignia stitched to his clothes. "Hey, there a manager here?" he called out, as he approached the front counter.

Shay went out to meet him. "That'd be me." Sort of; Shay had seniority over me.

The big guy held up a sheaf of photocopied pages. "Was wonderin' if you'd hang up this poster for me, in yer winda. M' brother Griffen vanished a couple nights ago. Went to a coven meeting, an' he never came home. Cops ain't been helpful."

Shay took the poster. I stepped out to look at it. A photo of Biker Guy smirk-glowered back from the page. "Sorry to hear about this, but I'll post it," Shay said.

"Thank you. Means a lot." Griffen's brother said, before buying a soda and leaving.

I managed to finish prepping that order. Once we'd hidden the spaghetti under a thick layer of sauce and cheese, I slipped them into the oven to heat for a few minutes.

Another call came in, this time for pepperoni bread sticks, among other things, something I could prep without trouble.

But when I had the pepperoni laid out on the strips of bread covered in garlic butter, my brain decided to crawl down into my spine. Those infernal suckers on that hideous gray tendril ...

"Irene, you're as white as a sheet," Shay said, in a tone that allowed no room for argument. "You need to talk to me about what happened during that delivery."

I started opening my mouth to tell him, when I lucked out. Saved by the bell a second time: the door opened, admitting Evan Chang, the college-aged oldest son of the Chinese family that owned and operated Chang's Chow next door.

"Hey there, kids," he said, grabbing a bottle of Welch's from the drink cooler near the front window. "Gotta fuel up. I have a delivery out in the boonies in Danvers."

The words fell out of my mouth. "Where in Danvers?"

Evan set the bottle on the counter and told me the address, as he handed his credit card over to Shay.

"Evan, don't go anywhere near that house. That's where I

delivered the other day, when that storm blew up. That place isn't right." And despite the increasingly concerned looks they gave me, I told them everything.

R.C. Mulhare was born in Lowell, Massachusetts and grew up in one of the surrounding towns, in a hundred-year-old house up the street from an old cemetery. Her interest in the dark and mysterious started when she was quite young, when her mother read the faery tales of the Brothers Grimm and quoted the poetry of Edgar Allan Poe to her, while her Irish storyteller father infused her with a fondness for strange characters and quirky situations. When she isn't writing, she moonlights in grocery retail. She's also fond of hiking in the woods of the White Mountains of New Hampshire and browsing the antiques shops one finds all over New England. A two-time Amazon best-selling author and member of the New England Horror Writers, her work has appeared in print with Atlantean Publishing, Macabre Maine, *FunDead Publications,* Deadman's Tome, *Off the Beaten Path Press, and* WeirdBook *magazine. She shares her home with her family, two small parrots, about fifteen hundred books and an unknown number of eldritch things that rattle in the walls when she's writing late in the night ....*

Find R.C. Mulhare on:

Twitter: https://twitter.com/MatrixRefugee
Facebook: https://www.facebook.com/rcmulhare
GoodReads: https://www.goodreads.com/matrixrefugee
Youtube: https://www.youtube.com/user/MatrixRefugee
Patreon: https://www.patreon.com/rcmulhare/posts

IF THE DEVIANT FITS ...

By N.L. Dalton

5:47 a.m.

Joe had been planning this for weeks. The girl, his target, was a loner; just the sort of girl he preferred. She worked as a waitress at Heaven, a nightclub about two blocks down the street from the bus station where he now stood. The woman worked four nights a week: eight p.m. to two a.m. waiting tables, and then until four a.m. cleaning up the club along with one or two others whose job it was to close the club.

She always came in on the 7:35 to work, and after her shift she spent the time between four a.m. and five at a diner across from the club. At five the trains started up again, and she'd be on the first one to her home about twelve stops down the line. It had taken Joe two attempts to follow the girl to track her to her apartment.

He had her now. The time was right: there were no passersby to witness what was about to happen, and from his earlier trips out, he knew that just a few blocks down the street was a deep, narrow alley. It was exactly what an enterprising rapist-murderer could want, especially one with a rather long, savage entertainment in mind for this evening. The thought of it brought a pleasurable rush from the small, half flaccid member stuffed in his underwear. It also brought on a flush and more flop sweat to mop from his forehead as he lumbered forward, his breathing becoming a bit labored. He couldn't afford that, and made an extra effort to bring his breathing back under control.

Less than a block from the alley, and he'd closed the gap

between predator and prey to about fifteen feet. His quarry had looked back once or twice as she covered the last two blocks, but he'd learned long ago to keep his marks solely in his peripheral … he never allowed their eyes to meet his if he could help it. It was far too easy to spook them that way. If you had to look forward, look past them. At the very most, allow a quick, polite nod if she looked directly at you.

He was going to kill her anyway; he always did, all the more reason not to spook them. Never leave a witness. He was a little closer now; ten feet, then eight. He extended his arms and surged forward … and never came close to his mark. He was shocked when he wrapped his arms around an armful of nothing and a cool, powerful hand clamped over his mouth, lifting him cleanly and silently from the pavement. The girl continued walking, completely unaware of the monster behind her … being carried into the alleyway by a far more dangerous beast.

7:32 p.m.

"Late again, Mr. Burrows."

"I'm sorry, Dr. Martin. I was in the front office talking to the day shift super about one of our bodies. I have this for you."

He gave Martin the form and waited while he looked it over. Martin let out an exasperated sigh and nodded. "Next time get word to me that you're upstairs, will ya? We're buried here, and you know it."

"I will," he said, then walked down the hall to the lockers. He waved to Harv as he passed his office and turned the corner to the locker room, a small area behind Exam A next to the bathrooms. Harv was waiting for him when he came out. The two men went into Exam A and each set about prepping the tables.

Harv went for the first body while Burrows set up the implement carts for each station. He was troubled for some reason he couldn't put his finger on. Not greatly troubled, mind you, just unable to concentrate on his work. A short pause to think brought his attention to the cheap portable stereo on a shelf near the office door. That was it … Harv and his fucking oldies, thought Burrows. Placing the bottle of disinfectant spray on the counter, he moved toward the radio.

"You best be keeping your damn hands off my radio, son!" came the raised voice of his super.

"Oh, come on, H …"

"Stow your BS and get back to that damned table, Goofy."

Harv wheeled in four bodies one after the other while Burrows finished setting up. The first of the group was a forty-year-old female named Elizabeth Allen. She was short, only about five feet tall, and slender. Blue eyes, blonde hair matted with blood, and rather plain-looking. The woman had fallen down her stairs some twelve hours prior. Rigor was well set in. Burrows removed and bagged the victim's clothing carefully, cutting as little as possible so as not to disturb any potential trace evidence. The lab boys could be real pricks if they wanted to be. It was best not to provoke them. Accidental deaths were autopsied just like homicides or deaths by unknown circumstance, whether the cause was obvious or not.

He had four to do for now, and more if Harv finished the autopsies before shift's end. The last one Harv wheeled in had to be Joseph Marcelli; at four hundred and fifty pounds, he was pretty hard to miss. A six-inch laceration ran from just under his left ear to the base of his throat where it met the shoulder. His clothing was old and somewhat grimy: loose khaki pants and an oversized blue tee shirt—a *really* oversized tee shirt with a sneaker logo on the chest. The coat and boots the man had been wearing were already bagged and sitting on the wire shelf under the exam table. He was about four days unshaven by the look of the brownish stubble on his jaw, and brown-eyed. Mouse-brown hair covered about half of his neck.

His fingernails and feet were especially filthy. Thick crusts of black dirt had built up between his toes, along the inside of his arches and along the edge of his heels. Obviously, the man had worn the boots for days without socks.

"Damn, this dude hasn't seen a bar of soap or a washcloth in years by the look of him. Mangy prick, eh Harv?"

"Well that's what you're here for, isn't it? Wash his grimy ass up."

"Ewww."

Needless to say, Burrows was not looking forward to washing the big man. Prepping bodies that had been filthy for extended periods of time was common, but something about Marcelli made him uneasy. He got the impression that even if he hadn't been so obese he'd still be, what was the word? Whatever, something was just plain wrong about him physically—he almost seemed lopsided somehow.

"Are you gonna get started or what?" Harv was getting impatient.

"Yeah, Harv, I will. I'm just a bit confused here. He just seems to be a little … off somehow."

"He's a big lardy bastard, of course he's off somehow. What kind of person walks around in mismatched clothing stinking to high hell in grubby boots without socks and a bootlace missing?" Harv shot back without looking up from his work. "Shit," he added, "Put a duck and a bazooka in the picture, and you get a *Far Side* comic."

Amused, Burrows glanced under the table at the clear plastic bag that contained Marcelli's boots. Sure enough, one of the boots was missing a lace. The other one was still where it should have been.

"Satisfied?" asked Harv, his impatience showing.

"Yeah, sure."

Making sure the body's clothing had been photographed, Burrows took a pair of surgical shears and sliced the tee shirt up the middle and peeled it back over the arms, stopping only to pull part of the shirt's hem out of the waistline just beneath the navel. Then he wiggled the shirt out from underneath the body a little at a time. Harv interrupted him.

"That is one hairy SOB."

"He sure is."

Harv was going to say something else but stopped suddenly, pointing to the waistline of Marcelli's pants. "You see that?"

"Yeah," said Burrows, now even more perplexed. He unbuttoned the pants and pulled them down to expose a long, nearly straight incision that ran about eighteen inches across the middle of Marcelli's abdomen. The wound was sloppily sutured together with the missing bootlace. The confusion that Burrows was feeling finally gelled into an answer.

"Harv, I think we're looking at a stuffed pepper."

Just then the body heaved upward and twisted violently to the left. Burrows and Harv jumped back, screaming in terror as what looked like taloned fingers broke through the open wound and sliced the bootlace. The body tumbled off the table and landed on its right side, then tipped onto its back a second time, twisting and undulating as something pushed against the skin above the wound from the inside. Slowly the stomach ruptured, and a large uneven mass of intestines and viscera pushed through and upward, the outer layers peeling back a few at a time to reveal a thin, bloody figure with long slender fingers. The man stretched his arms outward as he arched his back and drew in a deep breath. After a loud groan, the man twisted his head around, stretching his neck and then relaxing a bit, sitting back and breathing deeply and evenly.

"Al?" Burrows almost screamed. "What the hell are you doing?"

Suddenly tongue tied, Harv just stared incredulously and fluttered his hands toward the body.

"How ya doin, guys?" The man laughed. "Damn, it's good to be out of there. This is the first clean air I've had in fifteen hours."

The two men stared at Albert like he had two heads, which in a way he did ... sort of. They kept staring until Al leaned over and gently lifted Harv's jaw, pressing his mouth shut. "Vampires only breathe out of habit; don't you remember me telling you that? We only need to breathe to talk. It's a sort of camouflage."

"Oh, that explains everything," said Burrows sarcastically. "The hell it does. How ... why ... What the fuck are you doing in a cadaver?"

"Look, I don't mean to sound like I'm ignoring you," said the vampire apologetically, "but before I start, can you hand me that sprayer so I can clean up? I promise I'll explain everything afterward."

"Screw that, Al," said Harv, still utterly gobsmacked at what he was seeing, "Use the shower down the hall."

Twenty minutes and a clean pair of scrubs later, Al sat in the office with Harv and Burrows.

"So how have you two breeders been?"

The two men stared at him silently, making no attempt to answer.

"Oh, all right, you want me to tell you how I wound up camping out in Scummy the Whale. Will that make you happy?"

"Ecstatic," said Harv. Burrows just stared.

"Long story short, I ran out of time while hunting and needed a place to pass the day. The guy deserved it, trust me."

"How do you know that?" asked Burrows.

"I've been following him for a few days. Every once in a while, I go too long without feeding, and I wind up getting careless. We all do on occasion. So, we look for people who have it coming. That way, if we kill them, it's more likely to be overlooked. They tend to cause less of a stir. I know that sounds callous, but it works for us."

"Nice to know you guys have scruples," said Burrows sarcastically.

"Not all of us. Anyway, I picked him because he was about to grab a woman off the train. Just seemed the right thing to do, considering what I knew about the guy. As I was feeding, I ran out of time and had to improvise."

"So, you hid in a body?" asked Harv.

"After I dumped half his insides into a storm drain, yes."

"I didn't need to hear that," Harv groaned.

"I know you didn't," added Al with a sly smile.

Al stayed with Burrows and helped him clean up the mess, then hung around for an hour while Harv dried his sneakers in a cabinet sanitizer. As he was preparing to leave, he thanked them for covering for him again. Before going through the door, he turned around and said, "Be sure to run Marcelli's prints over to the police. I think they're looking for this deviant; he's been causing quite a sensation on Lake Street the last few months. That's why I chose him in the first place."

"The Plaza Killer?" asked Burrows.

"Joseph Marcelli in the flesh. See you around, guys."

N.L. Dalton is best known for writing horror and science fiction, speculative fiction, and dark-humored tales of various stripe. While working as an editor for Daverana Enterprises, it became apparent that she did her best work when she allowed a bit of her admittedly morbid humor to seep into her writing. Coincidentally, that's also how she managed to end a few of her relationships, but that's neither here nor there. Some folks just can't take a joke.

She has been a paralegal, legal assistant, laboratory technician/aide, construction worker, electronics inspector/programmer, and, funnily enough, a cosmetologist.

SCRIM AND SHAW AND THE HOUSE

FULL OF BONES

By Daniel Hale

Sister and brother, Scrim and Shaw lived in a house in the city boneyard. It was yellow in color and weathered in wear, as they were, and so effectively buried by mounds of old bones that Shaw and Scrim were obliged to use the topmost window whenever they wished to leave.

Not that they minded this at all; both brother and sister were quite unbothered by the skeletal wealth that surrounded them, and in fact had acquired a fond fascination for them. Every day they made at least one excursion into the yard to see how deep the mounds went, picking up whichever bones they fancied, trading them back and forth, fiddling and running their curious fingers over their yellowed membranes, before either tossing them back into the inexhaustible pile or tucking them under their arms to take home for further inspection.

Scrim and Shaw loved a bit of bone collecting, but each for their own reasons. For tidy Shaw, the bones were a puzzle to be reconstructed. He kept in his room a gallery of skeletons, reassembled like model kits through the application of wire (and occasionally glue) and all looking, but for the occasional overlong radius or mismatched phalanges, better than they'd probably looked alive, by Shaw's reckoning.

Scrim was not so tidy as her brother and had no patience for puzzles. She used the bones to make up new games to play, testing them out as bats and balls, riding them down the mounds, using them to dig tunnels or skipping them across the river. She danced with femurs, juggled clavicles and scapulae, took tea with skulls and skated on spines, played hacky-sack with patellae and washboards on ribcages.

All of which would have been fine, had Scrim and Shaw been anything other than brother and sister. Family squabbles: it is the way of family. Particularly, and most enthusiastically, brother and sister.

Many was the day when Shaw would awake in his bed to find that his skeletons were all a-jumble, and by evening Scrim would discover her bony playthings maddeningly sorted away by size and shape.

Sometimes the consequences were rough. One day, Scrim caught Shaw in the act of tying her spines in twine, whereupon she grabbed the nearest thighbone to hand and bashed him on the head with it. "They don't go that way!"

"That's the way they're supposed to go!"

"No, it isn't," Scrim protested. "Spines don't like each other. That's why everyone's only got one!"

"Don't be a moron. It's not as if you keep any of them as they're really supposed to go anyway. If you did, they wouldn't be lying around like this!"

"Like what, brother? I keep my bones exactly as I find them."

Shaw looked down at what he could see of his sister's floor, deep below the bone pile. Scrim's bed was down there somewhere under a carefully propped-up hollow. Sometimes he heard the pile shift in the night and wondered if his sister was being crushed to death under a load of parietal bones or something. He was seldom so lucky.

"Anyway, I'm not the moron," Scrim continued. "A moron tries to make the bones go back together when they don't want to."

"And how, sister dear, do you know that the bones don't want to go back together? Can you talk to bones?"

"Of course not, stupid. I don't have to talk to bones to see the way they let go of each other as soon as the skin's come off."

"That's just because the connective tissue falls apart as the body decomposes."

"Ugh!" Scrim stamped her feet, crunching several zygomatic bones. "You and your moron talk!"

And on it went until Shaw got fed up and took Scrim's thighbone away from her and gave her a conk on the head to match his own. There followed a long and protracted duel of hitting, poking, thumping, bonking, tugging, chasing, and generally throwing bones all over the house until the two of them tired out and went to bed.

The day it happened was Friday, when brother and sister would make their weekly expedition to the edge of the boneyard to watch the big trucks come and dump more bones. However, feeling more than usually annoyed with each other, they each decided to make the trip alone. Shaw took his usual route to the top of the house, where the big window opened on the highest bone peak, wondering vaguely if Scrim would go the same way and hoping he could see her see him ignoring her pointedly. He was momentarily disappointed when he did not run into her, then proceeded on his hike.

As it happened, Scrim left slightly earlier than her brother, giving herself time to dig deep into the pile and burrow her way to the trucks. She planned to dig a shallow pit to trap Shaw in for a few hours, giving her time to get back and scatter his bones all over the house. In her defense, Shaw was planning to tie her to a chair and show her an example of every single bone in the human body, slowly and clearly explaining its place and function until her eyes bugged out from boredom.

Neither sibling's plan would pan out. Though she was making fairly good time, Scrim was impeded by her digging. Shaw arrived a few minutes ahead of her as the first of the trucks arrived.

The boneyard lay some ways away from the city itself, at the other end of a long, narrow road that only the trucks ever drove on. They came slowly, their cargo piled high, occasionally spilling a bit on the ground. Then they'd pull up to a likely looking spot, turn around carefully, reverse and dump the load of bones onto the yard.

Once there'd been a gate and an office where the truck drivers had to check in before they got rid of the bones. Both gate and office and, indeed, the fence that once enclosed them were long ago devoured by the sprawling skeletal horde. Nowadays, the truckers simply checked in with whichever of the siblings they saw first.

Shaw nodded in what he hoped was a dignified manner to Mister Figgit, a doughy, stubble-cheeked trucker of a dour disposition, not uncommon in his line of work. He grunted noncommittally to the boy as he backed the truck up and pulled the lever to dump the load.

It was a significantly poorer haul than Shaw was used to, barely filling half the compartment. "So few this time," he remarked. "The city must be healthier than normal right now."

Mister Figgit scowled. The Shaw boy was marginally less creepy than his sister, but he insisted on talking as if he was normal people. "Not any healthier," he croaked. "People's dying just as they always do."

"Oh. Then why so few bones? Usually you're so full you can scarcely get to us before dinner time."

"They don't got as many now."

"Bones? People in the city don't have as many bones?" Shaw imagined people with randomly incomplete skeletons, dragging hollow legs or waving floppy arms like socks in the wind.

"Bodies. People in the city are getting rid of them a new way."

"How's that?"

"They burn them." Mister Figgit, job done, put the truck back in drive and pulled away without another word.

Burn them! The idea horrified Shaw. As if bones were firewood! Bodies in the city had always been left on the roofs, where the buzzards could get them and eat the rotting meat off the bones, which would then be hauled to the boneyard. That's the way it had always been. Surely Mister Figgit was mistaken?

Another truck was coming down the road, faster than Figgit's had been. Shaw hurried away, too troubled and upset to deal with more mystery, just as Scrim popped out of the pile.

"Hey, marrow brains! Where are you going?" But Shaw did not hear his sister as the next truck came to a groaning halt, and he ran off. The truck driver this time, Mister Golphene, slumped in his seat as he saw it was that horrible Scrim girl again. The child had a habit of showing him bones she'd dug up and dressed in doll's clothes. At least she did not seem to have any with her now.

"Watch yourself now!" Mister Golphene called as he brought the truck around. He pulled the lever before he stopped, counted the seconds as the bones rattled out. Then he heard something thump down in the back of the truck, run up and climb the cab. The Scrim girl's upside-down face appeared over the windshield, looking almost as alarmed as Mister Golphene felt.

"Mister! Mister! You've got no bones!"

Mister Golphene felt his face for any loose flaps or hollows under the skin. "What?"

"You've got no bones in the truck, mister! Somebody stole them!"

Golphene waited for his minor cardiac event to pass. "Ah, no, dear. That's all the bones there was."

"What! But there's loads of bones in people! And there's lots of people in the city! You should have scads more! What are they doing with them? Are they keeping them all to themselves? That's so unfair!"

"No, no," stammered Golphene. "They just aren't getting sent here anymore. Most people in the city are choosing cremation instead, you see, and …"

"Cream-ation? What do I care what people put in their tea? I'm talking about the bones."

"Er, no, you see. Ah, that is. They're burning the bodies now, dear." He switched gears, revved the engine meaningfully. The girl wasn't getting the hint.

"But what about the bones? Do they get burned too?"

"Well, yes. I suppose so."

Scrim looked at the worried driver a long, uncomfortable moment. Then her upside-down face retreated up the roof of the cab. Golphene released the brake.

There was the lightest creaking of springs in the seat next to him. The Scrim girl said: "They burn them all the way up?"

The rest of the afternoon was busy for Scrim. First, she had to figure out how to stop the truck after Mister Golphene fainted. This was easily done by steering it into the ditch that ran alongside the road back to the city. She couldn't pull the keys out to get the truck to stop growling, but she figured Mister Golphene could do that as soon as he woke up. She briefly considered resuscitating him with a bonk or two on the head, but she had no bones with her, and anyway he probably wouldn't like that, so she patted him on the head and went home.

It was dark when she crawled over the bones and got back into the house. Shaw was sitting in his room, a skull on his lap, sewing the jawbone back on. "No more bones," he said.

"Don't be stupid; there's loads more outside." Scrim eyed her brother's finished skeletons, lining the walls like soldiers at rest. She reached into a ribcage, carefully plucked a thread from a particular bundle of wire. The skeleton fell apart before her.

Shaw didn't seem to notice. "We'll make a record of all the ones that are left. We can bring a marker, sort everything by number and letter. Should be done with that in a few weeks. We'll need lots more wire. Have to clear some space in the downstairs rooms and work our way up. After that, we'll start lining them up around the house. Fill up the whole yard again that way. Be more organized."

"That's stupid. You'd be at it for ages. And don't think I'd help you. I have better things to do with bones than stick wire and glue on them that they don't want. Anyway, you wouldn't finish them 'cause there'd be a bunch left over. I suppose I can play with those …"

The skull flew into Scrim's and came apart with a crack. "You mustn't," Shaw screamed. "You mustn't, mustn't do that!"

"What was that for?" Scrim yelled back. She was no stranger to taking bones to the head, but that skull was weighted with screws and wires and things. Scrim's head was ringing.

"If you play with them, or act like we're happy with them at all, then they won't bring any more. They may even take the rest away. Why should they bring us any more bones if we look like we don't mind having a bunch of spares? We need to leave them alone; when they see that we can't make more skeletons …" Shaw tapped his chin with a spare jawbone, thinking. "Or, no. Maybe we can still use some of them. Make a bunch of half-done skeletons. Yes, I like that idea. Then they'll see we need more."

"I'm not letting you use my bones to make a bunch of idiot skeletons!" Scrim ripped the jawbone out of Shaw's hand. "Then they're won't be any left to play with."

"There won't be any left to play with eventually anyway, bone skull! They'll all rot sooner or later!"

There was, Scrim knew, a layer of bones deep at the bottom of the pile that had crumbled into dry dust. Sometimes she'd mixed the stuff with a bit of water to make face paint, but it wasn't good for very much else. "That won't happen for years and years."

"But it will happen, and then there won't be any left. Even the skeletons will turn to dust, and then what will we have? Just a load of wire and glue and a house full of dust." Shaw kicked a skeleton over, which knocked over the one next to it into a pile of limbs. Shaw began to cry.

Scrim didn't like it. She'd never seen her brother cry. Neither of them ever cried, even when they hit too hard or called each other names. She felt her own eyes tremble in sympathy but blinked away the tears and the doubt.

"Don't be stupid," she said, as gently as she could. "They'll not stop sending the bones. They're not really burning them. It's stupid."

"But what if they are?" Shaw whimpered. "What if they are just using the bones to light bonfires or whatever? I bet that's what they're gonna burn instead of trees from now on. The trucks will just start delivering them to the houses, so they can burn them all up and not leave any for us."

"They don't burn them in fires, marrow brain," said Scrim, feeling superior. "They're burning them in cream-ations. Anyway, how's making them back into skeletons gonna help? They'd just want to take those too."

"What? Why?"

"Cause then more people in the city could use them! I bet nobody there knows how to put bones back together. They'd probably line up for miles and miles to buy their skeletons back!"

Shaw had to laugh. "You are an idiot."

"Hmph." Scrim let it pass and hugged her brother. Shaw sniffled a bit longer before he calmed down. He regarded his ruined skeletons. "Look what you did. I'll have to put those back together now. I won't be able to sleep knowing they're all messed up."

"I'll help," Scrim said, not entirely reluctantly.

"Do you even know what goes where? I bet you don't know the difference between a tarsal and a metatarsal."

"I will if you tell me. Come on." She picked up a curved piece of bone. "Where does this bit go?"

Any warm feeling between brother and sister quickly fled over the hour Shaw spent trying to teach Scrim the basics of the skeletal system. As soon as Shaw showed her how to thread the wire, Scrim insisted on making a go at it for herself without taking into consideration what bone went where. They wasted half a spool of wire before Shaw gave up and went to work on one of the other skeletons. *She might as well have it now,* he thought.

It was another hour or so, when he got the skeleton back on its feet, that Shaw checked back in on Scrim. At first glance, it seemed the skeleton was still in a pile; Scrim was bent over it on the floor, gaunt face scrunched up in concentration, grey tongue sticking out the side of her mouth.

"Well?" Shaw asked.

Scrim barely looked his way before returning to her work. "It isn't ready yet."

"Obviously." Shaw pushed her away, then felt his jawbone drop as he took in the bizarre thing Scrim had been working on so intently.

It appeared to be a little hut, large enough for a cat or a small dog to use. But it was made of bones. The ribs formed a sort of archway and a latticework for the roof, between which vertebrae and carpus bones had been carefully slotted to close off the space within. Looking inside, Shaw could see humerus support beams held the whole thing up. It wasn't finished yet—there were gaps in the roof, and many bones were left over—but it was incredible, all the same.

Shaw registered something bony hitting the back of his head, and turned to see Scrim holding up an ulna to whack him with it. "Get away! I said, it isn't ready yet!"

"How did you do this?" Shaw squinted his eyes, tilted his head this and that, walked around the little hut, the better to see it from every angle. "They shouldn't fit together like this."

"Don't tell me what they should and shouldn't do, brother! I told you already they didn't want to fit the way you had them. I just put them together the way they want to go."

Shaw got on his knees to look inside the hut. You could fit a little dining room in there, with tables and chairs to seat a hundred mice.

"I couldn't make them go the other way," Scrim said. "I never could. They just ..." She clenched her hands, pressed them towards each other as though they were struggling against contact. "They didn't want to go together those ways. Or they didn't want the wire on them like that, and it'd go all twisty. So, I decided to show you the way they're supposed to go."

Shaw would have poked fun at his sister for such nonsense ... except the bones looked so right this way. So much more ... *made.* "That's not how bones go."

"Well," Scrim said, with self-satisfaction. "That's how these ones go."

Shaw looked at the ranks of his skeletons. What had once looked so perfect and neat to him now looked forced and rather grim. He could swear their smiles now looked strained, as if trying to hide some secret discomfort. "Can you teach me how you did this?"

Scrim scowled at her brother. "You aren't joking? You're not gonna call me a dummy or make fun of me or tell me I'm wrong?"

"No," Shaw said truthfully. "I just want to know how they fit together."

Brother and sister looked at each other a while. Then Scrim instructed Shaw to fetch some more wire, and the two set to work expanding the hut.

It wasn't as slow-going as Scrim had been, trying to learn the traditional way of bone reassembly; Shaw's fingers were adept at handling bones and wire, after all. Even so, it wasn't until the next morning that the two happened to sit back as one and really look at their work thus far.

Half the skeletons in Shaw's room had been deconstructed and incorporated into the new assembly, which was so big it nearly supplanted the whole space. There was one part where a new wall made entirely of bones covered the rotted wood original. At some point the little hut had been disassembled and expanded into a cozy little alcove that enclosed Shaw's window, complete with an in-built bench which would be a nice spot to read, once cushions were added for comfort.

Even Scrim was awed by what they had accomplished. The two looked up at the point where the bones did not quite touch the ceiling; neither of them could reach that high. Shaw began thinking of stronger materials to hold the bones together, support beams like the one in the hut to keep the room from falling in. He shared these ideas with his sister who giggled with hushed excitement and proposed replacing the floor with a pressed carpet of flat bones from the cranium and pelvis and sternum and rib cage. They could make a new staircase down to the ground floor, lined with banisters from the arms and legs, hang a grand chandelier from the ceiling made of vertebrae and sacrum and tarsals and ribs and skulls …

Scrim and Shaw didn't have much call to go in the city very often; most of what they needed could be found in the boneyard. As a result, there were few people who could claim more than a passing knowledge of the children, and fewer still the unhappy distinction of seeing them regularly.

Mister Bowshaw, of Bowshaw's Hardware Store, was one such unhappy individual. Every month or so, the boy would be in to order some wire and a bit of glue (or sometimes, because the house in the boneyard was very old, the odd bit of wood and nails). He was an off-putting sort of lad, but not nearly so as his sister, who'd once come along and spent the whole time staring at him. When Mister Bowshaw asked her what the matter was, she asked him how all the wet, meaty bits fit with his bones.

Bowshaw was quite startled to see both the siblings come into his shop; more so that it was Scrim who did the talking this time. Shaw was looking intently about the shop, occasionally scribbling in a little notebook he carried. When he was finished, he gave it to Scrim, who looked it over, nodded, and handed it to Bowshaw.

"We'll need this much wire and nails and tar," she told him authoritatively. "Also, some hammers and saws and tools to build stuff with. Any other stuff you suggest would be helpful."

Bowshaw read the notes incredulously, and started to explain that, even of the supplies on this list that he had in stock, he had nothing like the amounts they were requesting. But then Scrim stared at him like she was considering his meaty bits, and he told them instead he would make inquiries and have them delivered. This seemed to satisfy them.

The next few days saw the road between the city and the boneyard more alive with traffic than it had been in years, with Golphene and Figgit ferrying large spools of steel wire, vats of tar and crates of nails, hammers, saws, ladders, pliers, rulers, tape measures, and many other tools. Scrim and Shaw took them gratefully and sent them back with unsorted sacks of the old coins they used to pay for things, saved from the days when the boneyard had been more prosperous.

A month passed after the last delivery. Then another. By the third, most of the city had yet to stop speculating as to what those boneyard children were up to, but nobody was quite prepared to go and find out. By this point the bone deliveries had stopped altogether, so there would be no practical cause to visit the yard.

At last the mayor, who'd been feeling the dread of whatever was coming more acutely than practically anyone, decided it would be only right that a public official be seen to call on the poor boneyard children and see that whatever project they were undertaking was not a public nuisance (in fact, it was his wife who decided this, and who explained to him, rather emphatically, why he should go, but it amounted to much the same thing).

The people of the city saw their mayor off that morning, watching him walk alone down the road to the yard from behind the safety of their windows. It seemed he'd vanished from sight for only moments before he was seen to be running back, pelting away at quite a good speed for a man of his age. Several concerned citizens raced to meet him at the gate, and caught the puffing mayor as he collapsed, red-faced and exhausted, sputtering on his words.

"Come and see," he wheezed. "Come and see!"

For the first time in living memory, curiosity about what the boneyard children had done won out against public paranoia. The people set off, some more boldly than others, the most activity that road had ever seen. The menfolk walked in front (although their children shoved and bit for a chance to lead the way and be the first to see), then stood stock-still as they arrived at the yard. Their families shuffled and fanned out to see, till the whole city stood round the spot where the yard had once been and gawped at the ungainly thing now taking its place.

It was a house full of bones. A house *of* bones, huge and yellowed and knobby. Columns of tibias and fibulas bound together stood tall and proud over a femured archway that opened onto the yard proper. A road of skull plates marked the way to a door of ribs. Radius and ulna and humerus bones stacked and tarred and wired together served as walls; rows and rows of skulls fanned out along the exterior, marking the boundaries between floors. Spinal columns framed the glassless windows, which had their own elaborate bony balconies.

The city folk as one gazed at the house with something that was approaching both horror and awe. Subsequently none of them noticed when Scrim and Shaw stepped through the front door, until Scrim shouted at them. "What are you all doing here?"

Shaw was carrying two buckets overflowing with what looked like finger bones. He was red in the face but grinning widely at the stunned visitors. "Isn't it amazing? We've got most of the main hall completed and are set to start on the west wing. The roof is still patchy in spots, but we should have that all filled in soon." He tried to look for Mister Bowshaw in the crowd, but could not see him. "If you're there, Mister Bowshaw, thank you for everything," he shouted.

"It isn't finished yet," Scrim said firmly. "All of you go away. We'll let you see the inside when it's finished."

In fits and starts, the city folk regained their senses enough to begin marching back to the city. Nothing was said as the excited chatter of the brother and sister faded behind them and they all returned to their homes.

None of them ever went to see the bone house again. However, as the next few years passed and the old folks were on their death beds, more and more of them declared that their bodies were to be left out on the roof like in the old days, and the remains were to be sent to the bone yard for whatever use they could be put to.

If nothing else, they said, *at least it will keep them from finishing that* house.

Daniel Hale writes dark fantasy and horror. His first collection, The Library Beneath the Streets, *is available for purchase online. Find him at:*

danielhale42.wordpress.com

DO I FAT?

By Rob Smales

Flowers stared, fascinated, at the thick blue vein pulsing in the chief's forehead.

"Chief Bagley has determined," said Commissioner Greene, "and I support him in this decision, that you two are not to speak with any press. Therefore, it falls upon us to make any statements on your behalf. I heard the story from him, but I'd like to hear your version before I step in front of the cameras. Gentlemen?"

Carr's elbow nudged Flowers gently in the ribs, and Flowers tore his gaze from where the chief sat in the corner, returning his attention to the police commissioner's smooth, well-moisturized face.

"Well, sir," said Flowers. "It was like this: we caught us a serial killer. Case closed."

"Serial cannibal," corrected Carr. "A cannibal's worse, right?"

"Oh, yeah," agreed Flowers. "You usually get some kind of award for catching a serial killer, but a cannibal? We should get a commendation easy."

"Commendation?" said the chief from the corner of the room—a growl sounding more like a talking bear than a man. "Are you kidding me with this commendation crap? You guys were lucky she didn't …"

"Please, Chief Bagley." The commissioner held up a hand. "I'm just trying to hear their side of the story." Flowers glanced at the chief again. The man even *looked* like a bear: bulky, and with a penchant for growing hair just about everywhere he had skin. Except for his forehead, where that vein was throbbing *quite* prominently.

"But, sir," said the chief, beginning to rise.

"Please," the commissioner repeated, holding his stare upon the chief until the larger man sank, grumbling, back into his chair. The small, neat man currently standing behind the chief's desk gestured toward the two seated detectives. "Please, continue."

"It was," said Carr, "really just good old-fashioned genius police work."

Strangled sounds came from the chief, but Commissioner Greene's expression remained mild. "Please," he said. "Elaborate."

"Well, we walked into the establishment," said Flowers.

"Kappy's Liquors," supplied Carr.

"And, thanks to our years on the force, we noticed the perp acting in a suspicious manner."

"She flat-out asked you what wine goes with nine-year-olds!" shouted Chief Bagley. The commissioner held a hand up toward him again, eyes fixed on Flowers and Carr, nodding for them to go on.

"We engaged with the suspect to keep her busy while, uh, backup was called in."

Bagley shot to his feet. "The clerk was freaked out that you were helping her choose a wine, and he called 911!"

"Yeah," said Carr, turning toward Flowers. "Remember that rotgut Merlot she was holding? *That* was the real crime, that anyone would drink that stuff. What she needed was a nice Chianti."

"I understand that when uniforms arrived on the scene," interrupted the commissioner, "you already had your weapons drawn and IDs out?"

"Well, the dude behind the counter told us he'd called the police," said Carr. "So I said, 'We *are* the police.' He didn't believe me, so I flipped him the badge."

"I skipped the badge and showed him my gun," said Flowers, with a wink. "I've noticed people tend to show a little more respect if you show them the gun. The next thing we knew, Kappy's was full of uniforms, all showing their guns, too." He popped out a forefinger and thumb and finger-shot the commissioner. "It's good to see the younger generation learning from our experience. Makes me proud."

Chief Bagley was breathing like he'd just lumbered up five flights of stairs, and his skin, where you could see it through the hair, had gone a mottled, unhealthy-looking red. He raised his hands beseechingly toward Commissioner Greene, apparently unaware that his thick fingers were flexing spasmodically as if choking an invisible neck. "Do you see?" he said through clenched teeth. "Do you see what they've saddled me with? How do they expect me to run a department with …?"

"They were the first officers on the scene," said Greene. "They were the ranking officers on the scene, and they were identifying themselves as police officers. Even under these circumstances, I don't see how we can't give them the collar."

"But sir …"

"Do you want the union on you over this? Over *them*?"

The chief remained silent, jaw muscles bunching as he ground his teeth.

"I thought not. If this gets out, it'll make the whole department look like a bunch of idiots, and I won't have that. Not on my watch. And to that end …" He turned toward the seated detectives, leaning forward to plant his small fists on the desk blotter, and though his expression didn't change, his voice was suddenly ice cold and filled with menace. "If I even *think* you two have gotten within a mile of a reporter—and I don't care if it's just one of your own kids writing for the school paper—I'll see to it that you finish out your careers answering domestic dispute calls. In Guam. Am I making myself clear?"

Flowers said, "I don't have any kids, sir."

He didn't see the commissioner move, but suddenly the spare little man in the gray suit was around the desk, hands braced on the armrests of Flowers's own chair, and they were nose to nose.

"Guam. Am. I. Clear?"

Flowers gulped. "Yessir."

Commissioner Greene straightened and shot his cuffs. "Glad to hear it. Now, to help you two avoid the public eye, I'm assigning you to protection detail. Your prisoner apparently has some sort of health issue that may be life threatening. I don't know all the details, but there's a doctor in with her right now. You two handle it. This is the biggest case this department has ever seen, and I'm not going to have the damn perp die on me before she even gets to trial. Talk to the doctor, then liaise with the hospital. Do whatever needs doing to keep that old witch alive and healthy until we can give her a death sentence."

"But, sir …" started Chief Bagley, but the commissioner cut him off.

"With doctors and the hospital involved, how badly do you

think even *they* could screw this up, chief?" He addressed the detectives again. "Do it. Keep her alive. Do you understand?"

Flowers and Carr replied in unison: "Yes, sir."

"Good." He checked his watch. "Chief Bagley, the press conference is in fifteen minutes. Meet me downstairs in ten." Without another word, the little man swept majestically from the office. Flowers and Carr watched him go, then turned back to find the chief had finally left his corner and now stood before their chairs, his bulk uncomfortably close and looming.

"You heard the commissioner." Bagley's teeth were bared, though whether in a smile or a grimace, Flowers couldn't tell. "You two have babysitting detail. Go make sure your big collar stays alive."

"Okay, chief," said Flowers. "But I think …"

"*Think?* You *think?* Flowers, you don't get *paid* to *think!* You get out of here and do as you're told. I want nothing on your mind but getting that woman to trial, you understand me?"

"But …"

"I don't care if you see a crime in progress."

"But …"

"You see an escaped convict forcing a kidnapped woman to sell crack to the mayor's kid out the window of a stolen car while parked in a handicapped spot, you turn a blind eye, you get me? You're *babysitting!*"

"We had a prison break?" said Carr.

"*Out!*" the chief screamed, thrusting a finger toward the door.

They went.

"I still don't see anything about a jailbreak in here," said Carr, waving a copy of that morning's departmental briefing as they approached Interview Room Two.

"Not our problem," said Flowers. "Sounds like he's Narcotics' problem. Or maybe Crimes Against Persons. Whatever. All we have to worry about is the old lady's tissue."

"Issue."

"Huh?"

"Issue, man, the commish said she had a health *issue.*"

Flowers looked down at the box of Kleenex in his hand. "Oh. Crap. This might not be as easy as I thought."

They pushed through into Interview Two just as the doctor was packing the last of his equipment away, and he met them in the middle of the room.

"Detectives," he said, quietly. "This is a weird one."

"No kidding," said Carr, then gave the skinny old woman sitting at the interview table a little finger wave. "Hey, there, Mrs. Yaga. How's the cannibal business treating you?"

"Oh, Mr. Carr," she replied, her Russian accent thick, but understandable. "I am not good. Not good. I am so hungry. This is how police, they treat old woman? Lock her in little room for hours, with nothing to eat?"

"Why hasn't she ..." Flowers began, but the doc interrupted, voice low but intense.

"She's had two sandwiches, a half-dozen doughnuts, and four of those packets of peanut butter crackers from the vending machine in the hall, all in the past ninety minutes, and she's still complaining of hunger."

Flowers whistled as Carr said "Wow. But she's skinny as a rail—where do you think she puts it all?"

"Exercise," said the old woman, pronouncing the terminal E to make it four syllables. "I sweat. I work and I sweat. Is hard work, the baking. You think baker should be fat." She leaned back in the chair, spreading her arms slightly. "Do I fat?"

Flowers eyeballed her figure: like a broomstick in a housecoat. "No, ma'am, you do not fat."

"It's the strangest thing I've ever seen," said the doctor, keeping his back to Mrs. Yaga, as if trying not to be overheard. "I've been in here with her for almost two hours, and in that time, even with all she's eaten, she's actually *lost* weight!"

"So, what," said Carr. "She's all hopped up on diet pills or something?"

"You don't understand." The doctor looked a little wild-eyed. "I have a scale, and I weighed her when I took vitals, but I thought I detected a visible difference as I was trying to get a medical history, so I weighed her again. It had been barely more than an hour, and she'd been eating the whole time, but she was lighter by almost *six pounds!*"

Flowers grinned. "So, she took a big dump. I tell you, doc, the morning after Thanksgiving, I ..."

"There was no elimination. She never even left the room. But through observation and talking to her, I've developed a theory. It's crazy, but I can't think of anything else. For some reason—either natural mutation or some disease I've never even heard of—her ability to create fat cells is severely retarded."

"Retarded?" said Carr, looking past the doctor to the woman. "What, she's mentally disabled, or whatever they call it?"

"No, no," the doctor began, but the words seemed to run out of steam and he just stared at Carr for a moment, then shook his head. "No. What I mean is that her body doesn't seem to produce fat cells like a normal person, and her metabolic rate is off the chart. Our bodies use fat cells for fuel, but hers doesn't. With such a high metabolism, even when she's eating like this, her body's still cannibalizing itself to fuel her life functions."

Carr nodded. "So, what you're saying is she's a cannibal on a cellular level."

The doc stared, open-mouthed, before his gaze swiveled slowly toward Flowers.

"Don't look at me, doc." Flowers grinned. "I didn't understand a word of that."

Carr shrugged. "I seen a show on the medical network."

"Right." The doctor continued to stare for a moment, then seemed to shake himself out of a daze. "Well, right. Uh … so what I'm theorizing—and it'll take a bit of testing, but I think I can prove it—is that her own body's pushing her toward cannibalism. It's like when you're low on salt, so suddenly you crave potato chips."

"I love me some Pringles," Flowers said. "Like they say on the commercials, 'I bet you can't eat just one!'"

"Lay's," said Carr.

"Huh?"

"That's what they say on the Lay's chip commercial. Pringles says, 'Once you pop, you just can't stop.'"

"He's right," piped up Mrs. Yaga. "Pringles. Once you pop, no can stop." Her voice took on a whining edge. "All this talk of food is make me hungry. I have snack now? Maybe ham sandwich? Maybe with bacon?"

Flowers wiped drool from his lower lip. "Man, that sounds good."

"Her body knows what's missing, and is craving it," said the doctor. "Fat. Preferably, apparently, human fat. They said the witness, that kid she had in her 'larder'? She was trying to fatten him up."

"Wanted to get more bang for her buck," said Carr.

"Smart shopper," agreed Flowers.

"Yes, but with her metabolism, she wasn't wasting anything."

The doc was wide-eyed. "They didn't find any actual remains anywhere, but they should have. I think … I think she was eating them, bones and all, until there was nothing left."

"I still hear you," came the woman's voice. "And all your talking and talking is making me *hungry!*"

The doctor shuddered. "I have to get out of here. To the lab, I mean." They left the Yaga woman in Interview Two and followed him down the hall into the squad room. "I have some blood samples to have analyzed, quick as they can. At the rate her body's consuming itself, we have to find a way to get her what she needs, or she won't make it 'til morning, never mind all the way to trial."

Flowers thought of the chief. Specifically, he thought of those thick, hairy fingers, flexing like they were wringing a neck.

His neck.

"Hurry!" he shouted as the medical man hustled for the exit. "We'll be here. Let us know the minute you know anything we can do. Anything!"

The doc waved over a shoulder and was gone.

"So," said Carr. "Think we'll like Guam?"

"Shut up."

They went to their desk—one of those partner setups, a single desk with a knee hole and drawers on each side, so they faced each other—and sat. Flowers sighed. "You know, that Mrs. Yaga was right. All that talking about food made me hungry." He opened a drawer and began rummaging. "I got that bag of peanut butter cups. You want one?"

"Sure."

Flowers closed the first drawer and opened a second. "What the hell? I swear I put them right in here …"

"Don't worry about it," said Carr, standing and walking to the coffee station at the counter. "We're cops. We can always have doughnuts." His head swiveled left and right as he scanned the counter around the coffee maker. "Hey, where did the doughnuts go?"

"Dunno, man." Flowers was back to looking through the first drawer, taking things out and piling them on his blotter. "I'm kinda more concerned that someone went into my desk for my peanut butter cups. You don't mess with a man's …"

"Flowers."

Flowers looked up from his drawer. Carr had started to return to their desk, but had stopped, pointing to the floor. A trail of crumpled orange paper wrappers led away from the side of their desk like a peanut-butter-chocolate-scented dotted line. Flowers followed the line with his eyes until it ran smack into one of the visitor's chairs at a desk halfway across the room. Sitting in the chair was a kid of about nine, maybe ten, with a big round body, a red round face, and a nearly empty Dunkin Donuts box on his lap.

"Are those the doughnuts you're looking for?" Flowers asked Carr, then, without waiting, he raised his voice to address the kid directly. "Hey, kid. Those the doughnuts that used to be on the counter there?"

The boy nodded, still chewing.

"Wasn't it full?"

Another nod.

"Well they were supposed to be for everybody," said Flowers. "And we're pretty hungry. Would you mind if we …?"

The kid lifted the last doughnut from the box and, with a wide grin, took a big bite. Flowers grit his teeth in a rictus he hoped might pass for a smile and muttered, "Why, you fat little prick …."

"Well," said Carr, "that was rude. All he was asking was …" But the kid leaned forward, grin still wide. He opened his mouth, spilling half-masticated doughnut into the empty box on his lap, and pointed between his lips, nodding and raising his brows as if to say, *you want some?* Carr looked at Flowers. "What the hell is wrong with this kid?"

"He's a spoiled brat, is what it is," Flowers responded. "There's no discipline today. Kids just do what they want." He addressed the boy again. "And I suppose you went through my desk and took my peanut butter cups?"

He didn't nod, but the kid's smile widened even further.

"Not only is it rude as hell to go through someone else's stuff like that, but, seriously, you just don't mess with another man's cups."

The kid kept on chewing as he gave the detective the finger.

"*That's it!*" Flowers launched himself to his feet, thinking that someday, somewhere, someone was going to knock this little prick's block off, and right at that moment he really wanted to *be* that somebody.

Carr moved to intercept him, shouting "Flowers, come on! He's not worth it!"

Just at that moment a uniformed officer entered the squad room, read the situation, and hustled to the boy's side. "You ready,

Toby?"

"You know this kid?" said Flowers. "Who is he?"

The officer shuffled over until he was halfway between them and the boy, lowering his voice much as the doctor had when discussing Mrs. Yaga. "This is Tobias Hansel, the kid who was found in that old lady's larder? He's the lone witness against the cannibal."

"Seriously?" said Carr. "We better question him, then."

The uniform looked uncomfortable as, behind him, Toby Hansel continued to chew obnoxiously and flip off the detectives. "Well, sirs, I, uh, I can't let you do that. The chief said … well, the chief said not to let you within a mile of the kid. Ingemi and Fripp are going to handle all the interrogation."

Carr looked at Flowers. "So, what, all we get to handle is the old lady?"

"No, sir." The young officer looked even more uncomfortable. "Ingemi and Fripp are handling that interrogation, too."

"But it's our case!" shouted Carr. "How can *they* handle all the interviews on *our* case?"

"Because I don't think it's going to stay our case for very long," said Flowers, keeping his voice low, but unable to hide the anger in it. "It looks to me like they're giving it to those two kiss-asses."

"They are?" Carr looked crushed. "But … but what about the commendation? Will we still get the commendation?"

"Probably not."

"Jesus." Carr's voice sounded rough, as if he were on the edge of tears. "They get the case, they get the commendation … what do *we* get?"

Flowers glared across the room at the frosted glass set in the chief's office door, and murmured, "Babysitting duty."

"I *am* sorry, sir," said the officer, staring fixedly at Flowers and ignoring the wet snuffling sounds coming from Carr. "I'm just telling you what the chief said. Now, I have to put the kid somewhere until his parents can be located and brought to the station. Do you have any idea …?"

"If they're doing all the interviews," said Flowers, "then they'll be using Interview Room Two. Why don't you put the kid in there to wait, save Ingemi and Fripp some time?"

The officer smiled with a tight little nod. "Good idea. Thank you sir—and glad to see you're being such a good sport about this."

"Don't worry about it," said Flowers, then looked over the

blue-uniformed shoulder at the smug, doughnut-smeared face of the fat little prick who'd messed with his peanut butter cups. "See you later, tubby."

"It's Toby, sir," corrected the young officer.

"Whatever," Flowers said, turning to comfort his openly weeping partner.

"That's right, doc," Flowers said into the phone. "All charges were dropped. Uh-huh. What's that? You're gonna have to speak up, doc. Yeah, she walked out of here with her lawyer about ten minutes ago. Uh-huh. No, she looked fine. Strong and everything." He glanced toward the chief's office, where all the commotion was coming from. "Actually, doc, she looked like she'd gained some weight. I know, weird, right? Anyway, thanks for your help. Bye."

He hung up the phone and looked over at Carr, who was swiveled around in his chair to watch the play of silhouettes on the chief's frosted glass window. One huge, hulking shadow loomed over two smaller, seated ones, waving its arms in time to the chief's bellowing.

"Hey."

Carr looked over to him.

"You okay?"

Carr nodded. "I am now." He gestured toward the shadow show, where the chief was shouting "A *kid!* Just one goddamned *kid!*"

Carr smiled. "It's good not to be *in* there for once, you know?"

"I hear *that*," said Flowers.

"Weird, though, how Ingemi and Fripp lost the witness."

"Weird," Flowers agreed.

"I mean, the kid disappeared right in the middle of a police station."

"Disappeared."

"No kid, but they found his *shoes?* What kind of *X-Files* crap is that?"

Before Flowers could think of a response, the squad room door slammed open and the commissioner marched in, looking neither left nor right, but making a beeline for the chief's office. He entered without knocking, and everything went silent. There was some low murmuring in the commissioner's smooth tones, but Flowers couldn't make any of it out—at least, not until a single ejaculation that sounded like it came from a shocked Fripp:

"*Guam?*"

Flowers chuckled.

"You know," said Carr, "I almost feel bad for those case-stealing kiss-asses."

"Really?"

"Well, almost." Carr looked toward the door leading to the interview rooms. His eyes went blank, and then turned thoughtful. "Hey … that old lady?"

"Mrs. Yaga? She walked out of here healthy as a horse." Flowers rubbed his palms together with a grin. "Yup. Nobody can say we didn't do *our* job."

"Yeah," Carr said, sounding suspicious. "Yeah, about that. You don't think …?"

"Buddy," broke in Flowers. "I have it on high authority that we don't get paid to think. Now" —he rose to his feet— "let's you and me go see about buying that nice old lady a celebratory bottle of Chianti, shall we?"

Rob Smales is the author of Echoes of Darkness, *which garnered both a five-star* Cemetery Dance Online *review and a 2016 Pushcart nomination. With over two dozen short stories published, his story "Photo Finish" was also nominated for a Pushcart Prize and won the Preditors & Editors' Readers Choice Award for Best Horror Short Story of 2012. His story "A Night at the Show" received honorable mention on Ellen Datlow's list of the Best Horror of 2014, while "Death of the Boy" and "In Full Measure" made the same honorable mentions list for 2016. Most recently, he edited the dark humor anthology* A Sharp Stick in the Eye (and other funny stories) *for Books & Boos Press, and released the coming of age horror novella* Friends in High Places *with Bloodshot Books.*

POTEEN AND STOUT

By Stephen McQuiggan

Barry Bey hadn't seen Del Sparrow in years; they were on opposite shifts and, both being pathologically averse to overtime, their paths never crossed. That suited Barry just fine; he had hated Del on sight, long before the bad luck had kicked in, and found it hard to even pretend civility. They were like poteen and stout, that's what Barry's dad would have said (and Mr. Bey knew something about liquor); they just couldn't mix without a sickening conclusion.

For one thing, Del had a fat tongue. By the time his words had traversed that obstacle, they sounded annoyingly lethargic from their journey. The laziness of their delivery only served to highlight the misery of their content, a content Del was only too eager to share; he was one of those people who seemed to delight in relating his own embarrassing inadequacies.

Barry had almost forgotten him, though tales of him would drift back occasionally, causing him to shiver as he recalled Del's ratty eyes and the way he liked to punctuate every sentence with a wet hawking spit. Now Del was back, returning to Barry's shift, as part of some incomprehensible shakeup that Jones Bros, Ltd. liked to spring on their beleaguered employees every few months.

The thought of it was enough to bring Barry out in hives. Bad things happened whenever Del was around; bad things that mirrored the bad shit going on in Del's life. He would have been insufferable for his self-pitying monologues alone, but Barry was now convinced that by talking so openly about his problems, Del was actually passing them on.

There were too many coincidences and Barry didn't really believe in coincidences.

The supervisors put him on the machine right next to Barry's, an old piecemeal contraption (that belonged in a museum) which pumped out a fifth of what the others did, and you could believe that suited Del just fine. If Del had managed to wangle his way onto a clockwork antique to skive away the shift on, however, it seemed his bad luck had cranked up production and went into overdrive.

Over the roar and hum of the machines, Barry was treated to the *sturm und drang* of his colleague's misfortunes for twelve hours a day. He returned home each night exhausted; not from manual labor, but from the constant negativity and woe that Del assailed him with. When he showered before retiring to bed, although the grease and grime had been soaped off, Barry was sure a thin skin of despair still cloaked him: the kind of durable misery that could never be scrubbed off.

After a few weeks, he was convinced he could feel that misery surging thickly through his veins, and that the constant pitfalls that Del relished relating echoed mournfully in his own life. Barry began to listen to Del's moaning with a kind of superstitious dread, fearful that every word from that slack-mouth sibyl would soon be mirrored in his own experience.

One day Del was over an hour late. Just as Barry was beginning to think he wouldn't show and that he was about to have a stress-free day, Del turned up like the proverbial bad penny; chewing on his bottom lip, which had swollen up like a bicycle tube, and peering out at the world through two bulging and battered plum-colored eyes.

Barry could hardly keep from cheering. "What the hell?" he asked, trying to sound concerned.

"I got jumped by two guys on the way here," said Del, his voice even lazier now it had the extra obstacle of his lip. "They took my watch, my wallet ..." he trailed off as Barry made a mental note to shake the hand of the first guy offering to sell him some cheap watch down the pub.

By the halfway point of the shift, Barry had heard Del relay the story so often, had heard the number of attackers swell in ranks from the initial duo to a barbarian horde, that any joy he had felt in Del's suffering faded. His other co-workers seemed genuinely concerned, as if they actually *liked* him. Barry would not have been surprised to learn that Del had afflicted the injuries on himself just to get a pity fix. He clocked out ten minutes early in disgust, to get clear of the locker room before Del had one final captive audience.

He stopped at the corner store on the way home to pick up a pizza and, though he knew it would play havoc with his backwash, some chocolate milk. He was busy counting out his change when he walked, head down, into something solid. That something solid revealed itself to be a burly youth flanked by two gimlet-eyed, gum popping girls who bared their teeth and hissed wine-heavy breath in his direction.

"Sorry," said Barry, trying to maneuver around the colossal teenager.

"Hit him, Slinky!" spat one of the drunken girls, "he ain't got no respect."

"Yeah," echoed her inebriated clone, "deck the fucking creep!"

Barry smiled, put up a hand in a placatory manner and, just as he was about to explain his *total* lack of respect for their kind, and what a wholly inappropriate nickname Slinky was for such a humungous mound of shit, he let out a scream instead as the giant kraken of an adolescent crushed his fingers down into a tiny ball of exquisite pain and began punching him repeatedly, enthusiastically, in the face, pausing each time like he was indulging in a game of Whack-a-Mole.

Barry collapsed in a heap by his car. The behemoth boy stooped to pick up the coins that spilled from his mangled hand, then deftly relieved him of his wristwatch. That was the moment when the seed took root: the idea that Del was sharing his bad luck with him. That seed grew into an ugly billowing weed over the next week when Del came to him, tears in his bulbous eyes, lamenting the death of his beloved dog.

When Barry made it home, wincing as he put the key in the door due to his still-tender ribs, and saw his wife's sunken eyes, he knew instinctively that his own pet pooch had been shoved unceremoniously off this mortal coil. He took the rest of the week off work, not to mourn the mutt *per se*, but more to avoid Del.

He was fast cultivating a phobia of being anywhere in the vicinity of the Typhoid Mary of Tragedy; he would break into a sweat just thinking about what Del would tell him next, and subsequently unleash into his own life. He heard Del's thick voice in his head, in the wee small hours, constantly reciting a litany of disasters.

Barry became a tearful wreck. It frightened his wife, Julie, to see him like this, but he could not explain to her what was wrong because vocalizing it made him sound like a lunatic. He shunned his daughter lest he scared her too. He sheathed his fears in sorrow for the dog until

Julie got angry, told him to snap out of it, and get back to work; there were bills to pay, after all.

That first Monday back was an armistice of sorts—Del was off sick and Barry breathed easy until, as the evening wore on, he began to wonder exactly what was wrong with Del and if he were due to contract whatever ailed him, too. He was relieved to see Del, all smiles and leers, the following day, looking as hale and healthy (and eminently punchable) as he ever had. Barry managed to avoid him until lunchtime; Del caught and trapped him in the canteen queue.

"The wife's kicked me out," he whispered to Barry, as they shuffled their trays past the salad and toward the curry; he was still smiling, but his protruding lizard eyes looked haunted. Barry hoped he had misheard him. Suddenly, he did not feel hungry, not one little bit.

"Came home to find all my gear in a few plastic bags, heaped up on the doorstep for any passing fucker to steal," Del sighed, using his fingers to help himself to the last of the wizened sausages. "I'm staying at a mate's until I get myself sorted." He sucked on one the sausages thoughtfully. "Eighteen years, Barry, all gone in a flash."

Barry felt like crying. He and Julie had been together eighteen years, too. It was nonsense to think that she would ever dump him, that just because Del Sparrow had split with his wife. Barry laughed at the absurdity of the notion. He had been getting on so well with Julie. They were more in love than ever, and their beautiful daughter, Tabitha, only further strengthened the bond between them.

He was glad this had happened, for it would prove once and for all that bad luck was not contagious, he told himself. Yet, as the shift wore on, fears and doubts began to gnaw on him, like Del's yellow stumps on a sausage, until he could bear it no more. He went to his line manager, told him he had a migraine (not even a lie at this stage) and hurried home early to be with his wife.

He found her on the sofa with her skirt around her thighs and their neighbor between her legs. "I'm glad you caught us," she said defiantly. "I've been looking for a way to tell you for months. I was going to break it you last week, but then with the dog dying ..."

Barry fled to his sister's and drank himself into a stupor on her couch. Thank God Tabitha had been at school and hadn't witnessed the whole shameful, sordid scene. The thought of his daughter broke his heart, and simultaneously hardened the fractured pieces into razor sharp shards. Del had a daughter too; what if Del were to rock into work one day and tell him something awful had happened to his little girl, and then a phone call came through to tell him that Tabitha had—

"No!" he screamed, causing his sister, already frightened by his nonsensical ramblings, to spill her tea and burst into tears.

He spent the next day formulating a plan that made him cackle maniacally as it took shape. As night fell, much to his sister's relief, he took his hysterical laughter out to the car and drove off into the darkness. The Baby Bottle Bar was his destination: a rundown den in the worst part of town, a pub for the binge-drinking connoisseur.

He parked at the corner and walked the rest of the way, entering the bar through a badly scuffed, worm-eaten door. He took a seat by a burbling poker machine whose light provided the only illumination for several regulars drooling in their pints. Then he waited, checking his watch every thirty seconds or so.

Del drank here every night. Barry had heard him boast of it often enough, usually preparatory to some horror story of vomit and violence. No wonder Del's wife had kicked him out. Barry thought of his own wife, of his daughter, and checked his watch again. He couldn't back out now; he *had* to do this. Just as his resolve was weakening, Del staggered in, pinballing off several tables before reaching the bar.

The barman greeted Del like a revered guest (*and why not*, thought Barry, *he probably keeps the place afloat*), holding out his hand and asking, "Wanna leave your keys tonight, Mr. Sparrow?"

"No need," slurred Del, "damn car won't start. Like everything else in my life, it's fucked."

Barry noticed the barman pouring Del a pint of stout and his father's words, about how poteen and stout never mixed, came back to him so clear it was as if his old man was whispering in his ear. Del's tipple was a sign from on high, as if God was overriding Fortune and telling him his plan was justified.

Barry slunk quietly out and made his way back to his own car. He flipped the keys in the ignition and it started the first time. No doubt it too would not start in a few hours, but that would be the last piece of misfortune that Del would ever inflict upon him. Barry smiled as he slouched down in his seat to wait; yes, soon he would be rid of Del's curse once and for all. Tabitha would be safe and, hell, he might even be able to patch things up with Julie (the affair was Del's fault, not Julie's choosing). A knackered engine was a small price to pay for peace of mind.

The wait was not long, for there were three bars on this street alone and Del was keen to sample all their wares. Barry gunned the accelerator. The car growled, and Barry thought of his dear departed little dog and loosed the handbrake. When Del staggered across the empty road, the streetlights turning his eyes into bulging sodium pools, Barry sped off, aiming the car straight down the meat of his tormentor.

He ploughed into him as fast as the old clanking motor would allow; the windshield spider-webbed as Del's skull smashed against it, pulping like an overripe grapefruit, and he swore he could see that fat tongue fly free as Del's nicotine stained stumps clamped down on it in agony.

Barry brought the car to a screeching skid of a stop, peering at Del's mangled body through his rear-view mirror. He was done for, no doubt about it; "Del as a dodo," laughed Barry, a little too highly, speeding off in a cloud of diesel fumes.

He roared through the deserted streets, blasting his horn as the wipers smeared Del's blood over the cracks in the glass. He couldn't stop laughing. He felt so light he thought he might just float out the sunroof and sail up to the torchlight moon on the slightest breeze. He was still laughing as the car spluttered and squealed and ground to a clanking halt on a dark bend on the outskirts of town. His laughter stalled, too.

Ah, well, Barry sighed to himself, *enjoy your final petty victory, Mr. Sparrow. I hope you're already in Hell and reveling in the company.* He was about to get out of the car when a thundering rumble filled his ears. He covered his eyes as headlights lit up the road before him like a stage set. Through his fingers, he could see the grill of a huge juggernaut coming 'round the bend, bearing down upon him like divine justice.

They say that in your final moments your life flashes before you, but all that came to Barry were images of his workmate's splattered face. Barry had time to muse, "I never really thought this through properly," before he shared fates with Del one last time.

Stephen McQuiggan was the original author of the Bible; he vowed never to write again after the publishers removed the dinosaurs and the spectacular alien abduction ending from the final edit. His other, lesser known, novels are A Pig's View of Heaven *and* Trip a Dwarf.

A NEW SOURCE OF ENERGY

By Rosalind Barden

"It's a new source of energy. It will alter the world as we know it. Cheap, boundless," the young man said to his traveling companion on the commuter train.

The men were standing near Tabitha. She carefully kept her face disinterested, looking down. With furtive eye darts, she peeked at what manner of people the speakers were. She liked to eavesdrop. It made her daily ride to work on the train more interesting as it zoomed through its dark tunnel.

The other man was older, but not by much. He and the talking man dressed in the same casual, but studied fashion favored by confident young things aiming to rouse the world, at least ones Tabitha noticed on the train. This listening man rubbed his shadow of blond beard and nodded thoughtfully, interested.

Encouraged by the nod, the talker plowed on. "This has been crowdsourced up the wazoo. People are excited. People are buzzing." The talker carried a briefcase that looked heavy by the way he leaned his trim form to favor the side he held it from. He hefted it slightly, nodded his chin toward it, and raised his eyebrows. "It's compact, too. Fits seamlessly with the new minimalist lifestyle that I—like you—value."

The listener mirrored the talker's raised eyebrows. The talker rewarded him with a quote from a trendy online lecturer: "Life is minimum, but living is maximum. Minimize the maximums, and you will maximize the minimums." The listener threw back his head, slightly, and laughed, softly, in a mutually understanding way.

The train slowed to a jerking stop and the doors popped open. As the talker chattered more about buzz, new lifestyles, minimums and maximums, he and his listener poured out with a crowd of sleepy commuters.

It wasn't Tabitha's usual stop, but she hated to miss out on what was shaping up to be an interesting conversation. She wasn't sure, but she had a feeling it could be a close runner-up to last year's intense, whispered discussion at the back of the train between two apparent co-workers about whether their boss was in fact some sort of shaved gorilla: "The proof being that hat. Have you ever seen it off? No. Hides that pointed head all gorillas have. Says so on the nature shows. Gorillas have pointed heads. That's science."

Deciding she'd tell her work that the train broke down (which it did from time to time and could again any minute, so her excuse might not be completely untrue), Tabitha joined the tide flowing out the train.

She had to rush to catch up to the fit and fast young men as they strode through the underground train station and stepped up the escalators, as if they were stairs, to the world above. She hadn't quite reached them when they strode up the final escalator rising to the busy downtown sidewalk, but she saw their moving heads silhouetted by the morning light. Their voices carried down the escalator: "And the metrics? You wanna know about the metrics, you say?" the talker asked rhetorically. "Oh, man, they are smiley face metrics—no joke. Smiley face!"

The listener made an impressed, yummy-humming sort of sound as they arrived at the sidewalk. Then he suddenly stopped, making the talker stop too, oblivious they were blocking where the escalator disgorged its passengers. When the escalator deposited Tabitha onto the sidewalk, she had to do some fancy footwork to keep from slamming into them.

They didn't move, so she couldn't move lest she risk missing their conversation that she was missing work to follow. So, Tabitha stayed close, adding to the escalator blockade. In hopes of looking less suspicious, she rustled into her bag, like she might have forgotten something important and had to stop to find it on the spot.

More commuters coming off the escalator made rude remarks as they dodged the obstacle of Tabitha and the men. Tabitha sustained an angry elbow jab to the back. Her listening hobby had its risks sometimes. The men didn't notice the rushing tide of annoyed people and continued their conversation.

"I'm excited. I won't lie to you about that," the listener said in a cool, deep voice. "But, wow, that's a hefty share you're asking us to chip in."

"I get it. I feel you. We're on the same zone about this."

The listener made a sigh that sounded vaguely impatient. "Umm. But there is so much we don't know about this project. The name, ZACK—what does that even stand for?"

The talker bowed his face and said intensely, "There's a personal, deeply personal story about that." Then, brightening, "Hey, there's that indie coffee startup I've told you about, The Minimal Bean.' Only been open since last week, but already, everyone asks, 'How could we have survived all this time without The Minimal Bean?' What say I tell you about ZACK and everything else inside?"

The listener stared inwardly with fondness at the thought of this happening establishment, and said, "Yeah, great idea."

Then they were on the move again, apparently to the coffee shop. Tabitha followed, keeping a cautious distance behind.

Turning off the crowded sidewalk, they reached the coffee shop of the moment, hidden down a once seedy alley. Its black metal and glass exterior was blank with no identifying signage. A maze of streetscape planters filled with cacti and left shoes made getting to the cafe door challenging. A sign announced the planters were the work of artist Half-WhyNot.

Tabitha waited a tense 60 seconds after the two slipped through the planter maze and into the coffee shop before following. Once her eyes adjusted to the dim interior, she saw the men were involved in placing their orders at the counter: black pepper and turmeric lavender lattes, plus organic, locally sourced berry and basil buns with a cinnamon non-glaze glaze. Or at least that's the best she could determine, because the men spoke in broken French-Spanish-English to the grim coffee artistes who spoke only what sounded possibly like French.

She watched enviously as the artistes, glowering and huffing with annoyance, prepared and presented the fancy coffee drinks and hot, cinnamony buns to the men. Tabitha was tempted, oh so tempted to order something, but by the posted numbers she assumed were the prices, she'd spend her train ride home money. She didn't speak French, either. So, she ordered nothing and found a shadowy little table near where the men sat. She hoped the coffee artistes were too busy staring at one another with distain to notice.

As the men perched on hard, three-legged metal stools that served as the cafe's chairs, the talker explained the high risk suffered in harnessing the new energy source. His voice breaking, the talker said, "Someone died in the process. Someone close to me. Zack. We named the energy source in his honor. We all knew the danger, and sadly for Zack, he drew the short straw."

The listener nodded but raised one eyebrow that seemed to say, How sad, but do I really care?

Sensing the disinterest, the talker's voice became upbeat again. "This energy, we believe, does not function in isolation, but in fact tends to move in clusters. So now that we have one unit, we are confident the rest of the 'tribe,' as it were, will follow. Then, with all units harnessed, wow." He smiled and spread his hands expansively.

"But these 'units,' what are we talking about?" the listener asked, squinting at the earnest talker.

"Yes—what? I mean, it is totally innovative, never been unleashed or, rather, leashed in this way before. Hard core maximizing the minimum!"

"Are we talking quantum physics? Nanoparticles? Fusion? What, exactly?"

"It could involve quantum physics. That's a possibility. There's a lot we don't know about how the mechanism manifests, exactly. But manifest it does."

A slight frown darkened the listener's face. "Perhaps this technology is too new. It doesn't sound like it's quite ready, and may be too far from a practical launch. You understand that increases our risk factors. Even without our team crunching the probability cost ratios, I can say off the top of my head that the exposure numbers must be substantial. I'm not seeing that it will pencil out for us, to put it plainly."

The talker held out his fingers, as if to put a stop to this penciling-ratio talk. "I hear you, totally, and I don't mean to put a stop to your penciling-ratio talk, but this is not exactly a 'technology' we're dealing with here. ZACK is a tried and true, existing, traditional, if you will, type of maximizing resource."

The listener's frown deepened, and his head moved back as if sensing something odious. "Do you mean coal? I don't know that we could be on board ..."

"No, no, no," and the talker smiled in a dismissive way as if this was the silliest thing he'd heard all week. The listener's face did not smile back, remained guarded. In response, the talker carefully toned down the amusement in his voice and explained, "I—like you—are concerned and am on board with the concept of renewable resources—maximizing the minimums—minimizing the maximums. This resource doesn't need renewing. It is biologic."

The listener's face lost its cloud, became interested again, eyebrows shot up. "Bioscience?"

"Ah, I suppose ..."

"But gene manipulation is controversial. Here we'd need more specifics. Understand, the investors abhor negative publicity, or any publicity at all."

"No gene manipulation or splicing or dicing. None of that. No worries there."

The listener sat back, waiting.

The talker chuckled, though nervously, and added, "It's a pre-existing organism. Very rare, but positively pre-existing."

The frown came sharply back to the listener's face and his fingers pressed the table top as he half rose to leave. Tabitha, with a pang of longing, noted he'd barely sipped his steaming drink, and had taken nary a nibble from his berry- pocked bun.

"Endangered species? Out of the question!" the listener's deep voice declared. "We have policies. Our investors have donated a proportionate ratio equal to point oh oh one and one fourth the projected return fractional monetizations to save the quagga zebra. I hope you know that is a significant sacrifice to the calculated percentages—all crowdsourcing aside." He made an unhappy huffing sound, not unlike a displeased horse. "This ZACK is absolutely not who we are."

"Oh, no, no, no!" the talker reassured, a rising note of panic in his voice. He reached out his fingers again, as if willing the listener to stay. Frowning, suspicious, the listener complied. He sat back down on the metal stool, arms crossed, one leg crossed over the other, ignoring his barely touched drink and untouched bun (Tabitha noticed).

"Rare, yes, but by no means endangered. Not even close."

"So, what are we talking about? A fungus?"

"No."

"Bacteria?"

"Um, no."

71

"Bioluminescent slime."

"Not per se. No."

"Then what?" The listener did not hide his annoyance.

"Well, you see, it's, ah, you see it's ..."

"What?"

"Meaning to say, ah, well, to be blunt ..."

"Well?"

The talker responded with an inaudible whisper.

"A what? What did you say?"

Slightly louder, but still so low, Tabitha had to lean her head toward their table to hear: "A leprechaun. It's a leprechaun."

"Oh, man, I don't think so. Ridiculous." Shaking his head angrily, the listener started to get up from his stool.

The talker held the other man's arm lightly. "Hold a moment. Just a moment. I'll show you. Please." The listener kept angrily shaking his head, but he sat back down on the stool.

The talker cracked the briefcase open a sliver. Tabitha saw what looked like an angry wrinkled face, yellowed with age, glaring out.

"Oh, my God! Is that, is that really?" from the listener. He put his hand close, and she saw the creature opening its mouth filled with dozens of sharp teeth points. The man held his hand at bay, yet kept leaning forward, tipping his cafe stool so it stood on only one leg.

Relieved at the reaction, the talker resumed his spiel enthusiastically. "Not only do they generate unlimited energy—somehow—and we haven't figured out how yet—they make money appear. It's crazy but it's a win-win-win situation for you and your investors." The talker smiled with satisfaction, sensing the pitch went home. "Like I said, we think they like to cluster. So, imagine what will happen when we have all of them. Truly, the world will be ours."

The listener, all high-minded thoughts of minimizing maximums gone from his face, was awestruck with naked greed.

Sometimes Tabitha had a mischievous streak. Maybe it was the fancy coffee she couldn't afford, maybe it was all this talk of hip things owning the world, but she moved her foot to nudge the listener's tipping stool, nudge it just so the listener's hand moved forward within snapping range.

The creature lunged, bit. The listener screamed, thrashed his arm about, knocking over the briefcase. In a flash of red hair, the thing was out and whirled about other patrons, making them join in screaming, until it flashed out the door.

The listener hurried out too, along with half the cafe.

The artistes stomped to the talker, who was sobbing in disbelief at his now empty briefcase. All French forgotten, a man who appeared to be the head artiste declared, "You can't take no damned crazy cats into this establishment. We have signs posted!" and he jabbed his thumb to point at a "*La Servico eu La Animalas Le Only-la*" sign. "You get yourself outta here. Now!"

"But you don't understand! Zack. Oh, poor, poor Zack. I switched the short straw and for nothing. It's all lost."

But the artistes loomed over him until he and his tears slunk out the door with the empty briefcase.

Though the cafe's windows, Tabitha thought she spotted the wizened face staring from the shadows of the artfully arranged streetscape planters. She didn't know why, but she smiled and gave it a thumbs up. In an instant, the red hair darted deep into the maze of planters and she couldn't see it anymore.

That was the most interesting eavesdropping experience she'd ever had. But all amusing things must end sometime. Time to head to work. Sigh.

As she stepped out the door, she stepped on top of a brand new $20 bill. No, not one. There were two more twenties neatly tucked under it. How about that? People do drop money. Maybe it was her lucky day. Or maybe a little thank you from the leprechaun?

She headed back into the cafe. This time, because the artistes hadn't yet reverted to French, she brought herself a fancy coffee (biggest size available), and a hot steaming breakfast bun (to take back to work). Or maybe not. She decided her work could wait a bit longer. She returned to her seat in the cafe and took her time savoring her hot drink and the tasty bun.

This is Rosalind Barden's fifth story in the Strangely Funny *series. Mystery and Horror, LLC has also included her stories in their anthologies* History and Mystery, Oh My! *(FAPA President's Book Award Silver Medalist), and* Mardi Gras Murder.

Sparky Of Bunker Hill *and* The Cold Kid Case *is her humorous Young Adult mystery novel set in Depression-era Los Angeles. Dozens more of her short stories have appeared in print anthologies and webzines, including the U.K.'s acclaimed* Whispers of Wickedness.

Ellen Datlow selected her short story "Lion Friend" as a Best Horror of the Year *Honorable Mention after it appeared in* CERN Zoo, *a British Fantasy*

Society nominee for best anthology, part of DF Lewis' award winning Nemonymous anthology series.

TV Monster *is her print children's book that she wrote and illustrated. Her satirical novel* American Witch *is available as an e-book. In addition, her scripts, novel manuscripts and short fiction have placed in numerous competitions, including the Writers Digest Screenplay Competition and the Shriekfast Film Festival. She lives in Los Angeles, California. Discover more at:*

RosalindBarden.com

SPONGEWORTHY

By Stacey Longo

"Your Nana Millie's dead," Erika's mother Judith announced. "And she left everything to *you*."

Her mother's inflection on that last word made clear the woman found this preposterous and unexplainable, as if Nana had left her possessions to a houseplant, or a turd in the toilet.

"What? How'd it happen? I just saw her, like, two weeks ago." *Okay, maybe it was two months*, Erika thought with a guilty cringe. "She looked fine."

"It looks like she mixed up her medication," Judith said. "Took too much of something. She was sixty-nine, for goodness sake. People start losing it at that age."

This from the woman who still takes Zantac instead of Zyrtec when her allergies act up, and swears the heartburn medication is the best antihistamine on the market. But Erika let the remark pass. After all, her mom had just lost *her* mom …

"Anyway, now that you're independently wealthy, can I borrow sixty bucks? I need a manicure before the funeral."

So much for grief.

The weeks that followed were overwhelming and absurd. They buried Nana, got the official death certificate listing hemorrhagic stroke due to an overdose of blood thinner, and they learned the horrifying truth: Nana had probably been dead for close to a week before she'd been found, collapsed on the kitchen floor, Scotch-Brite sponge clutched in a death grip. Her dinner dishes were still in the sink, a testament to her last meal of tuna noodle casserole.

Judith had met with a lawyer, and though Erika suspected it was to see if her mother could contest the will, the nice probate attorney who'd handled Nana's affairs assured them both the paperwork was ironclad. Erika debated giving her mother half the estate anyway; Judith had invested in a pool installation startup company not long ago, and the owner had promptly disappeared with Judith's substantial savings.

But the attorney advised against it: "Don't make any major decisions yet. Grief does funny things to the mind, and you might regret it later."

The last step was figuring out what to do with the house.

"I'll just move in," Erika said, though that final image of Nana decomposing in the kitchen for a week was hard to shake. But Erika had graduated college that past May, spent the summer working as a bartender on Martha's Vineyard, and was ready to try the *being a grownup* thing. Plus, it sure beat living with Judith, which was her only other choice now that Labor Day had passed on the Vineyard and tourist season was over. The probate lawyer gave her the key, she packed, and voila: here she was, climbing the three steps to Nana's side door, the proud new owner of an early 1950s ranch house.

Erika took a deep breath and stepped inside.

The hallway with Nana Millie's bookshelves looked disheveled. Erika frowned, then walked farther in, turning the corner to peek into Nana's bedroom. Some of the dresser drawers weren't quite shut, and the closet door was wide open—something Nana never did. Erika had asked her once about this fastidious habit of always keeping the closet shut. "Afraid of the boogey man?" she'd joked.

"Mice in the attic." Nana had glanced up. "Easiest way down from there is through the door in my closet ceiling, and I don't need rodents running around the bedroom."

Someone had been through Nana's things. Erika's heart sank. *Judith.*

Erika loved her mother, but didn't like her very much. Judith was still furious that Erika had inherited everything in Nana's estate, save for a $20,000 CD gifted to Judith, which was a pittance compared to the bank account and annuity—and the house. Though small, it was located in a nice neighborhood in an upscale town. Erika had no doubt that her mother had used the spare key to rifle through Nana's belongings, probably looking for tucked-away bills, pawnable jewelry, and anything else that might be of value.

Erika inspected the top of Nana's dresser. There were rings in the dust where Nana's crystal perfume bottles had sat for years. She sighed.

I have enough, she told herself. *Mom will never change, and really, it's not hurting me. It's more sad than anything.*

She slowly explored the rest of place, poking her head in Nana's spare room, noting the absence of the Hummel statues Nana kept displayed on a small table in the corner. "Sure, the woman can't remember the difference between Benadryl and Beano, but when it comes to a name that might have value as a collectible, damned if she doesn't have the memory of an elephant," she muttered.

A moment later, she caught a whiff of vanilla, a scent reminiscent of the madeleine cookies she and her grandmother baked together when Erika was young. She took it as a sign of Nana's approval, and smiled.

Erika had been avoiding the room where Nana died, but the vanilla served to remind her of happier times in the little kitchen. She straightened her shoulders and headed in.

The funeral director had been kind enough to discreetly hand her a business card after Nana's closed-casket funeral. *AFTERMATH: UNATTENDED DEATH CLEANUP*, it read, and tears had pricked Erika's eyes in gratitude. They'd done an amazing job. The vinyl flooring hadn't looked so shiny in years; the counters were spotless. It looked like they'd even laundered the curtains. The sink was polished, with a bright new sponge patterned with fat pastel flowers waiting on the rim. *I gotta mail them a bonus*, she decided.

Her eyes settled on Nana's prescription bottles, sitting next to a container with each day marked in a different color. The days were subsequently split into squares labeled *Morning, Noon,* and *Bedtime.* Unlike the silverware drawer, these looked untouched. Erika picked up a bottle, read the label, and raised an eyebrow. Oxycodone. Even she knew it had to have some street value. "Of course," Erika mused. "Mom probably thinks it's for acne. Bet she didn't even touch the prescriptions."

A sudden stench assaulted her nose hard enough to make her gag. It wasn't death—she'd been sent up to Nana's attic a time or two to clean up a dead mouse over the years—but something sour and rancid, like rotting lemons soaked in cat urine. She swallowed down the rising bile and looked around for the source. The garbage can? She flipped the lid, but there was nothing inside, save a fresh new liner. Next up was the refrigerator. That too was empty.

She sniffed, coughed, and followed the scent to the kitchen sink. Nana didn't have a garbage disposal, so it wasn't coming from there. The sheen of polished steel winked, mocking her.

The sponge.

Erika picked it up, and in one gut-puckering sniff, found the source. Between forefinger and thumb, she walked it out the door, tossing it on the lawn. *Oh, God. What if that's the sponge Nana was holding when … they wouldn't* leave *that, would they?*

There was no other plausible explanation. *So much for that bonus.*

Her stomach churned at the thought of returning to the kitchen. She grabbed her keys and headed out for Chinese and a six-pack instead.

The sponge was back in its spot the next morning.

Erika blinked at it. She'd wound up drinking the full six-pack before passing out on the living room couch. *Was I so hammered I went outside and retrieved it?* She remembered crying a bit, feeling sorry for herself being so utterly alone in Nana's house. And hadn't she had a weepy jag thinking about all the stuff her mother had stolen? It wasn't the value; there was one Hummel of a little girl in an apron, stirring a mixing bowl full of batter, that Nana Millie had always said looked just like Erika whipping up a batch of madeleines. It was a sentimental thing.

Could she have gone outside, thinking the sponge was another connection to Nana she just couldn't part with?

She eyed it warily as she rummaged through the cabinets for coffee filters and Maxwell House. Being outside seemed to have cut down the stench, though, and for that she said a silent prayer.

As the coffee pot perked to life, she opened the fridge, then shut it again with a groan. "Don't suppose you have any powdered creamer hiding around here, do you, Nana?"

A faint whiff of vanilla.

Mom always says I have an overactive imagination. But still—she opened the cabinet where she'd found the filters and started pulling things out. And there, tucked in the back: a plastic container of non-dairy, powdered creamer. "Thanks, Nana."

The scent grew stronger. And damned if it wasn't coming from the sponge.

Goose pimples tracked up Erika's arms. She knew this was crazy—had scoffed at campfire ghost stories, and prided herself on never once watching a single episode of those stupid paranormal reality shows, but oh, she missed her grandmother so much, and …

She picked up the sponge: "Nana?"

This is stupid, I must look like an idiot—and the tiny kitchen filled with the rich scent of butter and vanilla. If she closed her eyes, she'd swear a batch of the sponge-cake cookies was baking in the oven right then and there. Erika's vision blurred with tears and she held onto the little scrubber with two hands, babbling. "I miss you so much! I'm so sorry I didn't visit more—I meant to, but being out on the Vineyard, it was so—I'm sorry, that's terrible. I should've made time." The heady fragrance changed slightly, a hint of lemon now in the mix, and for Erika, it was as comforting as her nana's embrace. "I love you," she finished with a squeak. The aroma was a buttery kiss: *I love you, too.*

Erika was giddy with the thrill of her grandmother's presence, and talked to the house all morning. "I'm sorry I got drunk last night," she offered as she wiped water rings off the living room table. She paused mid-wipe. *What do I do if I want to have a guy over? Nana doesn't need to see that.* "Uh, but I *am* an adult now," she added, but thought she could detect a tinge of sour lemon in the air. *Guess we'll just have to go to his place*, she decided.

She retreated to the kitchen for more coffee. Her eyes studied the cabinets, then the floor. Her grandmother had died in this room. Amiable ghostly presence or not, the thought was still creepy. Erika cleared her throat. "Nana?" she whispered. "I'm sorry it took so long for the neighbors to find you."

Light vanilla. *It's okay.*

"It should've been me. Or Mom."

The stench of rotting lemons and urine rose so quickly Erika spat out her mouthful of coffee. With a sob, she fled from the house.

It wasn't okay. *Nana's mad*, Erika thought glumly, heart breaking, because there was nothing she could do to change the past now.

She killed a few hours at the grocery store, then headed back home. The only scent greeting her came from the Pledge used to wipe down the table earlier; still, her hands trembled unloading groceries in the kitchen. "Sorry," she whispered when she was done, and the tang of vanilla teased the corners of her mouth up into a smile.

Relentless banging on the door woke Erika. She was still sleeping on the couch—she wasn't ready just yet to move into Nana's bedroom—and she shuffled past the bookcases with a yawn to find her mother's face peeking through the window of the door.

"What's up?" Erika asked, letting her in.

"Did you change the locks?" Her mother held up a key accusingly.

"I think the attorney said he'd hired a guy," Erika mumbled, though she'd done it herself yesterday afternoon to prevent any further looting by the woman standing before her. "Is something up?"

"I wanted to see how you're settling in," Judith said, flip-flops slapping as she breezed past her daughter. "Thought we might do breakfast."

"Uh ... sure?" It was wholly unlike her mother to take her out for a meal. "You feeling okay?"

"Perfectly fine, dear," Judith said. "Except don't look at my feet. I think I picked up athlete's foot at the gym. I've been soaking them in Anbesol for the past three days, but it's not working."

"You mean Lamisil, Ma?"

"Don't be silly. Got any coffee?"

Judith strolled into the kitchen, then stopped short as if she'd hit a brick wall. "Jesus H. Christ! Have you been scouring a septic tank in here?" She spun and ran, holding her throat like a choking victim. "Rain check—you can buy me breakfast tomorrow morning! And for the love of all things holy, clean *up* in here!"

Erika put a hand over her nose, watching her mother's retreat. She took a few tentative steps into the kitchen. "Is it Mom? Why? I mean, I know she's self-absorbed and greedy, and I'm still pissed about the Hummel."

Rotting lemon.

"Is it the Hummel?"

Rotting lemon.

"I don't know if that's a yes or a no," Erika admitted, then coughed. "Think you can clear out the raw sewage smell while we try to figure out a system?"

After opening some windows, Erika sat down with pad and paper. The first hint of vanilla had been when she'd been griping about Mom's looting. Erika'd taken it as a sign of Nana's approval. But of the theft or the criticism?

More vanilla when she'd asked about creamer. And Nana had dialed it up to eleven when Erika had told her how much she'd missed her. "I think we should go with vanilla for yes," she muttered, then glanced at the sponge. "Sound good?"

The sponge responded with a wisp of warm cookies.

The eye-watering stench had been when Erika was looking at the prescription bottles. Then when she'd apologized for not finding her grandmother's body. And the septic tank—that was one hundred percent because Judith had showed up. "Okay. And stinky means no. Can we keep it to rotting lemon, though?"

You bet, the Nana sponge said in its own distinctive way.

Erika looked at her list of spiritual smells again, trying to find the connection. The theft. The prescription pills. The apology.

Wait: she'd apologized because it should've been her *or Mom* who'd discovered the body. "So, it's definitely Mom you're upset with?" Erika asked.

Vanilla.

"But *why* is the question, and I'm not sure how we get to that," she muttered. "Is it because she's a bitch?"

At first there was no change in the air, then lemon, both sweet and spoiling. "What the hell does that mean? Yes *and* no?"

Yes.

Cloe studied the list again. The pills. The theft. A chill tightened her chest. "Is—is Mom doing drugs?"

No, came the scented reply.

She chuckled. "I guess that *is* ridiculous, now that I hear it out loud. Did you hear her this morning? She's putting toothache gel on her toes! Can you imagine? The woman can't tell an aspirin from an enema."

Rotting lemon filled the kitchen all at once, then escalated to cat-urine levels, then sewage.

No, no, NO!

Erika felt like she was choking on her own tongue. "Stop! Okay—please!" She dashed outside, clearing her lungs with several deep breaths. *What the hell, Nana?*

She turned the reaction over in her mind, mentally looking for a button that would unlock the answer. *It's Mom and the pills.* But what?

She needed to look at those prescription bottles, figure out exactly what Nana was taking.

Erika stood in the kitchen. There was still a hint of rot around

81

the edges, but when she started picking up bottles and reading the labels, she asked offhandedly, "Am I getting warmer?"

Sweet tendrils confirmed her instincts.

Oxycodone Hydrochloride, 5 mg. Take as needed for pain. She shook the bottle; it was quite full. *At least Nana wasn't in pain that often.* She felt a stab of guilt—Erika had no idea what pain Nana had been in that she'd need anything stronger than Tylenol, and that was on her, for not calling as often as she should.

Lipitor, 10 mg. Take once daily, in the morning. Yes, that made sense. Nana had been pretty ticked off that her cholesterol numbers had come in over 250 at her last physical.

Apixaban, 10 mg. Take one before breakfast and one before dinner. "Apixie-what?" she muttered. She was stricken with the reek of skunk so strong that it wouldn't have surprised her if one had sprayed the sink when she wasn't looking. "Okay! Was that a *no* or a *bingo*?"

A whiff of butter. "Yes? This medication has something to do with Mom?"

Vanilla.

Erika pulled out her iPhone and Googled the drug. Brand name Eliquis, it was for treating blood clots. Nana had been hospitalized with clots in her legs this past spring.

Erika's fingertips went numb, and the bottle nearly slipped from her hands. "This was the drug that killed you."

Yes and no.

"It was a different drug?"

No.

Erika glanced at the pill organizer and its tidy little squares. She opened each day. Monday morning, evening, and Tuesday morning were empty. Tuesday night still held one tiny white pill. Which was odd, because she was supposed to take it before dinner, but Erika could still see the probate attorney's smile when he'd told her it looked like Nana'd eaten tuna noodle for dinner. It had been one of Nana's favorites.

One of Judith's, too, now that Erika thought about it.

"Oh, no. Are you saying Mom ... she gave you the overdose?"

A bakery full of sugary vanilla clouds filled the room, so sickeningly sweet Erika fell to her knees. "But how? She can't even— she's numbing her toes, for chrissake!" A darker thought crossed her mind: *which would make the perfect alibi. The woman's constantly screwing up drug names ... but if it's important enough to her ...*

Her mother was greedy. And cold. And, after the pool installation fiasco, dead broke. "She did it." Erika knew it to be true even as the words rolled off her tongue.

But what to do next? Call the cops? She couldn't prove a thing, and how would she explain the spirit sponge? They'd lock her in the nuthouse, and Judith would likely be named her guardian ... giving her access to the cash that had put this all in motion in the first place.

She finally called the only person she could think of that might be kind enough to listen to her. And when the probate lawyer heard her story, he patiently agreed to come over and see this miracle sponge for himself.

Two skunk sprayings and three batches of baking madeleines later, Holland Powers was convinced. This kid had a ghost on her hands, and her carnivorous mother likely did it.

"Can she" —he glanced at the sponge— "uh, can you ... what I mean is, how can we use this to our advantage? We have no proof. But if we could maybe catch her in a lie, or somehow prove she knew ..." he turned to Erika. "Like, for example, I can't stand the smell of onions. Gets me queasy every time. Your mom got anything like that?"

A sly grin slowly spread across Erika's face. "White Diamonds perfume. Mom says it smells like old lady. Gives her a headache every time."

One puff from the sponge confirmed the trap was set.

"Sure you don't want any coffee?" Erika asked over her shoulder as she unlocked the door. Over breakfast, Judith had asked her daughter for money. No surprise there; if Judith was capable of murdering her own mother, then certainly she'd have no qualms about leeching off her daughter. It worked out perfectly, though: Erika protested at first at the $10,000 request, but when Judith reminded her Nana had left her $109,260.72 in savings—*sure, when it's important, she can remember to the exact penny*—Erika insisted she'd have to call the probate lawyer to meet them at the house, since he still had to authorize any payments out of the estate. And of course, Mr. Powers was happy to oblige.

"Here's the lawyer now," Judith said impatiently as a silver Camry pulled into the driveway. "At least he's punctual."

The trio exchanged greetings and went inside, sitting at the kitchen table. "Now," Powers said, pulling out a small recorder, "I need to get this all on tape, to prove it's all on the up-and-up later. Erika, you want to give your mother $10,000?" He arched an eyebrow at Judith. "The CD wasn't enough?"

Judith pulled a Kleenex from her neckline and dabbed at dry eyes. "I've fallen on hard times. You see, I was conned out of a lot of cash not long ago ... oh holy Christmas, is that White Diamonds?" A manicured hand went to her temple. "*Instant* migraine. Erika, sweetie, can you get me an enema?"

"On it, Ma." Erika moved to Nana's pills, then the sink, filling a glass with water. "Take these."

Judith popped the pills with barely a glance, chasing it with the water. The perfume dissipated, and after a moment, Erika's mother offered a weak smile. "Thanks. But that's not what I normally do for a headache." She gestured toward the seat of her pants. "What did you give me?"

Erika's lip twitched. "One of Nana's medications—they're supposed to be good for headaches, and I figure, why not use them up?"

"Which one?" Was Erika imagining it, or had her mother's face lost color?

"Apixie-something."

"Apixaban?" Judith shot from her chair, eyes darting maniacally before finding the sink. She shoved a finger down her throat, clearly no longer worried about her nail job. She retched into the sink. Surely the influx of more White Diamonds helped.

Judith wiped her mouth, then whirled toward her daughter. "You could've *killed* me, you twit! Don't you know what that stuff *is*?"

"No?" Erika blinked innocently.

"That's the same stuff that killed Nana Millie! I think I need to go to the hospital. Drive me," she said, snapping her fingers and heading to the door. "And bring the lawyer with the checkbook!"

"Are you *sure* that's what killed her?" Erika asked, trying to keep concern in her voice. "How do you know?"

Judith stopped dead in her tracks, then slowly turned to face daughter and lawyer. Her eyes narrowed to slits. "I just do," she hissed, and stormed out the door.

"So, Mom's still in jail awaiting trial." Erika took another pull at the beer in front of her. "They found her fingerprints on the pill bottle, and some interesting stuff on her computer search history, so it's not looking good." She glanced at the handsome young hipster sitting to her left. He wore a polite smile, but his eyes were glazed. Still, he was cute. "Wanna go back to your place?"

His eyes brightened. "Yeah, but it's kind of a mess. Can we go to yours?"

Erika shook her head. "Can't. I live with my nana, and she gets super mad when I bring guys home. Trust me, you do not want to be there to smell that."

Stacey Longo is the author of My Sister the Zombie, Ordinary Boy, Secret Things: Twelve Tales to Terrify, *and dozens of short stories appearing in numerous anthologies and magazines, winning awards that likely nobody save her mother cares about. She's rumored to be a former runway model. That she started this rumor herself should be of little importance. Her popular book series* Longo Looks at … *is based on her past humor columns for the* Block Island Times *and her current weekly humor blog posts found on staceylongo.com. She lives in Connecticut but doesn't recommend it.*

PAPA'S PRIMO DELI

By David Bernard

We always called the owner 'Papa'. The last five owners hadn't lasted long enough to change the name on the neon sign out front, so now the name Papa's Primo Deli Italiano was traditional. What was also traditional was that matter how good the grinders, how popular the menu, Papa failed spectacularly. Not the business—Papa himself.

The original Papa had a building constructed on a small vacant lot at the end of Mattanit Road for his sandwich shop. He always planned to concentrate more on take-out and deliveries than sit-down, so there weren't many booths inside, and even Rhode Island drivers couldn't squeeze more than five to six cars into the gravel parking in back of the building.

It seemed like a good design for what he had in mind, but he didn't last long enough to see it. He died when the gas line to his bread oven leaked and asphyxiated him. Somehow, it didn't actually explode, so Papa #2 took over as a turnkey business. He lasted two weeks. Papa #2 got locked in the basement after closing one night, the same night the main sewer line burst on Mattanit Road, directly in front of the building. Officially he drowned when the floor drains backed up, although the coroner's report never specifically said what he drowned in.

Papa #3 had a run in with fatally off-balance meat slicers, Papa #4 tried to dust an improperly installed (and surprisingly sharp) ceiling fan, and of course, poor Papa #5, who tripped carrying a hotel pan of freshly made mozzarella, knocked himself out and suffocated face first in the cheese. He trended on Facebook for weeks, which probably would have helped business, except for the whole "already dead" thing.

The new Papa, a nice Greek fellow named Papadopolous, knew about the Primo Deli's reputation. He considered it a good omen that the name of the restaurant was his high school nickname. He also knew the shop wasn't designed for a sit-down crowd and concentrated on deliveries. Not that he had a choice—by this point, just entering the store for takeout made people nervous.

I got a job delivering for Papa on evenings and weekends. The pay was lousy, and good luck getting decent tips out of the cheapskates in this town … Trust me, Kittonqua went beyond traditional New England frugality and was deep into "just plain cheap." Still, it was all I could eat and just enough cash to pay my phone bill and keep gas in the car, vital parts of high school life in a small town. And when school let out in a few weeks, lunch orders would go up, meaning more hours.

My girlfriend Patsy, on the other hand, was absolutely horrified by my job. Patsy was convinced Papa's was cursed. Everyone knew about the store's run of bad luck, but my argument was that yes, there had been five rather unpleasant deaths, but they were the owners. The delivery boy survival rate was still 100%. Patsy was unconvinced. Her parents were old hippie flower children, so she was raised amongst cleansing crystals, candle magic, and militant veganism. She was prone to believe in bad karma and evil spirits (although the vegan thing ended the moment she walked into Papa's). Unfortunately, she also didn't buy into that whole "peace, happiness, and free love" thing. Trust me, I tried. On a quiet night at Arrowhead Lake, you can still the echoes of me being slapped.

We were sitting in one of the deserted booths late one afternoon. I was waiting for the evening orders to start coming in. Patsy was attempting to see how many Buffalo wings she could eat before Papa began charging me for food. Suddenly, there was a crash in the back. I ran into the kitchen, with Patsy close behind. Papa was pinned under the metal shelving he used to stack the grinder roll dough in proofing pans. I was able to leverage the shelf up high enough for Papa to crawl out. Together, we were able to stand the shelves back up. Patsy kept looking at the shelves while Papa quickly brushed off the dough and put it back in the pans.

"You didn't see anything if the health department asks," Papa said as he put the last pans back.

"I didn't see a thing. I was distracted by Patsy's ass. It happens all the time," I said. Patsy turned and gave me a withering glare that was usually reserved for my unsuccessful attempts at getting lucky at Arrowhead Lake.

After she glared at me long enough to be certain my testicles had receded and were hiding in fear behind my pancreas, she turned to look at Papa.

"Ignore him," she said, jerking her head toward me. "How did the shelf fall over? It looks pretty sturdy."

Papa tried to shrug and winced. He grabbed his shoulder and rubbed it. "I don't know. One minute I was standing there, and the next minute I was on the ground. I'll have to anchor it to the wall." He walked away, still rubbing his shoulder. Patsy watched him go with a frown.

We walked back to the front. She sat down in the booth and pushed away her wings. That was concerning. Normally, she'd finish the wings and then gnaw at the bones on the remote chance a stray subatomic particle of meat had escaped her the first time around.

She looked at me. "Phil, this place has a bad vibe. I don't know if it's haunted, has bad Feng Shui, or negative Hartmann lines, but it's been going on too long. Five deaths are proof the energy is imbalanced."

I nodded but didn't comment. I had learned not to say anything when I recognized less than half the words.

Papa stacked a bag of wrapped grinders on the counter. "Order out!"

I stood up. "Okay Patsy, you do what you think is best, but clear it with the boss." I grabbed the order and headed out to my car. As I left, I heard Patsy asking Papa if he had ever considered a professional exorcist.

A week later, Patsy had set off the smoke detectors burning sage, tripped a circuit breaker when she hit an outlet while spritzing salt water along the baseboards, and had tucked healing crystals in various corners, including one in the men's room that fell off the urinal when I flushed and nearly gave me a heart attack.

I didn't see Patsy for most that week. That was unfortunate—I liked to spend my rare nights off making out at Arrowhead Lake, which really required her participation. On the upside, it had been a week without getting slapped for trying to sweet-talk my way into her pants.

When she walked into the shop, she was loaded down with

books and notes. This did not bode well for my plans for an after-work marathon makeout session at the lake. She dropped the books and notebooks in a booth.

"This town is cursed," she announced. Even Papa stopped and looked at her.

She tapped an ancient looking book. "The History of Kittonqua just says the town's name comes from the Narraganset Indians."

"Pats," I said trying to sound soothing. "A lot of towns in Rhode Island have Indian names: Woonsocket, Pawtucket, Chepachet …" She gave me that look again. I shut up.

She pulled another book out and waved it around. "The Language of the Natives in New England gets more specific. The Narragansett word is Kitonckquêi. It translates to 'He who is dead.'

"The street we're on, Mattanit Road? Mattanit is the name of the Spirit of Evil. It's another name for Hobomock." She paused and looked at us. I wasn't saying anything out of self-preservation. Papa just shrugged.

Patsy did not look happy. "In Narragansett legends, Hobomock was the Manitou of death. After the missionaries showed up, Hobomock was identified with the Devil. What I can't figure out is why the names were used. Naming things after the dead and the Devil is not a good thing."

The landline rang, meaning the evening rush had begun. I left Patsy to her books to see if I could help with the order. When I went to deliver it, she was muttering something about deed searches. Fortunately for Papa, it was looking like a busy night, so he wouldn't need to actually listen to her.

Papa had more accidents. He tripped behind the counter, narrowly missing the open oven door. Another time, a filleting knife fell off a counter and into his foot. What was odd was that Papa didn't know he even owned a filleting knife. When the circuit tripped the basement lights while he was halfway down the stairs, he started to believe Patsy was on to something. He hung a large crucifix on the wall, only to trip over it the next day—overnight, it had somehow fallen off the wall in such a way to crumple into a ball.

Patsy brought her homework to the shop, just to keep an eye on Papa while I was out making deliveries. After the crucifix thing, I think he appreciated the company. And she always had some sort of oddball toy she conveniently "happened to have with her." One night it was a Geiger counter, which I suspect she "borrowed" from the old Civil Defense shelter at the school. Another night, she swiped my phone and installed something she called an "electronic voice phenomena app". I would have argued about that one, but Patsy's parents were convinced cell phones were just another way Big Brother could track you and forbade her to have her own.

On Monday, I had just stepped into the shop for my shift when Patsy burst into the shop with another armful of papers. "I was right; this shop is cursed!"

Papa walked in from the kitchen. "You're telling me?" The side of his face was a swollen bruise and there was a row of stitches over his eyebrow.

"Papa?" Patsy looked as horrified as I felt.

Papa tried to smile. "I'm told it looks worse than it is. I was reaching for something on the top shelf and one of those gallon jars of pickles came down on me."

A timer went off, and Papa ducked back in the kitchen.

Patsy looked at me. "Phil, it's getting worse."

I glanced at the kitchen door. "Accidents do happen in a kitchen."

Patsy gave me the "You're an idiot" look. "Really? Okay. We both know those gallon jars are so heavy and clumsy that Papa keeps them on the bottom shelves. Explain to me how one of them got on the top shelf."

She ignored my blank look and pulled out a notepad. "During the American Revolution, Loyalists from Newport were exiled and ended up out here. The town history says they bought land from the Narragansett and lived in peace and harmony ever after. However, the county history says the village of Kittonqua was already here. The Narragansett chief said they could have the land if they wiped out the village. The God-fearing Christians saw no problem with wiping out a few extra pagans, so they torched the village and slaughtered everyone."

This was not the town history Mrs. Price had taught in third grade. I saw Papa listening in the doorway.

Patsy pulled out another page of notes. "What the Narragansett didn't mention was that they hated this village because they were death walkers—a cult that offered live sacrifices to Mattanit, the Spirit of Evil. The new settlers buried all the bodies in a pit where the sacrifices took place."

Patsy was creeping me out. "Pats, this is fascinating, but what does it have to do with Papa's accidents?"

She shot me the "You're an idiot" look again. "Remember Kittonqua translates to 'He who is dead?' Mattanit Road was literally the road to the Mattanit sacrificial altar. This is the location of the altar. We're standing on a mass grave of death-worshipping Native Americans."

Papa cleared his throat. "Okay, let's assume that you're right. You're saying that all these accidents are caused by evil spirits?"

Patsy flipped to another page. "In 1830, this lot had a church on it, which burned down an hour after it was consecrated. In 1889, a livery stable opened here. It lasted two days before a horse went mad, trampled the owner to death, and then kicked over a lantern and burned the stable down. In 1929, someone built a social club on the property that was really a speakeasy. The Revenuers raided the place about 6 months later. They busted up the barrels of bootleg booze, and accidentally cut an electric wire that fell into the alcohol puddles and electrocuted twenty-seven people. It's like every fifty to sixty years, the next generation forgets about what happened and just sees an empty lot to build on. Like Papa #1 did."

Papa looked at her, then walked away. I knew well enough to know he was processing the information. Fortunately, it was a quiet night, because he seemed distracted.

It took another three days, but after that accident, Papa started getting skittish—taking an order of toasted grinders out of the oven, his paddle snapped into three pieces and the middle chunk flew at him. If he had been standing 6 inches to the left, it would have impaled him in the heart instead of leaving a hole in and out of his tee shirt. I saw it happen, and that pole didn't fly off at an angle I would have expected. Then again, I barely passed geometry, so calculating angles were not my strength. Fortunately, Patsy was at the historical society double-checking her deeds or something. Otherwise, she'd have had Papa taking a bath in holy water or some sort of thing.

"Papa," I said, as he examined the jagged wood pole, "Go home. It's quiet and it's late. I'll make this trip and we'll figure it out tomorrow."

"You may be right, Phil. As much as I like your girlfriend, she's got me thinking every little incident is *matiasma* – the evil eye."

I nodded and picked up the bag of grinders. "Go home, Papa.

Maybe have a little of that nasty Greek licorice booze and call it an early night."

He gave me a look that almost reminded me of a Patsy glare. "It is anise flavor, and it's a nectar from the gods called ouzo. Now go make that delivery while I lock up."

A flat tire on the way back meant I didn't return from the last delivery until after 11. Papa's was dark; he had actually taken my advice. I had a key, so I'd let myself in, drop off the cash, then go home. I got out of the car and Patsy was waiting. That was no surprise. She planned on getting a ride home after her research, and without a cell phone, I had no way to tell her we were shutting down a little early.

What was surprising was the odd look in her eyes. I had expected her "annoyed" eyes because she had to wait. I was far too familiar with her "You're an idiot" look, and her "If you don't move your hand, I'll rip it off" glare. This was different, even odder that "psycho eyes," which I'd only seen the one time I managed to unhook her bra when she wasn't paying attention (That slap knocked a filling loose). This was different. I didn't recognize the look, and it made me a little uneasy.

"Phillip, I believe I have the solution to our dilemma."

Patsy's ideas never gave me a warm fuzzy feeling, but none had resulted in stitches, at least lately. Cautiously, I asked, "You know how to exorcise a field of evil ghosts?"

She shook her head. "No, the process would be too complicated for we mere teens. But I know another way to lay these poor spirits to rest—sacrifice a virgin."

I looked at her. "Pats, I'm pretty sure human sacrifice is illegal, even in Rhode Island."

She smiled. It was not a reassuring smile. "The books do not specify who sacrifices the virgin or how the virginity is sacrificed. It can be symbolic." She pulled off her shirt and dropped it to the ground.

"So, here I am, sacrifice me! Take me right here and now, in the parking lot."

Hormones aside, something felt wrong. After all the months of fighting me, this seemed too easy. She saw me hesitating. She undid her jeans and slid them off.

"Phillip, I always said I wanted our first time to be memorable. What could be more memorable than sacrificing my maidenhead to give eternal rest to a field of troubled spirits? Let us join as one and release the spirits!"

93

From behind me, I heard a familiar voice. "Seriously? I leave you alone for a few minutes and you're ready to bang some slutty doppelgänger?"

I wheeled around. There was Patsy, looking as angry as when I went for second base.

I had angry Patsy behind me and Pasty in her underwear in front of me. "One of you is fake."

They both looked at me with the same "You're an idiot" look.

The clothed version looked at me. "Seriously, when did I ever use the term 'maidenhead'?"

She pulled the neck of her shirt off her shoulder and pointed. "Scar from an archery accident at summer camp in 8th grade." She pointed at her less-clothed double, "No scar."

The half-naked version shrugged. "Oh well," and vanished.

The clothed version came over and punched my shoulder. "Idiot, you're a virgin, too. You fuck that ghost, and the virgin sacrifice would release the spirits from the grave field."

I got a little defensive. "She looked like you. She sounded like you. And with all your mystical mumbo-jumbo, it made sense."

"You should have gotten suspicious when I offered to put out. Plus, my ass does not look that big. Trust me, you'll see the difference, sooner or later." She dug into her pocket and pulled out a really ugly medallion. It was an oval of dark metal with some sort of figure waving at a cloud.

"Put this on. It's a symbol of the Manitou followers of Wetucks, the Narragansett hero. He intercedes for mankind on behalf of his father, the Great Spirit."

I nodded at the few words I understood and put the medallion around my neck to avoid an argument, then tucked it inside my shirt so no one would have to look at it. We walked toward the building.

"Patsy, one thing seems odd." She stopped and looked at me. "Why are they picking on me? I don't see them trying to talk you into being a virgin sacrifice."

For a second, she looked like a deer in the headlights. "Well, about that—um ..."

I shrugged. "I know, it's because I'm easier to convince."

"Exactly. Boys are pigs and are always easy to seduce." She seemed to say it very fast.

I nodded. "Makes sense. You certainly have more self-control than I do. No one's going to rush you into anything."

She nodded quickly. "Exactly, no lapses in judgment in a hayloft that I might regret almost immediately. Can we get inside, before you try to dry-hump the next dead but willing thing to cross your path?"

We went in and I put the receipts in the safe. "Pats, something the demon Patsy said bothers me."

She looked at me. "Can we call that evil spirit something else besides "Demon Patsy?"

"Fine, you come up with a name. Right before she flashed her demon bra, she said the process would be too complicated. That means there must actually be a process, right?"

Patsy looked thoughtful. "I suppose it does, but I still don't know how we do it."

We locked up the shop and headed for my car. She was silent on the way back to her house. I pulled up and she gave me a quick kiss.

"Try to avoid getting lucky with any undead spirits. I'll check a couple of sources tomorrow. And watch out for more "demon bras." She snorted and got out of the car. I drove home wondering which Patsy was the evil one.

The next day, I was out making a series of deliveries when I got a call. The phone ID said it was Papa. That usually meant an order mix up. I gritted my teeth and hit the button.

"Phil, get back here." It was Patsy. She sounded frantic. "It's Papa."

I got back just in time to see an ambulance pulling away. Patsy was waiting by the door. She ran over to me and sobbed on my shoulder. From what I could hear, she had come in as usual and Papa was already on the floor. He started floating, glowing red. She tried to run over but was pushed back by something that wasn't visible. The hand hit her square in the chest and she shrieked in pain. Then Papa fell to the floor. She called 911 and the ambulance came.

We walked into the building, so I could make sure everything was shut off and lock up. While I was in the back, I heard Patsy yell. I ran out. She was coming out of the restroom, with her shirt in her hands. She was terrified. She ran over and stuck her chest in my face.

"Look!" She said. Of course, I already was looking. Instinctively, I double-checked the scar on her shoulder before attempting to memorize every inch of that bra and the terrain within.

"Not at my boobs, you idiot—Look!" It was not her happy voice. She pointed at her cleavage, where her copy of the ugly medallion rested. There was a burn mark around it. Nothing serious, and it was already fading. At first, I thought it was a handprint, but I had seen enough of Patsy's handprints on my face after a visit to Arrowhead Lake to realize it looked more like an x-ray of a hand. Whatever had pushed her had skeleton hands and didn't like her medallion. She still looked a little spooked, but Patsy didn't like playing the victim. As she put her shirt back on, she walked back to a booth where there was an old paperback book.

"I went through my mother's collection of magic books and found this one. It's an old 70s how-to book of Wiccan witchcraft. I'm not sure if Wiccan magic is compatible with Narraganset evil spirits, but it's all I can find."

My phone rang. It was my father. I put the phone on speaker.

"Phil? This is your father. Did you know something happened to Mr. Papadopolous?"

"Yeah, Dad. I'm at Papa's now, locking up. I don't know anything. Patsy was here and found him on the floor. They took him to Central Hospital by ambulance. Did the police say anything about how he's doing?" I decided to skip the glowing and floating parts for now.

My father paused. "The police said he was in some sort of coma and they're running tests. But the doctors say he's just fading away."

"I'll be home as soon as I shut everything down here."

I hung up the phone and looked at Patsy. She looked a little teary, but her teeth were clenched.

"Phil, we need to do something."

I looked around helplessly. I looked at her notes. "Pats, all of these other buildings were destroyed pretty quickly. Why not this building? It's been standing for almost three years."

She looked at the list. Then she flipped to another page. "There's no pattern—the church burned in November. The stable fire was in August. The speakeasy raid was in May."

She flipped through a few more pages. "The only pattern I see is that all owners here died in the late spring. Papa #1 died in early May. Papa #2 died 2 weeks later. Papa #3 died in April the next year and Papa #4 in June. Papa #5 died last year in March."

"I remember that last one. It had been such a mild winter, one of the paramedics got fired for joking that the ambulance company was going broke because there were so few heart attacks from old-timers trying to shovel out their driveways that winter."

Patsy glanced at the paperback book and her eyes widened. "Give me your phone."

I handed her the phone. She dialed a number. "Hi Marge, it's Patsy. Can you do me a big favor? Go to the reference shelves and look in The History of Kittonqua. See if you can tell me what year they paved Mattanit Road. Sure, I'll hold."

I looked at her. She tapped her forehead. "You gave me an idea." She went back to the phone. "1928? Perfect. I owe you one, Marge." She handed me back my phone.

She pulled me across the table and kissed me. "The speakeasy took 6 months to be destroyed. It was the first winter after Mattanit Road was paved."

From the way she was looking at me, I assumed she felt I should have the faintest idea what she was talking about. She was wrong. She saw the blank look.

"What do you do to a paved road in the winter when it snows?"

That one I knew. My father was a plow contractor. "You plow it."

She nodded encouragingly. "Yes, and after you plow it, what do you do?"

I was still wasn't sure where we were going with this. "You treat it with sand and salt."

She nodded like I had said the correct answer. The tone she was using sounded like if I got another one right, I'd get a gold star and a cookie and graduate kindergarten.

She opened the book and pushed it toward me. It was a chapter on purification rituals. Then I made the connection—a salt circle to purify anything within.

I looked at her. "A salt circle?"

She nodded. "Think about the weather. We had a late blizzard; they were still salting the roads in April. The salt goes into the ground; that's why my parents keep protesting its use along the river. The salt here on Mattanit Road gets washed off into the dirt under the gravel in the parking lot. Salt purifies—the salt runoff weakens them. That's why the deaths take place in the spring. The salt leaches out of the ground into the water table, and they get powerful again."

As if on cue, it thundered outside. I looked out the window. One of the massive thunderstorms that form out in the bay was rolling this way.

Patsy stood up and looked out the window. "That's what we need. We put in a salt circle around the parking lot and it will trap the death-walker spirits. And then the rain will wash the salt into the ground and purify it, along with any bloodthirsty ghosts."

I wasn't sure if that was her plan or if she was thinking out loud. "Pats, we don't have time to find go buy enough salt, get it back here, and then make a giant circle before it rains. And if you're right, we need to finish the circle before it rains. Otherwise, we're going to make a lot of ghosts very angry."

Patsy glanced at the storm. "Your father said Papa is fading. We don't have a choice. Go look in the cellar while I move your car out of the lot."

"The cellar?"

She grabbed my car keys and shot me the "You're an idiot" look again. "Hello? Winter supplies? Rock salt?"

Now I got it. All the Papas kept rock salt in the cellar. In New England, you really don't have a choice unless you like getting sued by someone falling on an icy sidewalk. I looked under the stairs. There was a stack of six 50-pound bags. I could handle a 50-pound bag, but six trips up a flight of stairs toting fifty pounds of dead weight was going to be rough. Let's just say I was never going to college on an athletic scholarship. I thought of Papa in that hospital bed, and grabbed a bag. I tossed it on my shoulder and staggered up the stairs, and dropped it next to the building. Patsy picked it up with no effort, cut off the corner with a lethal-looking hunting knife I'd never seen before, and started pouring an uninterrupted line along the edge of the parking lot. The wind was picking up, and I could see lightning in the distance.

I went back for the next bag. This trip, I tried slinging a bag over my shoulder and carrying another one. I got them upstairs, but my shoulder was numb and my back was already aching. When I dropped the next two bags off, my back was in agony. The thunder was deafening. Either it was the worst storm in months, or something buried under the parking lot had figured out what we were doing.

When I picked up the last bag, I felt something pop in my back and the bright light in front of my eyes was not lightning. Fighting through the tears, I got the bag up the stairs. Patsy was beet red and breathing hard. I tried to straighten up. I did, but the pain was so bad I doubled over again. But I saw Patsy emptying the last bag but we were at least four feet short of completing the circle. The middle of the parking lot was bulging in several spots. Something was coming up, and I didn't think it was a welcoming committee.

I yelled over the wind for Patsy to run. We didn't have enough salt, it was going to rain any moment, and we were in deep shit. To my horror, she ran back into the building. My back was on fire, and my legs were pins and needles. I made my way toward the door. I wasn't sure if I could make it inside, so trying to force Patsy to safety was going to be a problem. She came running out with a tray. Running past me, I saw it was filled with salt shakers. Papa still kept the booths set up, on the remote chance someone dared to dine in. I watched as she unscrewed the caps and poured the salt shakers on the ground. I knew she didn't have enough, but she gave me an idea. I staggered into the building. On the supply shelves were most of a 25-pound bag of table salt that one of the previous Papa's bought to refill the shakers that no one used. I wrapped my arms around it and ignored the white pain lancing through my lower back. I made it as far as the edge of the building before my legs went numb and I went down to my knees. It was dark as night, but Patsy saw me during a lightning flash and ran over. She grabbed the bag and took two steps and then came back and kissed my forehead.

"Go!" I screamed over the wind. "If it doesn't work, just keep running. We're out of time."

A skeletal arm burst up through the gravel and lunged at her as she went by. But Patsy was no stranger to being lunged at and just went around it. She poured salt and stepped out of the closed circle. The rest of the skeleton climbed out of the ground, and it wasn't alone. I still wasn't sure if the salt circle would even work, and now Patsy was betting her life on it.

The rain came down like someone turned on a faucet. I clawed my way onto my feet using the side of the building, and saw the salt circle dissolving in the rain and soaking into the ground. Suddenly, there was a howling that drowned out the wind. The inside of the circle turned red, and then black. One of the skeleton death walkers reached out across the salt and grabbed Patsy. It tried to pull her inside the circle.

A tree branch slammed into my back as it blew past. The pain drove me back to my knees. I looked down and saw the outline of the pendant she made me wear outlined against my soaked clothes. I clutched it and whispered "Wetucks, I don't know if you can hear me. Hell, I don't even know if you exist. But she believes. Help her."

It thundered again, but it sounded different. I looked at Patsy—she was glowing white. The hand tugging at her shriveled to dust. Suddenly, the black in the circle turned white and above the wind, I heard hundreds of screams echoing in the distance.

The storm stopped. Patsy was standing there, looking confused. I stood up before I remembered my back. To my amazement, nothing hurt. She ran to me and we hugged.

"Is it over?" I asked.

"I think so. Come on, let's call the hospital to check on Papa. We can lock up the shop and get the hell away from here." We stepped into the shop. Patsy headed to the phone on the counter, while I locked the door and pulled the blinds. I killed the lights.

Patsy hung up the phone.

"Papa suddenly began improving. The doctors don't know why. If he keeps improving, they may let him go home in a day or two. Maybe things will get back to normal now."

She looked around. "You know, this place is kind of cozy in the dark."

She walked over and stood close to me. "I guess we did it."

I leaned in and kissed her. She grabbed me by the hips and pulled me into to kiss. Without thinking, I reached around and grabbed her ass.

It wasn't the hardest she's slapped me, but it was in the top ten. She glared, spun around, and headed out the door. I followed, checking that she hadn't knocked any more fillings loose.

Things were definitely getting back to normal.

David Bernard is a native New Englander who hightailed it to South Florida as soon as he was informed that grown-ups can live anywhere they want, and that despite opinions to the contrary, he was considered to be an adult. He does still keep an ice scraper by the door, because you never know. In addition to appearances in several of the previous Strangely Funny *books, his previous works include short stories in anthologies such as* Snowbound with Zombies *(Post Mortem Press),* Legacy of the Reanimator *(Chaosium), and* The Shadow over Deathlehem *(Grinning Skull Press).*

EYEWEAR OF THE DAMNED

By C.D. Gallant-King

My optometrist sold me cursed eyeglasses.

Yeah, I know, we've all had crappy glasses. Sometimes they don't fit right and they rub the back of your ears, or pinch your nose and leave those ugly red marks. Sometimes the prescription isn't quite right and stuff is fuzzy, or the floor kinda bends toward you weird. I know a guy who once got new glasses and the shop screwed up and put plain glass lenses in them. Who does that? If your whole business model is selling prescription eyeglasses, how do you forget to do the one thing you're in business to do? That would be like Domino's sending you a plain disc of dough without cheese or tomato sauce on it, or a hooker taking your pants off and then walking out the door.

Okay, maybe not exactly like the hooker thing. I know a guy who gets off by paying hookers to do just that.

But see, this thing with my glasses, this is not a normal screw-up. How do you "accidentally" sell someone eyeglasses that can look through the veil of death to show you ghosts and demons and other fucked-up critters from another world? Was there some kind of exorcist with the same prescription as me, and the lenses got mixed up? Or maybe, by some million-to-one chance, my exact prescription just happens to be the exact right cut and angle to create an inter-dimensional vortex into another plane of existence? It sounds crazy, but I know a guy who bought a bag of oranges and found a turtle inside. Sometimes these weird things just happen.

I don't think this one was an accident, though. I think I got these glasses for a reason; I just haven't figured out what it is yet.

I saw a guy get beheaded on the subway yesterday.

I'm not sure if the reason I got the glasses was to prevent deaths like his, but I'm sure he would have appreciated a heads up.

Sorry, that was in terrible taste.

It was a freaky accident. There was a crowd in the station waiting for the rush hour train uptown to take us all home after a long day of soul-crushing work in the big office buildings downtown. We heard the train coming down the tunnel; you always do, because it's a giant metal snake in an enclosed space rocketing along at 50 kilometers an hour on a rusty old metal track. You can't *not* hear it, even if you were wearing earplugs and had your head stuck in a bucket of cement. But this middle-aged guy in a dark blue suit, he leans over and looks down the tunnel to see if the train is coming. The problem is, he leans a little too far, or maybe he lost his balance or something, but the next thing you know there's a screech of steel as the train tries to brake. The screeching drowns out the sound of a watermelon exploding, but it sure as fuck doesn't drown out the sound of fifty people screaming as they're sprayed with blood, brains and bits of bone as blue-suit guy's head bursts from the impact of the train like an overripe tomato thrown at a brick wall. Then, the headless body falls over and gets caught in the gap between the train and the platform and dragged the length of the station leaving a bright red smear the whole way down, dropping an arm here, a leg there. People are screaming and running away, and I can see the therapy bills of all those poor people climbing higher and higher as the train rolls to a stop.

I know a guy who works for the transit commission, and he says that whenever there's an unexplained subway delay it's usually because someone jumped in front of a train and they need time to hose off the tracks. The maintenance guys have gotten pretty efficient at cleaning it up, and apparently they have a little contest every time to try and break their record for getting the trains running again. Their record is under ten minutes, but this time they had to shut down the whole station for the rest of the day to clean little bits of this dude out of the grout work of the tiled walls.

The whole thing was grotesque and sad and everything, but the weirdest part was that I knew something bad was going to happen right before it did, because I saw the little black snake fuckers flying around at the edges of my vision.

O-O

I should go back to the beginning.

My first mistake was buying eyeglasses in Chinatown. Not that there's anything wrong with buying glasses from Chinatown or anything, as long as it's from a licensed optometrist. The one I went to … I don't think they were. Something about the cat sleeping in the exam chair threw me off. I know a guy who told me to go check this place out. He said they sold really nice, cheap knock-off glasses that cost a fraction of the retail price; he himself had bought these gold wire-framed Cartier frames for under a hundred bucks that made me more jealous than I care to admit. Sure, "Cartier" was spelled with an extra "i," but nobody's going to look that closely at your glasses, right?

I walked into this shop in a basement under a grocery store, and the whole place smelled like fish. It felt like I was stepping into the shop from *Gremlins* where the dad bought the furry critter. Sure, there were eyeglass frames in the window and on racks, but there were also jars of herbs on the counters and ornaments hanging from the ceiling and a half-dozen censers full of burning incense around the room. I suspect they were trying to mask the fish smell from upstairs, but it wasn't working. I did get a sudden craving for smoked salmon, though.

I half-expected an ancient old man to walk through the beaded curtain to greet me (okay, maybe more than half), but instead a young, attractive woman in a white doctor's coat stepped out. She wore a pink blouse, a black pencil skirt, and very high heels. Her black hair was neatly piled on the top of her head except for one exquisite curl that floated down over her stylish thin purple frames so perfectly that there was no way it was an accident.

She asked if I had an appointment, and I said no, I had a prescription and just wanted to look at the frames. I showed her the script from my last eye doctor and she *tsked* and shook her head, and said it was outdated and I should get my eyes checked again. I'm sure she just wanted my eighty bucks, but who am I to argue with a beautiful woman who wanted to press her face close to mine and stare into my eyes?

She introduced herself as Doctor Liu and took me over to her examination area in the corner. That's when she shooed the cat away.

103

The little furry bastard hissed at me like I had eaten its offspring. Whether it was just pissed because I stole its seat or because he could see some kind of dark shadow hanging over my soul, I have no idea. Animals have never much liked me. When I was a kid, a dog chewed my pinky toe off when I fell asleep at a park.

She did all the regular eye exam stuff, asking me to read letters with one eye closed and all that, and everything was fairly straightforward. Except for some reason I got the crazy idea that she was into me. Maybe it was the way she smiled, maybe it was the way her boob brushed against my arm and I convinced myself she did it on purpose, or maybe it was because I haven't been able to get a date in months. Whatever the case, by the end of the exam I had worked up the courage to ask her out.

"So, you just spent the last twenty minutes staring into my eyes," I said. "How about we go out for a drink some time, so I can stare into your eyes for a while?"

She laughed, but it wasn't a flirty, cutesy laugh. It was more of a snort, like she had just choked on paint thinner. I've been told I'm a bit slow at taking a hint, and instead of just smiling and backing away, I saw this as a challenge and doubled down.

"Your lab coat is too long," I said. "You should get a shorter one that shows off your ass. It's quite nice."

She looked at me with such disgust I was afraid I'd shat in her chair and didn't notice. I gave a furtive sniff of the air just to make sure I hadn't left any surprise packages. I have never seen a woman turned off so fast, and I had once thrown up on a girl in a bar mid-pick-up line.

Thinking back, I may have figured out why my optometrist gave me cursed eyeglasses.

I was so embarrassed and eager to get out of there, I didn't think at the time how strange it was for her to immediately pull out a pair of frames, already loaded with my exact prescription. I didn't think it odd that the thick black frames fit me perfectly, and looked damn good, too. No, the strange and odd came later when I started to see snakes and monkey demons following me around everywhere.

O-O

It's like catching a glimpse of something out of the corner of your eye, like somebody walking through your peripheral vision. But whenever I turn my head, there's nothing there. At first I didn't think much of it, then I started wondering if there was something wrong with the glasses, like they were throwing off my depth perception or something, playing tricks on my eyes. I could never focus on the black spots that flickered at the edges of my vision; as soon as I tried to look at them they were gone, like those ladies sunbathing topless at the park.

After the first couple of times, I realized they weren't just shapeless blobs, but were twisting, worm-like ... *things*. It freaked me the hell out, but not as much as when I realized what they could do.

Like last week, when I saw the black, snake-like demons in the corner of my eye while stepping out of the supermarket with an armload of groceries in hand. At this point, I was getting used to what that sign meant, so I immediately stopped and looked around for whoever was about to bite it.

Was someone in traffic, in one of the dozens of cars zipping by on the crowded street, about to be mangled in a horrible, fiery wreck? There was nothing I could do if it was. Was that hipster couple in matching plaid shirts, walking down the sidewalk arguing about vape flavors, about to get mugged? I didn't really want to stop them to say anything. I knew I guy who once accidentally started a conversation with a hipster about music and the next thing he knew, he found himself in an organic fair-trade coffee shop/barber shop with a fucked-up haircut, a latte, and a bill for sixty-four dollars.

Was it the young mother in the active wear stretch pants walking her baby in a stroller? Fuck, I hoped not, but maybe I should try to warn her just in case.

There was a dog tied to a bike rack outside the supermarket, yapping its ugly little head off. It was a Shih Tzu or some other fuzzy little white bastard that vibrated and yipped non-stop. I usually dislike animals, but I especially want to punt those little fuzzy pricks.

The dog kept barking and growling, and I got distracted from chasing down the woman in the stretch pants. My vision jumped back and forth between her and the traffic and a crane atop a condo building down the street that could fall and kill dozens of people at any second. I felt sweat on my forehead and more running down the back of my neck. I started to shake, just like the dog, feeling paralyzed and trapped and unsure of what to do. Who was about to die? Every time I glanced around at another potential victim I saw the black swirls out of the corner of my eye, those strange manifestations that disappeared the second I tried to focus on them or turn my head toward them. Just like the dog, I wanted to scream out in frustration, to try and warn everyone at once.

And then a giant fucking wolf came out of nowhere and ripped the dog in half.

Maybe it wasn't a wolf. Maybe it was a coyote, or a Rottweiler or something. All I know is that this giant dog the size of a horse leapt over a fence and pounced on that poor ugly little Shih Tzu and snapped its neck with one bite of its massive jaws. The sudden and abrupt halt to the yipping seemed to plunge the world into perfect silence, and I watched in awe as the Hound of the Baskervilles whipped that little bastard like a rag doll back and forth in its powerful maw so hard the thing ripped in half, its head flying into the air like a pop fly at the Rogers Centre and its body hurtling into traffic where it bounced off the hood of a blue Toyota Camry. The driver hit the brakes and was rear-ended by an SUV. The kayak that was strapped to the roof of the SUV came loose and shot into oncoming traffic like a missile, blasting through the front windshield of another Toyota, causing it to swerve, jump the curb and plow through the front doors of a Starbucks.

All of this had taken just a few heartbeats, but by the time I had pondered the apparent popularity of Toyota Camrys in the neighborhood, the wolf had already disappeared, leaving me holding my groceries and my shoes spattered with Shih Tzu gore. I was trembling worse than before, and I couldn't catch my breath. I felt like I was going to faint, and my knees gave out. I slumped to the ground and dropped my groceries, breaking a very expensive bottle of olive oil in the process. I watched the oil soak through the paper bag while I pondered what the hell I was going to do with my life and these goddamn glasses.

O-O

Spoiler alert: The glasses end up killing me.

I went to the terminal cancer ward at the hospital, just to see what would happen. As soon as I walked through the door I saw the black swirls I couldn't catch, but they didn't seem to be as fast or as fleeting as the other times. But they were more prevalent, more constant. Death here wasn't as quick and violent and random, but it was inevitable. The spooks were just hanging around, waiting inexorably.

The black swirls were too maddening, and I had to leave after a few minutes. Listening to someone's last dying gasps from a nearby room didn't help. As I stood outside in the hall, trying to catch my breath, a nurse stopped and gave me a concerned look. Maybe I looked like I had just lost someone. Maybe I looked like a mental case, with dog blood on my shoes and oil stains on my shirt.

"Can I help you?" she asked. She was a middle-aged woman with graying hair and piercing eyes. Working in this part of the hospital, those eyes had probably seen a lot of pain. But they looked at me and she seemed utterly perplexed.

I shook my head no and quickly excused myself. Maybe I should have asked to see a doctor. Maybe I was crazy. Maybe I needed some therapy and a good dose of meds. I know a guy who was all kinds of loony, and judging by his Facebook posts I thought for sure he was going to end up on the news for shooting up a bank or an old folks' home, but he found the right doctor and the right prescriptions and now he was a city councilor. But I didn't think it would work for me. I knew this shit was all real, and no amount of drugs or therapy was going to make it go away.

But what was it there for? Why had the woman in Chinatown given me the ability to predict death? Was I supposed to use that to help people? Or was it just to torture me, to ruin my life and drive me mad?

Sweet mother of god, a couple of bad pick-up lines wasn't worth this, was it?

O-O

The very first time I saw the black swirls was just after I left the optometrist in Chinatown. This was before I realized what they were, what they meant. I just thought there was something funky about my new prescription and it was just going to take some getting used to, when I walked up the steps and I kept seeing these little spots out of the corner of my eye that I couldn't quite focus on.

At the time, I didn't make the connection between the glasses and the poor sanitation worker who was loading up those stinky garbage bins outside the Chinese grocer, who got his sleeve caught on the pneumatic arm of his garbage truck and was hoisted, screaming, high into the air before being dropped along with forty pounds of rotting fish into the truck's garbage compactor. I watched in horror as he fell into the back of the truck with a thud, his head hitting the rusted metal side and silencing his terrified screams. I thought "there has to be some kind of safety" just before the hydraulic door closed and the truck went through the full crushing cycle. I think he regained consciousness briefly because I'm sure I heard one quick, abruptly cut-off scream, but that might have just been my imagination.

I stood frozen with revulsion jellying my knees and the crushing weight of mortality pressing down on my heart. I know a guy who, in high school, had driven off a wharf on a bicycle and got sucked into the engine of a motorboat, but I hadn't actually seen his slapstick, freakish demise. I had never seen anyone die, and I didn't know how to cope with it. After all this time, it hasn't gotten easier.

I felt awful for the poor guy in the truck, but little did I know how shitty my life was about to become.

Not to diminish the shittiness of getting crushed in a garbage truck.

O-O

I decided to get rid of the glasses the night after the subway incident.

I estimated that, by that point, I had witnessed close to one hundred people die in horrifying ways in just over a month, and I had been unable to do anything to stop it. As I lay in my bed staring at the ceiling, I just couldn't understand what the point of it all was. These glasses should be a boon. If they can predict tragedy, surely they must be able to help prevent it, right? But time after time, they had left me frozen and horrified as I watched people die in grotesque, cartoonish ways.

Then it hit me. I had never seen anyone die—let alone be mangled in freak accidents that made me think God must surely be one sick fuck—before I got these new glasses. Maybe the glasses weren't showing me something I couldn't see before. Maybe the glasses were what were *causing* the accidents.

It made sense. Instead of the glasses making the invisible visible, maybe the black swirls were inside the glasses. Maybe *I* was the one who was causing all those gruesome deaths by wearing the cursed glasses around town.

I looked at the offending eyewear sitting on my nightstand.

They looked so innocuous, so ordinary, just sitting there. Those thick black frames were starting to look a little douchey to me, anyway. Anyone could have mistaken then for ordinary eyeglasses. It wasn't my fault all those people died. How could I have known that simple metal and glass could kill people just by me looking at them?

I had mostly convinced myself it wasn't my fault, but I knew that if I kept wearing those damned spectacles, any further deaths *would* be my fault. I would knowingly be unleashing some evil hot optometrist's curse onto the world. I immediately decided I had to destroy the glasses, jumped out of bed, and smashed them with the heel of a shoe.

I was shocked by how quickly it was over, and how undramatic it was. I don't know if I expected a spirit to rise from my nightstand, but all I was left with were smashed lenses and bits of twisted metal. It was nowhere near as cathartic as I hoped it would be.

Worse, I realized I had lost my old frames, and now I was completely without glasses and half-blind. I would have to call in sick tomorrow and go back to the optometrist—my *regular* optometrist—and get a new pair. Even if they cost an arm and a leg, getting some non-demonic eyewear would be worth a few hundred bucks.

I slept better than I had in weeks and rose bright and early to head downtown. I put on some jeans and a clean shirt and the very same shoes I had used to smash the glasses from hell, and stepped out into the warm morning air with a smile on my face and a bounce in my step.

And then, half-blind, I walked out into the street and got hit by a bus.

O-O

As I lie dying on the asphalt, I feel something coming out of my eyes. At first I think it's just oblivion creeping into my vision as I slip into unconsciousness, but I quickly realize the black worms are coming out of my eyes, crawling onto my face and across my field of vision. Black, twisting worms like small snakes made from shadow that had always been there, that the glasses had somehow allowed me to see.

Black swirling evil that was now crawling away, looking for another host to infect, for more lives to destroy.

I scream and the people around me think I'm in pain. I try to

109

explain that they're getting away, that someone needs to get the glasses and find the black worms.

The witnesses just think it's the mad ramblings of a dying man.

I scream about the eye doctor in Chinatown. About the woman who tried to show me I had demon snakes in my eyes. About the guy I know who claims he found a devil in the glove compartment of his Kia that made him drive off the road and mow down a pair of Swedish tourists, about how it's all real and he wasn't just texting like the cops said. I see sad, anxious faces all around me. They think I'm crazy. There's blood everywhere and I know it's mine, but I can't feel anything below my neck. Someone holds my hand. I'm trying to warn them, but no one will believe me. An old man in a brown coat tells me that it's okay, that everything is going to be okay now.

I try to tell them *nothing's* okay.

I can't make words anymore, but I can just see the black worms out of the corner of my eye. I can't look directly at them because I can't turn my head.

After everything, I still can't see them.

Then I can't see anything.

C.D. Gallant-King wrote his first story when he was five years old, and he made his babysitter look up how to spell "extraterrestrial" in the dictionary. He now writes stories about un-heroic people doing generally hilarious things in horrifying worlds. A loving husband and proud father of two wonderful little kids, C.D. was born and raised in Newfoundland and currently resides in Ottawa, Ontario. There was also a ten-year period in between where he tried to make a go of a career in Theatre in Toronto, but we don't talk about that.

ACCIDENT PRONE

By Gwen Mayo

The dragon yawned, purposely tilting his head to allow the torchlight to glint off his razor-sharp teeth. Lenora knew she was supposed to be impressed. She might have been impressed if Parker's allergy to reptiles hadn't picked that exact moment to act up.

Being stuck in the body of a hound had enhanced Parker's senses, worsening his allergy attacks. Lenora watched in horror as a powerful sneeze erupted from Parker's droopy hound dog jaws.

The nearness of a reptile as large as the dragon magnified the impact of his magical sneeze. Tiny particles of enchantment flew explosively out of his mouth and nose, attached to the sandstone walls of the cave, and sent ribbons of enchantment running in blue-green streams along the cavern roof. The stone immediately began to crumble along the glowing lines of power. Fragments of sand and rock rained down on them.

Lenora wanted to escape before the whole cave fell in. Unfortunately, the dragon stood between her and the exit. They were trapped, at least she was; in dog form, Parker might have gotten past the beast. But Lenora never doubted that he would stay. That was one of the reasons she loved the big lug.

Her husband wasn't the brightest guy her father might have chosen for her, but he was loyal. These past few days had tested their love more than she cared to admit. She glanced briefly at the droopy-eared hound at her heels and sighed.

"Parker, you owe me big-time for this," she said.

He whined in response.

"Don't look at me that way. This is all your fault. Now come on," she said, taking to her heels.

She ran deeper into the cave, hoping to find a way out somewhere beyond the dragon's reach. She and Parker spent the next several minutes running for their lives as the cavern crumbled around them. Worse, the sharp stone fragments loosened by Parker's uncontrolled magic kept striking her, leaving her cut and bleeding. The dragon ignored the falling shards of stone, which were nothing more than a nuisance to him as he chased them.

Nearly exhausted, Lenora darted into a long narrow passage with Parker hard at her heels, his ears swinging wildly as he ran.

The dragon was too large to follow, but the angry beast sent a breath of fire coursing along the walls. Lenora ducked behind a boulder to escape the flames. Parker dived in after her. It wasn't the perfect shelter. A flaming piece of brimstone burned through her skirt and two layers of petticoats before she could shake it off. The flames singed Parker's tail.

Parker barked his protest to the painful burn, alerting the dragon to their survival.

"Stop it!" Lenora yelled, as the dragon pounded the walls of the cave with his long tail. "Can't you see that your barking is only making him mad? Are you determined to get us killed?"

Deep down she knew that she shouldn't have scolded him. But, like the falling rock, their visit to the dragon's cave was directly connected to one of Parker's magical accidents. No, "accident" wasn't the right word. Parker had deliberately turned himself into a dog. He thought it would be a great surprise to have one really good spell to show off at their wedding.

If he had thought through the consequences of his spell, Parker might have realized that as a dog he wouldn't be able to say the words that would return him to human form. But, Parker wasn't good at thinking things through. In fact, her husband wasn't good at much of anything requiring deep thought.

Everyone, including his father, knew Parker wasn't brilliant, but as the only son of the most powerful wizard in all the Lower Kingdoms, no one would dare say that he was dumb. At least, no one said it to his face. But, Parker was not so dumb that he hadn't realized the reason their fathers had arranged a match between them was in the hope that their children would get his power and her brains.

Lenore wondered what the two old schemers would do if their grandchildren turned out to have her lack of magic and his wit. With the present state of affairs, there was no danger of that happening. They had spent what was supposed to be their honeymoon trying everything they could think of to change him back to human form. Together, they had gathered the ingredients for more than a dozen potions. Nothing had had worked.

Parker was grasping at straws. Yesterday, he had discovered a formula for a powder that was supposed to reverse any spell. He had come into their chamber, tail wagging, the ancient text clutched in his teeth. The big lug had been so happy he could hardly contain himself. She'd cringed when she read the ingredients. The most important part was a large quantity of freshly ground dragon's claw. It was their attempt to obtain the necessary claw that had led to their present difficulties.

Finding the dragon wasn't hard. With his improved sense of smell, Parker had easily located a dragon cave, but the reptile allergy had kicked in almost immediately. His first sneeze alerted the dragon to their presence. The first sneeze hadn't been too bad, just a little half sniffling affair that bounced along the floor of the cave sending up a cloud of dust—just enough to wake a sleeping dragon.

Another blast from Old Brimstone Breath jarred her from her musing. The flames danced around her, and she clutched Parker tightly.

Thinking about this, Lenora sighed. "I'm sorry," she said, feeling a little guilty about the hurt look in his big, watery, doggie eyes. "I'm trying to be reasonable, but if you don't do something about that allergy, you are going to get us killed."

She wasn't sure about him, but she didn't envision spending her dying moments stuck in a cave with a dragon that wanted to have her for dinner. The air was ripe with the mingled stench of brimstone, smoke, and burned dog hair.

"I am hardly able to breathe for the stench. The last thing I want is another blast of dragon fire."

The dog didn't think much of Lenora's apology. He growled at her in reply. That was the last straw. She was only there because she was trying to help him.

"Oh, shut up," she snapped. "You're the one who got us into this mess. It is bad enough that you enchanted yourself into being a dog. But really, pissing off dragons is just plain stupid."

He lay down on the floor of the cave, covered his ears with his paws, and gave her another pitiful whimper.

Parker must have gotten dust up his nose or another whiff of the dragon, because he started sniffling again.

"Don't do it," Lenora yelled, half a second before he let loose another enchanted sneeze.

She cringed. But this time, instead of the roof caving in on them, some sort of doorway opened.

"Way to go, Parker," she said, trying to get a look at what lay on the other side of the opening. "It doesn't look like home, but it has to be better than being trapped with a dragon." She picked her husband up and stepped through the portal into the village on the other side.

Instantly, the portal vanished behind them, leaving the two of them alone outside a seedy little inn. "Well," she said, "this place doesn't look like it will have all the comforts of home, but maybe they won't object too much about my having a dog with me. Shall we give it a try?"

Parker wagged his scorched tail, and then whimpered.

Now that we were outside where she could see him better, Lenora could tell that the burns on his tail were pretty bad. She knew it hurt, but the little blackened hairless tail looked so comical she had to laugh.

"Oh Parker, what am I going to do with you?" Lenora said, as she scratched him behind his big droopy ears until he stopped being offended. "You are more trouble than a nest of dragons."

The dog put his front paws on her shoulder and licked her chin, which was as close to a kiss as he could manage in his present state.

Lenora smiled at him, and then headed toward the inn.

The inside of the inn was as seedy and rundown as its exterior. There was an unfamiliar game of chance going on in one corner of the room. One of the players glanced at Lenora in a way that made her skin crawl. Two rough looking men stood drinking by the fire. She could feel their eyes following her, but carefully avoided looking directly at anyone as she made her way to the counter. Behind the bar was a greasy, weasel-faced man in a soiled apron. He smelled of sour sweat and stale beer.

"I need a room for the night," she said, moving a little closer to Parker.

"We don't allow dogs," he said.

Inwardly, she groaned. In a village this size, there was little chance of finding another inn. The thought of spending the night in the streets frightened her, but her face betrayed nothing.

"I'll pay extra," she offered.

The innkeeper was silent for a moment, as if weighing the prospect of a hefty profit against the pleasure of watching an attractive young woman plead for a favor from him. His beady eyes narrowed above his long, pointed nose. Lenora could tell that greed had won him over. The innkeeper named a sum three times higher than what the room was worth. Lenora paid it, without comment, and headed up the narrow stairs.

The room was small and had the same scent of soured sweat and stale ale that permeated the rest of the establishment. Still, there was a bed and a basin.

"We can manage," she said as she dropped the bolt into place and set Parker down. It was late, and she was tired enough not to care how stale the bed smelled. Not bothering to undress, she stretched out to get some sleep.

The dog climbed up beside her, but she pushed him off the bed. "I don't care if we are married," she said, "you are not sharing my bed until you are back in your own form again. It is hard enough to be married to a dog without having to sleep with one."

Parker sat there staring at her, his woeful eyes and droopy ears resting on the edge of the bed. She shook her head and tossed him one of the pillows.

"You're impossible," she said, scratching his head once more before turning over and going to sleep.

Lenora was not sure how long she slept before she was awakened by a cold nose pressed into her cheek. Irritated, she pushed him away. "Get off the bed, Parker," Lenora hissed through clenched teeth.

He whimpered and nudged her again before she pushed him to the floor.

Too late, she realized he had been trying to warn her.

There was a loud crack as the bolt splintered, and the door flew open.

She recognized the intruders as the two men who had been talking by the fire when they arrived. She screamed as the scar-faced one burst into the room and rolled her in a blanket. Her struggling amounted to nothing; the kidnapper threw her over his shoulder and carried her to the alley behind the inn. Tangled as she was in the blanket, there was nothing she could do, only scream for help. It infuriated her that no one in the village came to her aid. The scoundrel tied her across the back of his horse and rode away.

She wasn't sure when she fell asleep, but it was well past midday when the kidnappers stopped and roused her. The blanket was wet with sweat, her own and the horse's. Hours of bumping along across the back of a horse in the hot sun without food had left her bruised and ill. Lenora's captors didn't seem to care as they pulled her roughly from the horse and carried her to a small tree.

The scar-faced kidnapper tied her to the trunk, still wrapped in the soiled blanket.

Lenora leaned back against the bark of the tree, grateful for the shade it gave her, and tried to figure out what they wanted with her.

Neither of her kidnappers had shown any personal interest, which ruled out sex as a motive.

They could have taken her or her purse easily enough at the inn. Nobody there had made any attempt to come to her rescue. This ruled out robbery.

She considered ransom, but her family was neither highly placed nor rich enough to make her a target for a ransom kidnapping.

She shuddered at the one thought left to consider: slavers. A woman of her age would bring a handsome price in the western slave markets. The thought made her regret her eagerness to escape the dragon. There were, she realized with a shudder, fates worse than being dinner for an angry dragon.

A moment later, she wished she had not thought about the dragon as his wide-spread wings blotted out the sun. The beast flew in an arc around the campsite before lunging toward them.

Her captors grabbed their mounts and raced for cover, leaving her tied helplessly to the tree.

She struggled to free herself from the ropes as the dragon drew closer. But, to her surprise, the dragon ignored her and chased after the two men riding away. Lenore watched in horror as flames scorched the earth along road consuming everything it touched. When the smoke cleared, all that remained of her captors were cinders.

It was taking all her willpower to keep from retching as the mingled stench of brimstone and burnt flesh clung to the back of her throat.

Lenora closed her eyes and pressed against the trunk of the

tree, afraid to even wonder what had happened to her husband. She was surprised to realize how much she missed the big lug, even if he was responsible for the mess she was in. Hot tears welled up in the corners of her eyes as the full impact of her situation hit.

Just as she was about to give up hope, she felt a tug on the ropes. Her heart flip-flopped as Parker's cold nose pressed against her hands.

"Parker! You followed us all this way!"

A small tear formed in the corner of her eye as he licked her hand, then continued trying to untie her ropes with his teeth.

"Hurry!" she urged as the dragon returned.

Lenore realized that Parker must have seen the shadow looming overhead. They both knew he would never get the knots untied before the dragon attacked. Lenore screamed as the dragon's talons sank into the branches of the tree. Parker clamped down on the knots with his teeth as the dragon pulled, uprooting the tree and carrying it and the two of them away.

Just when Lenore thought the situation couldn't get any worse, she heard her husband begin to sniffle.

To his credit, Parker tried valiantly to hold back the sneeze. The sneeze that resulted was the worst Lenore had ever heard. She could feel the lines of power strike her. Her hair stood on end as magical powers coursed through her body and spilled from every pore.

Lenore had never experienced anything like the magic Parker released. She could see the lines of power as they ran along the branches and roots of the tree. Streams of energy ran along the dragon's talons and over his scales.

A scream unlike anything Lenore had ever heard erupted from the dragon's maw in a stream of blue fire, as he struggled to free his talons from the branches of the tree.

Bolts of lightning rained from the tips of each branch and shot toward the ground from every root. Heavy clouds were drawn to the storm, adding their fury to the enchantment.

Lenore was sure that at any moment the lightning would strike, disintegrating both of them. Then she realized that Parker was no longer clinging to the ropes. The sneeze must have made him lose his grip on the rope.

"Parker!" she shouted.

There was no answer.

Around her, his magic showered light and color, but she was

oblivious to the enchanted spectacle. Her eyes pressed closed to hold back the tears at the thought of Parker tumbling alone toward the ground.

"Oh, Parker," she sobbed as his magic flowed through her, held her, allowed her to drift slowly to earth on a cushion of magically charged air.

The dragon no longer struggled; even his heavy scales could not protect him from the relentless blasts of power flowing through the tree. His limp body drooped from the tree, touching the ground before the smallest root sizzled its way into the soil.

Rain fell nearly as fast as Lenore's tears. She touched the ground lightly as the tree sank deeper into the soil, but her heavy heart made her knees buckle. Behind her, she could feel a slight give in the wet ropes. Slowly, she managed to work one hand free, then the other.

All Lenore could think about as she worked on untying the wet knots was finding Parker. She had to free herself. She had to find him, alive or—no, she wouldn't think about that.

Just then, there was a familiar sniffle followed by a small sneeze.

Lenore sighed and plucked a daisy from her ear.

"Oh Parker," she said. "What am I going to do with you?"

"I can think of a few things," he said, slicing through the ropes holding her to the tree.

"Parker! You're you."

He stepped from behind the tree and took her in his arms.

"Yes, the enchantment is broken," he said, plucking another blossom from her ear. "Now let me fix that."

Parker mumbled a few words and touched her ear before she had time to protest.

A small green sprout wilted and fell away.

Sniffling again, her husband pinched his nose tightly.

"Can we get away from that dragon before something else happens?" he asked in a nasal voice.

Lenore grabbed his hand and ran.

Gwen Mayo grew up in the hills of Eastern Kentucky. Her home state's colorful past forms the backdrop for her Nessa Donnelly historical mysteries, Circle of Dishonor *and* Concealed in Ash. *She is a graduate of the University of Kentucky Department of Political Science, and is an active member of Sisters in Crime, including the Florida Gulf Coast, Derby Rotten Scoundrels, and GUPPY*

Chapters. She currently lives and writes in Safety Harbor, Florida. Since relocating, she has teamed up with humorist Sarah E. Glenn to write the Three Snowbirds Mysteries: Murder on the Mullet Express *and the forthcoming* Murder at the Million Dollar Pier. *Her numerous short stories have appeared in anthologies, webzines, and micro-fiction collections.*

Learn more about her at: gwenmayo.com

HOW A VAMPIRE GETS A TAN

By Paul Wartenberg

I stand at the sliding glass door of the hotel patio, wearing only a beach towel and covered in three layers of suntan lotion. The morning sunlight is moving into the day, leaving little time left before the building casts a shade on where I can sit.

"Very well, Minette." I whisper words of courage to myself. "You know how this works. Ten minutes. You can do this in ten minutes."

A deep breath and then I slide the door wide open, keeping it that way. In case the sun burns. The ocean breeze wafts into the room, scent of sand and salt making me aware of how this is Florida and not New York City, my domain of night and shadow. Just inches away from sunlight now …

I scurry to the patio bench facing the beach, sitting in the sun. The heat of summertime beats against my face. I can feel the slow burn already, but steel myself to make this last. The desire to see myself with any kind of a skin tone instead of my vampiric pallor is too tempting.

The noise outside deafens me, but not because of my enhanced hearing. I hear the roar of the crowd cheering the musicians of a beach concert, sounds echoing against this hotel. I dare not take even a moment to look over the railing. Besides, it is not the music I prefer.

I cast off the towel with a wave of my hand, draping it over the lounger, leaving every inch of me exposed. I never enjoy seeing tan lines on my lovers and am not about to become a hypocrite upon the matter now. Besides, I am twenty stories above the beach with a concrete balcony. Few should see me naked here.

I collapse onto my back atop the towel, arms stretched out.

Daring the sun to burn me as I feel the heat like dagger tips against my flesh. Even with the darkest tint sunglasses, I keep my sensitive eyes closed to the bright light above. No, sunlight does not kill me. I am Dhampyr, blood born instead of cursed, arisen Revenant, and I can walk in the day. But it hurts.

I breathe again, and fumble at the smartphone in my hand. Blinking my right eye open, squinting away from the sun, I find the Music app already opened to the short playlist I am using as my timer. The album version of Gloria Gaynor's "I Will Survive" at 4 minutes 56 seconds to tone my front side, Lady Gaga's "Do What U Want Kronic Mix" at 5 minutes 12 seconds for my back. As close as I can dare to be this exposed. I should not burn, I may sear, but I can recover. I know I can ...

Settling in, unable to rest with my skin feeling the warmth all too well, I take a minute to muse about why I was even in Daytona doing this. Megan, my current lover, attending her professional conference with fellow museum archivists, was so eager for this trip and so eager to take it with me.

"But why a hotel at a beach?" I asked her, in between sessions of packing for the trip and sessions of lovemaking whenever we modeled our revealing swimwear. "Should not your profession have you going to places with, well, museums?"

"You obviously never been to conferences," Megan giggled after a particularly playful evening. "The whole point of one is to attend one presentation, maybe sometimes host your own, and then spend the rest of the weekend goofing off, getting drunk, or getting a tan." She grinned as she moved her finger from freckle to freckle along her body where her sunning attempts had left her spotted. "Anyway, I'm curious about you. I've been with you long enough to see you can walk around in the day just fine. But I wanna know how a vampire gets a tan. I'd love to see you warmed up."

I smile at the memory, so recent and so pleasing. She is at the conference now, performing her demonstrations on how to counter ancient curses on Sumerian finds. Yes, for her sake more than my own vanity, I am risking this briefness in the sun.

Oh no. I hear a patio door nearby slide open. I did not pay attention if there were occupants next door, too focused on the effort to tan. If they are downwind to me, while I'm sitting here in the nude getting all hot and all sweaty ...

The thing about Vampires seducing Normals, you see, doesn't

have anything to do with hypnotic eyes. It is in the scent, the pheromones of attraction that boost the interest and eventually the libido of a person within range. The person we want. It is usually not powerful enough to hook anyone's attention past a few meters.

Unless we make ourselves perspire, like I do when I'm on a dance floor. Or if I am in the sweltering sunlight right now trying to work on a ten-minute tan. In these moments, I cannot control my own body. All this lotion painted onto me will not mask my scent.

And I think the tanning is making my aroma stronger than ever. Making it more potent.

More dangerous.

A man's voice shouts across the short distance between balconies, cutting into Gloria's song as she laments the pieces of her broken heart. "You are a work of art, my beautiful *femme*. Such loveliness, such perfection. You must talk to me, *ma chérie*."

Damnation. I press the pause on my app. I need to hurry back into the room.

I rise from the bench with a dancer's grace, reaching for the towel beneath me and wrapping myself with a swift gesture. I turn to stand in the voice's direction to see who it is I have attracted before I run for cover.

I see an aging, waddling man with more hair on his stomach than his head, and the hair he has covers lumpish skin paler than mine own. Barefoot, I still stand taller by inches and I know I am no Amazon. In my two hundred years of nightlife, I have never seen a man both decrepit and obese. My father's warning from before the First World War calls out from the deepest memory, about the tragedy of a Dhampyr's longevity. He is right: You will live to see every horror that Divine Thought can imagine.

Without a word I rush off the patio, embarrassed yet hoping I can avoid any further confrontation. If my scent did not fully overwhelm him, with luck the breeze will carry my addictive aroma away.

The hotel room walls may separate me at the moment from that man; they do not protect me from the sounds now coming next door. I hear another voice, then two more. The old man is not alone over there. The voices become shouts, the shouts become orders. I understand the language from my early years of wandering Europe during the days of the continental wars. A mixture of French and Slav. I recognize one particular order in French. "Saisir." *Seize her.*

123

Within seconds, the noises move from next door to the front of my hotel door. A knock. Several knocks. Another man's voice, barking in harsh English. "You there, naked woman! The boss likes you! Open the door. Open the door!"

I stumble away from the noise, finding myself back on the patio. Considering my options. And no, turning myself into a giant bat to fly away is not an option. I never understood where that false myth ever arose.

That old man remained at his spot, his face expressing desire in the worst way. "Ah, *chérie*. Ah, beauty. Your perfume intoxicates, the curve of your breasts entice, your …"

I snarl, knowing my canines will shine in the sunlight. "Shut up and call off your dogs. I was not doing any of this for your enjoyment."

The banging at my door gets worse as the grotesque on the neighboring balcony makes a lewd gesture with his tongue, all the while holding up a bag of powder in one hand and an over-sized semiautomatic pistol in the other.

I think to myself in the most sarcastic way possible. Of course Megan and I had to book a hotel room right next to a vacationing drug lord. You cannot plan such misfortune.

The banging turns to thumping. I worry they are going to shatter the door down. An additional cost on Megan's bill, I fear. That will not do.

"Very well, gentlemen." I turn to face the monster leering at me from a few meters away. "I did not come on this trip for this, but I dread I will have to do what I do best."

I let go of the towel, flicking it away as I raise an arm to pose. The slimness of my arms and legs for all to see as I hop onto the ledge to make the jump across. The eyes of the perverted old man widen in delight. It will be the last joy he knows.

For a Dhampyr, a jump like this is easy. In my youth, before I aged into my eternal womanhood, I could jump across the length of entire castle walls. The problem now is the obstacle in my way. What looked to be two hundred kilograms of flab. I can likely kick him onto his arse, but I would bounce off and fall to twenty stories below. It would not be to my death, but I would land awkwardly. Naked. Sweating. Surrounded by a hundred more Normals immediately aroused by my presence.

No, I have to do this just right. No more attractions or distractions. A return to the silence, before the sun flays my skin into

124

painful crispness.

I jump.

I move quicker than he can react. With one arm outstretched, I wrap myself around the pervert's thick neck, using him as an anchor and letting my body slide feet first past him. My own weight would never have been enough to knock him down, but my momentum works to my favor.

My arm around his neck becomes a vise. I grip my free hand around my wrist, tightening my catch. My body turns just enough that I can turn his head faster than his spine can handle.

My feet touch his patio just as the crack of his neck can be heard. The pervert is not dead, not yet. It will take some seconds for his life to ebb.

As I land, letting the weight slip from my arms, I can see into the man's hotel room. A mess of bedsheets, open suitcases, a set of rifles on a dresser, one youthful bodyguard standing at the front door looking at me with stunned eyes both excited and horrified. "The boss!" the boy shouts in Croatian, raising a gun in one hand. "She's over here! She's choked him! Get her! Get her!"

He stumbles at me, leaving the door open for two more men, both of them older and grizzled with scars from earlier battles, to follow him. The eyes of both men light up as they see me naked and enticing, but the adrenaline of the moment urges them to charge with guns drawn as well.

It takes me thirty-seven seconds to deal with them.

I return to my hotel room by jumping back across the patios. I did not have my room key, after all. I try to wipe my feet on the concrete, but I am dripping with splattered blood, so I realize the carpet is doomed no matter what. I walk towards the bathroom to the front of the suite, but pause to look at myself in the dresser mirror.

There is blood from my right shoulder down to my hip. The left forearm covered as though I dipped it into a vat. I notice droplets across my right cheek, a vivid marking, but I refuse to taste it. I do have standards ...

I sigh with the realization that blood and suntan lotion do not mix. My tanning effort may be done for the day.

I should wash, but I cannot wait for the discovery of what I left behind next door. I find my phone and choose my Contacts list, dialing the one person who can assist me now.

Every Dhampyr has a Handler, thanks to the treaty between us and Normals. We do odd jobs for them, they keep us off the news. Since my kind does not need to hunt for blood anymore, we have become useful monsters to them, reducing their intent to hunt us with weapons we can no longer adapt against. I have never met my Handlers in person, due to the risks of ... interpersonal persuasion. The current one of the last eight years only goes by a phone code name: Aegir.

Aegir answers my call with a prompt statement. "You're still in Daytona."

"Yes, as arranged with your department."

"What is your situation?"

I glance to the wall separating me from the scene of my crime. "I had a confrontation. Four men. We need a recovery team, crime unit, and a cleaning crew before the hotel's staff discovers the scene."

"We need?" Aegir echoes back to me. "You need, to clean up your body count."

"This is a good thing," I sigh. "The men were armed drug smugglers." I close my eyes to recount what I spied during the fight. "I noticed two suitcases each containing thirty-six bags of heroin. Five semiautomatic rifles in plain sight; there may be more at the scene. One open laptop, although I did not secure it, so it may go into sleep mode. Ten different phones, three of them still in packages. I also ..."

"Enough." Aegir tends to focus on a primary concern. "You do realize this is not a sanctioned hit. You had no mission assignments. This is you going rogue."

"This was an accident."

Aegir takes five seconds to connect cause to effect. "You were sunbathing, weren't you." It was not even a question from him.

"I was unaware the hotel room next to me was occupied at that moment." I defend myself. "This was not a planned target."

Aegir said nothing for a minute.

"I should not be the least of your concerns at this moment," I continue. "Consider these men are, very well, were, carrying that much in weapons and drugs. It takes two parties to make any deal. You at least need investigators here to follow up on that."

I hear typing from Aegir's end of the call. "Dispatching a cleaner and investigators. Notifying the hotel so they have no concerns. For all they'll know this is a deal gone bad, and they'll want it hushed up for convention season. In the meantime, Minette, you are on notice. No more kills until you get debriefed by us within the next twenty-four hours."

"Thank you."

"You are not welcome." Aegir beeped his phone off.

With that, I take a shower with the bathroom door open, so I may listen to all noises from the hallway. Considering it a lesson learned. The droplets of water cool my skin as it washes away the blood-mixed lotion. I think of the stories about vampires and running water and shake my head. As though water could harm us, outside of drowning just as Normals would. One day my brethren should stand before the world and explain all the things the humans get wrong about us. Then I remember what my father warned me about humans. They would simply invite us onto the late-night talk shows and have us perform Stupid Vampire Tricks. Which is sad; I would rather play the cello for them instead.

The hotel door rattles. It is too soon for Aegir's team to be here. My awareness attunes to the noise, picking up the comforting slide and click of a keycard to open. Thank the Gods. I push the shower curtain aside, so I can turn and watch my lover enter.

I see Megan is not in the best of moods. Her professional clothes are in bad shape: one sleeve nearly ripped free, odd scratches and hastily improvised oriental wards inked onto her face and hands. The rolling cart she uses to carry her papers and displays seems more loaded than when she left this morning, but with broken pieces of something that should be better off as dust. That lovely auburn hair of hers no longer in a ponytail, but dangling over her shoulders in bitter, desperate victory. She sees me from the stall watching her, and even with me naked and inviting, she can only glare back with a lifetime's worth of frustration and ire.

I take a moment to decide what to ask with prudence and an open mind, hoping not to upset her further. "So. Ah. How did your morning conference presentation on cursed artifacts go?"

Megan scowls at me, as though I should not have asked a single thing. It takes almost a minute before she relents and shakes her head. "Not as well as it should have. Some idiot brought samples."

I catch myself raising a hand to my lips to suppress a giggle. I make the effort to lower the arm to where the hand rests above my belly button. "You have my sympathies. Would you care to join me and relax?"

"I shouldn't," Megan sighs. "I just need to collapse for an hour. No, make it a day. Besides," she gives me an appraising look. "I think you're needing to wash all that blood off."

"You can tell?"

"That, and the small army of troops gathering downstairs in the lobby." Megan steps away from the bathroom, still talking as she reaches toward the bed. "I take it you had to work on a body count this morning as well?"

"I did not mean to," I answer her, "but I did not consider how my presence would affect others while I tried to get a suntan."

"Oh ho, so you tried that." I think I can hear Megan smile as she collapses onto that comforting bed. "So, did we find out how a vampire gets a tan?"

I shake my head and resume showering. "Yes, we did. It turns out the Beatles knew the answer all along. I have to do it standing in the English rain."

Paul Wartenberg is a full-time librarian who never worked on a tan. He has, however, worked on a lot of short stories that have shown up in previous Strangely Funny *collections. Other stories can be found in his short story collection,* Last of The Grapefruit Wars. *He recently received Finalist consideration for the Florida Writers Association's Royal Palm Literary Awards in the Short Fiction category. You can find out more at wittylibrarian.blogspot.com*

A TERRIBLE THING TO WASTE

By David Perlmutter

I.

It was a harrowing experience, to say the least.

You could say that about all of my adventures, but it was particularly true of this one. Especially since my mind, which typically helps me deal with everything, nearly cracked—and could have taken me with it.

For those of you not familiar with me, allow me to introduce myself.

My name is Cerberus, and I am the most powerful puppy in the universe. I don't like to brag, but my speed, strength, physical endurance, and, above all, intelligence, are unmatched among any other canines. You can probably tell because I'm writing to you now, and most dogs can't master that, what with having no fingers and all.

Well, technically I'm dictating it, and my *computer's* writing it. But that's beside the point.

I am the consequence of a union between a normal Earth Dalmatian and a member of a race of super-powered alien canines known as the Perros, who originated in the solar sphere around the dog star, Sirius. Apparently, my father the alien got around a bit, because I seem to have a ton of half-brother and half-sister relations among the dogs and puppies of the world. Many of them have super-powers as well, but not to the degree and the totality which I am fortunate enough to possess. Although we're all good for helping each other out in a pinch.

When not on duty—either solo or in various team configurations with my heroine gal-pals—I adopt the secret identity of "Cuddles", the mild-mannered pet of the Parker family, and the object of the excessive affection of their kindergarten-age daughter, Gudrun. But, when evil strikes, I emerge in my monogrammed T shirt uniform to fight it. Whatever form it takes, and however long it takes to subdue it.

On the occasion which I am about to relate, though, it didn't seem, for a long time, that I had any chance of subduing anybody. I was lucky to get out of it alive.

II.

I wasn't entirely correct when I said all the children of the Perros on Earth were dogs. Some of them preferred the species related to us—wolves, coyotes and foxes—for copulation desires. I don't get along well with the beasts that emerged out of that line of the family at all. For good reasons.

On this particular evening, I had retired to my doghouse after Gudrun had spent most of the first part of the night entertaining herself with me, until she had to go to bed. Tired beyond belief, but still intact, I had hoped to catch up on my reading, but it was not to be.

For what should face me as I arrived at my destination but a doughnut-shaped hole in reality, spewing the icy-cold winds of space right at me with gale force. Trouble with a capital *T*.

I quickly shifted to hero mode by ripping off the false pelt I wear over my shirt, and flew as quickly as I could over to the hole as the winds would allow. Fortunately, I was able to grab hold of an edge of the doughnut with each paw. Then I applied my strength, and compressed the doughnut into a small, unthreatening pinprick. It was an immense assertion that left my body feeling completely drained of power.

But I had done my duty and saved the universe.

Or so I thought.

At that point, a small and very cunning creature, all red and white fur and yellow eyes and black feet, emerged from behind a conveniently placed boulder.

"Very good," she said, with mock sincerity. "Your might has not deserted you since our last encounter, Cerberus. What about the rest of you?"

"*Kit Vixen!*" I growled, spitting out the name of my hated

mortal enemy to show I had not forgotten her.

"In the flesh," she responded.

"Am I to assume," I asked, "that you just escaped from your last place of imprisonment via that wormhole?"

"In a word, yes," she answered.

"And I'll bet you did it so you could resume your desired conquest of the universe—which I only so recently thwarted. Correct?"

"That's about the size of it, *sis.*"

I became livid.

"Do not call me that!" I snapped.

"Oh, come on," she barked. "No matter what you say, we are related."

"We are not."

"Maybe I'm not one of your precious half-dog siblings, but I have Perro blood in me that's just as pure and true as yours."

"That, I do not doubt. But the fact that you use the powers derived from said blood for evil, rather than good, has soured me on your side of the 'family'."

"As if being good really gets you anywhere."

"Trust a villain to say that. But the fact remains that, according to Linnaeus, foxes are not canines. You are not listed under the genus *canis* but under your own separate one—*vulpes.*"

"Get your head out of the laboratory, scientist. Foxes have the same behaviors and instincts for survival that wolves and coyotes have. And what you *dogs* would still have if you hadn't sold out to the human beings."

"We did not "sell out"! They offered us eternal food and eternal friendship, and we accepted."

"You really believe that fake news?"

"Enough of this!" I ordered. "Make tracks, Vixen—before I smite you."

"'Smite'?" She laughed. "What century did you pull that line from?"

"My point has been made."

"Then let me make *my* point."

She clicked her tongue, and …

We were no longer on Earth as I knew it. Instead, we were in a completely different place.

"Hey!" I said, surprised. "What's going on here?"

"Finally," said Kit. "Something you don't know."

131

"How about you enlighten me, then—before I decide to get rough?"

"Certainly. As you probably guessed, this is not the universe we both came from. This is a dimension of an entirely different construction. Chiefly because it is the creation of my own mind."

"I see. You didn't exactly have this ability before. How come you do now?"

"Partially, due to you. Your defeat of me led to my banishment away from Earth, and thus to me traveling between alien worlds for a time. All through that time, I had my mind set on vengeance against you. You are, of course, a formidable adversary, given all your gifts of strength, speed, intelligence and whatnot. So, if I was to defeat you, I would have to make myself superior to you in some area. And so, I ask: are *you* capable of creating entire dimensions with your mind alone, dictated entirely by your subconscious? And can you harness that dimension to enhance your own magical powers?"

"Well … no … but I could …"

"Good. All that time I spent learning how to do this wasn't spent in vain."

"I've had enough of your showing-off, Vixen. Get me back to Earth before I …"

"*You* fail to understand the gravity of this situation," she shot back.

Before I could do or say anything further, something resembling a third eye appeared at the top of her head, and it emitted a long beam of light not unlike a laser. Which proceeded to hit me and knock me to the ground, practically senseless.

That's normal protocol for me. I typically am able to shrug such things off and carry on.

But not this time.

My body, usually invulnerable to such tricks, had been unable to protect me. I had been gravely and severely wounded for the first time in a very long time.

Somehow, Kit had figured out a way to make herself mighty and reduce me to being merely mortal.

Or so it appeared.

"What … just … happened?" I sputtered, as I got up with what was left of my strength.

"Just a little show of force to remind you who runs things here," said Kit. "This is *my* dimension. My mind, my ball, my rules."

"So?"

"Don't you get it, Cerberus? You're my prisoner."

"*What?*"

"That's right. A small price to pay for disrespecting me."

"Why, you treacherous ... "

I rose to attack her again, forgetting my reduced condition. She caught me in the midst of jumping at her and knocked me down again with the eye beam. Then, a doughnut-shaped hole not unlike the one I'd shut down earlier opened behind me, with the winds inside starting to pull me towards it, and me now powerless to resist them.

"I could snap your bony little neck and put you out of your misery easily," said Kit. "But, as you're not your usual self, I'll be merciful. This'll be tit for tat. You exiled me from Earth; I'll exile you from it likewise. You'll stay in here forever! And I can take over Earth unopposed!"

She used another shot of the light to push me through the doughnut, and I was sent to what appeared to be my doom.

III.

I seemed to fall to the ground for an eternity, until I finally hit land with a loud, painful crash.

At that point, it was apparent that I was at the bottom of an enormous pit of coal-colored blackness, with no beginning or end, no entrance or exit. And thus, no way to escape.

Not that I was capable of doing that at the moment.

I had been deeply humiliated—and severely weakened—by my enemy and was feeling the effects of both. Now, I'd been humiliated and smacked around by enemies before, but my superpowers and great intelligence had previously allowed me to escape with only minimal damage to body and pride. Here, however, I had been broken in both body and mind, and felt it deeply. There seemed to be no end to my pain, nor likewise to the length of my punishment.

Kit projected herself in front of me as a two-dimensional transparent image. Where she was now, for real, was another matter entirely.

I was so worn out and defeated that I resorted to something I had sworn I would never do with an enemy.

I begged.

"Please!" I shouted. "Get me out of here, and I will never oppose any of your schemes again!"

"Well …" she said, pretending to consider my plea.

"Consider it, at least!"

"Oh, for God's sake. You are pathetic without your powers, you know that?"

"Have you no compassion?"

"Don't be so childish."

"*Childish?* How dare you!"

"Honestly, Cerberus. You could really use a rethink on being a heroine, 'cause you sure can't handle a defeat very maturely. Your whole *modus operandi* proves that."

"How?"

"Isn't it obvious? Your body is small, but your powers—and thus, your ego—are big. The powers compensate for your lack of size, and make you super effective as a fighter and as a brain. But, take them away, and you're nothing."

"You can't just reduce me to a Freudian cliché like that."

"I can do anything I want in here. Remember, this is my dimension."

"You are the most mean and spiteful creature I have ever met!"

"Not the best thing to say to your new mistress!" she snapped, revealing the eye and giving me another blast to shut me up. "Just for that, it's going to be even harder for you to get out of this joint, you so-called Princess of Puppies!"

And, with that ironic parting shot at my superhero nickname, she was gone.

And I was trapped in oblivion.

IV.

I don't know how long I was there. It could have been an hour, or it could have been days, weeks, months or even years. Time was utterly meaningless in that space.

All I knew was that, having suffered intense physical pain, I was now undergoing the worst kind of mental torture imaginable. Kit had beaten me already; now she was trying to break my mind.

The pit in which I was constructed was an ingenious act of capricious sadism on her part. She'd constructed it so that it seemed impossible to escape, but easy enough to get into. She showed this when she constructed some demons with her mind and dropped them in there with me. Of course, I had been robbed of my strength, so I had no way of resisting them. They beat me soundly and then departed, leaving me in constant dread of when they might return.

Otherwise, Kit showed restraint, compared to what she could have done with me. She easily could have killed me right away. But she felt it was easier to let my own mind kill me instead—with worry and fear.

Gradually, I could feel my mind slip away from me as what passed for time passed. I found myself going insane. Imagining things and becoming preoccupied with them instead of my reality. I was becoming a mad dog, although because of something other than rabies.

Finally, I could bear the tedium and isolation no longer. The stoic mask that is usually my face disappeared, and I laughed and cried in mental distress.

"Vixen, you fiend!" I spat. "Stop tormenting me! I can no longer resist you. Finish me off, here and now, and be done with it, already!"

"No!" another voice, resembling mine, suddenly shouted. "You will not surrender yourself in such a fashion. I forbid it."

I turned around and was suddenly face to face with a doppelganger. She looked exactly like me, except that she wore a white dress and had a halo hovering above her head.

"Who are you?" I asked. "Did Kit send you to off me, or …"

"Don't be absurd," she said. "I have nothing to do with that monster."

"Then who are you?"

"Gad! For a supposed mental 'genius', you have some big blind spots. *I* am your conscience."

"Then it's true!" I said, cackling like a loon. "You're supposed to be a metaphysical thing, not a physical one. Therefore, it's obvious: I am going completely stark-raving mad!"

Her response was to give me a brutal slap in the face that hurt me more than any of Kit's previous attacks, which was saying something.

"Do not disrespect me!" she thundered. "I am a patient creature, but I do not tolerate insolence. Is that clear?"

She was me, all right.

"Yes, ma'am," I said, adopting a submissive body pose.

"Get up!" she ordered, and I obeyed.

"One question," I requested. "How is it that you are taking corporeal form like this? I thought that was merely mythology."

"Nonsense," she said. "I have always existed this way to help

135

you, Cerberus. As I said, I am your conscience. I live within you, through your words and your deeds, as one's conscience does in every being. But the Perros are not typical that way, as they are not typical otherwise. At the most perilous times in the lives of their hosts, the consciences of Perros can assume this form, when they are on the verge of death or seeking it out. We then persuade—*insist*—that you banish these thoughts and go back to living."

"Living?" I still doubted her. "What have I got to live for? I've been completely humiliated and defeated by an enemy who has shown herself superior to me. Besides which, I have been imprisoned here, in this place where there is no time or space, and no means of getting out. How do you suppose that I *live* here?"

"You fool. Stop doubting yourself. You are her superior physically, so battling her should not be an issue. She simply used … shall we say, extra-legal means to defeat you. But you yourself have equally formidable abilities that she does not have—and will never acquire."

"What are you implying?"

"Use your head, you idiot!"

The words stung, but they made their mark on me right away, as soon as I considered the implication.

"Of course!" I said. "She's not familiar with absolutely everything I can do. Maybe physically I can't match her if she has the advantage here, but there's nothing that says all of my abilities are useless in this realm."

"Exactly," she answered. "She was used to fighting you physically before then, so the … higher end … of your abilities wasn't necessary with her. Perhaps it is now."

"Perhaps," I agreed, already pondering.

"Well, my work here is done," she said, preparing to depart.

"Wait!"

"What?"

"Usually, if a conscience manifests itself in this way, it takes both angelic and demonic forms."

"So?"

"What happened to the devil me?"

"She quit. You gave her absolutely *no* material to work with."

And with those words, she was gone.

V.

Remembering now a particular resource I could use to my advantage, I sat down on the ground in a pose resembling a Buddhist monk in prayer, grasping it tightly in my lower paws. Then, after a warm-up of chanting, I felt an intense surge of energy build up inside of me, almost as if I were on fire.

This was the most complicated—and flashy—of my super-canine powers. If it didn't help me free myself from Kit's grasp, nothing would.

"Fabricated illusions!" I shouted. "In the name of all that is righteous at my command, I order you to cease deceiving me at once, and return me to the place and time where I truly belong!"

Flames flung themselves out of my paws and eyes, and hit the coal black darkness with full force, burning it up, while leaving me unharmed. In a matter of seconds, it was obliterated ...

And I was back where I started, back on Earth, and feeling not only smart, but strong anew.

Kit lay down on the ground in front of me, looking as if she had suffered a massive injury to her head. Which, to all intents and purposes, she had.

"What did you do to me?" she shouted. "I thought I was unstoppable with what I had."

"That was your mistake," I responded. "You assumed you knew who I was when you attacked me, Kit. But you didn't realize the extent of what I have. Neither did I, until I was finally able to clear my head and rediscover it again."

"I suppose I deserved being undone by your trickery, since it was me tricking you that started this whole thing. But it still doesn't mean that what you did was fair—or just."

"Oh, please," I said, dismissively.

"But," she grinned cryptically, "at least I got you to beg me for something."

Outraged, I grabbed her by the scruff of her neck and held her aloft.

"Just this once," I snarled, "and never again. Good night, Kit."

Utilizing my strength for the final time that evening, I threw her as far as I could, hoping that she'd never come back to torment me again. Then and only then was I finally able to retreat to my doghouse and get some much-needed sleep.

David Perlmutter is a freelance writer based in Winnipeg, Manitoba, Canada. He is the author of America Toons In: A History of Television Animation *(McFarland and Co.)*, The Singular Adventures Of Jefferson Ball *(Amazon Kindle/Smashwords)*, The Pups *(Booklocker.com)*, Certain Private Conversations and Other Stories *(Aurora Publishing)*, Honey and Salt *(Scarlet Leaf Publishing)*, Orthicon; or, the History of a Bad Idea *(Linkville Press, forthcoming), and* The Encyclopedia of American Animated Television Shows *(Rowman and Littlefield). His short stories can be read on* Curious Fictions *at* Curious Fictions/David Perlmutter. *He can be reached on Facebook at David Perlmutter-Writer, Twitter at @DKPLJW1, and Tumblr at* The Musings of David Perlmutter *(yesdavidperlmutterfan).*

SKUNKNADO

(or Every Disaster Movie Ever Made)

By B. David Spicer

I.

Chet smashed the accelerator and pulled off the freeway onto a little dirt road that had no name on the map. The black clouds hung above the van as he fishtailed over the gravel.

"Hurry up, Chet! We've got to get the imager in place before the funnel forms!" Bree kicked the back of Chet's seat for emphasis.

Chet peered up at the clouds through the windshield. "Have you ever seen a squall line like that before? It's immense!"

Dr. Redmond clung to his laptop in the passenger seat. "It's absolutely unprecedented, easily the largest and most unstable airmass I've ever seen. We might be looking at the Mother of All Storms."

Bree poked her head forward from the rear of the van, her uniquely rebellious purple mohawk artfully disarranged on her head. "The imager's all set. Find a funnel, and I'll fire the laser so we can hurry up and win our Nobel."

"How's that thing work again?"

Bree threw a pen at him. "Seriously, Chet? It's a super-complicated device that fires a laser beam into a tornado and gathers the most accurate data ever collected on what goes on inside the thing. It's the sort of thing that every member of this team should know backwards and forwards without asking, or at least should have asked before the very moment when we're chasing down the largest tornado ever seen in North America. Discussing it now just seems oddly extraneous."

Chet nodded sagely. "I guess I forgot."

Dr. Redmond traced out their route on a roadmap with a finger, even though he had a perfectly usable computer right there on his lap. "We should be coming up on the highway."

"Which highway is it?"

"*The* highway." Dr. Redmond moved his finger over the map. "The town of Harmond is just a few miles away."

Chet's brow creased. "Isn't Harmond the center of the nation's skunk-ranching industry?"

"Why, yes." Dr. Redmond smiled. "My father was a farmhand on a skunk ranch. We were poor, but we had dignity. From those humble origins I, with a supreme amount of hard work, raised myself to my current, lofty heights of academic achievement."

"Uh, Dr. Redmond ..."

The van careened down the road, rolling onto two wheels as Chet hauled over the steering wheel without slowing down. The van made the eighty-mile-per-hour turn on two wheels, then settled back onto four wheels without deleterious effects. Chet hooted and hollered as he beat out a frantic rhythm on the steering wheel. "Woo-hoo!"

"Dr. Redmond ...?"

"I remember when I was just a freshman at the University of Princeton. Several of the older boys made fun of me, not because I was in any way intellectually inferior, no indeed, for they recognized in me, even then, the seeds of genius. Rather, they disliked me because, having been raised on a skunk ranch, naturally my sense of smell was painfully acute, and I could tell when they had been indulging in the sinful and filthy habit of reefer-smoking."

Chet gasped. "Surely not!"

"Oh yes, my friend, they indulged their depraved desires nearly every day, and I could always smell the stink on them. They were reprobates of the worst kind. They all died of reefer-madness, alone and destitute, rotting in the gutter."

"Dr. Redmond!"

He frowned and turned to look at Bree. "What is it, Bree?"

She pointed out the windscreen. A pitch black, whirling funnel tore its way through the stockyards just outside of Harmond. Thousands of unfortunate skunks, representing untold millions in valuable breeding stock, were snatched up and hurled into the towering gyre of the tornado.

Chet slammed on the brakes and the van lurched to a halt, stalling the engine. He slowly and dramatically removed his sunglasses, which he wore despite the near blackout conditions, and stared slack-jawed at the tornado. "That's not just the Mother of All Tornadoes, it's the Great-Grandmother."

"So, anyway, I turned in those older boys for their life-destroying habits …"

"Dr. Redmond! This is not the time for nostalgia!"

"Fine, Bree. Let's just *not* impart our hard-earned wisdom. Let's do what *you* want to do."

"I'm firing the laser!"

Chet pointed out the side window. "We've got another one! It's at least as large as the first one!"

"One over here too!" Dr. Redmond looked out the window to his right. "They're all three going to collide!"

Bree frowned and leaned forward to see the twisters. "That's not possible."

"They're combining into one huge tornado!" Chet futilely tried to restart the van's stalled engine.

"That's not how weather works, Chet!"

"It is now. It's a thousand percent bigger, at least!"

"That's not how math works, either!"

"It is now!"

The three massive tornadoes swirled into one another, increasing the size of the original by several orders of magnitude. Now it towered far above the horizon, bearing down on the town of Harmond. It crashed through the Skunk Rancher's Mercantile Exchange and sucked up the innumerable thoroughbred skunks from their expansive pens.

Chet put his sunglasses back on and tried to restart the stalled van. "When did the van stall? I don't remember that happening."

"Oh my God. The skunk-ranching industry is going to be devastated." Dr. Redmond shook his head sadly. "All those poor skunks just flying around and around and around, yet somehow never falling to the ground. It's heartbreaking."

"It's a Skunknado."

Dr. Redmond frowned at Bree. "We don't coin any neologisms without putting them through the neologism committee, you know that, Miss Dammett."

"We do now."

Chet ground the engine, which stubbornly refused to turn over. "I've never seen an F5 before."

"This one, Chet, is at least an F11."

"The Fujita Scale stops at five!"

"Not anymore, Bree."

She threw him an exasperated sigh. "I'm firing the laser. Unless you see more tornadoes coming to join the party. No? Okay."

Bree aimed the imager at the monstrous twister. A bright red, clearly visible, laser beam streaked across the skunk-infested air and pierced the tornado. "I'm receiving data! This can't be right!" Bree slapped the side of the computer monitor. "It's impossible!"

"Not anymore." Dr. Redmond peered at his laptop, also seeing the data as it came in from the imager. "The large volume of skunks within the tornado has stabilized the airmass. The motion of the swirling skunks will keep the tornado active, acting like a dynamo, perpetually spinning and keeping it from dissipating."

"For how long?" Bree slapped her computer again.

Dr. Redmond closed his laptop, removed his glasses, and rubbed his eyes. "Indefinitely."

"I think you pissed it off, Bree!" Chet pumped the gas pedal as he tried desperately to restart the van. "It's headed right for us!"

"Get us out of here!" Bree cried.

"I'm trying!" Finally, the engine started, and Chet threw it into gear. He tore down the road directly into the town of Harmond. Debris of every sort (but mostly skunks) hurled through the air, slamming into the van and denting the sides. The twister seemed to follow them, turning onto the highway and staying on the asphalt. Chet accelerated as much as he could, but the Skunknado wouldn't give up the chase. It bore down on them as they raced through town.

"We're not gonna make it!" Chet fought to keep the van on the road, but skunks were bouncing off the windshield at such a brisk pace that visibility became difficult.

Bree jammed her finger out the window. "There! In that building!"

Chet aimed the car toward a small, sturdily built auto repair shop with an open garage. He came to a screeching stop inside, leapt out of the van, and slammed the steel garage door closed. "Good thing this building was here. With an open door. And not a soul in sight."

Dr. Redmond placed his laptop on a tool bench and peered

intently at the screen. "If these readings are correct, this storm could just sit here, virtually unmoving, for a long time. We're trapped."

"That's it. I'm calling in the big guns." Bree fished her cell phone out of her pocket and tapped in a number. She held it to her ear. "Daddy, I need help."

II.

Jack Dammett clambered toward consciousness when his phone rang. He staggered toward it, kicking empty beer bottles out of the way. He looked like Arnold Schwarzenegger, Jason Statham, and Bruce Willis had each contributed DNA to create the perfect meteorologist. How he managed to spend eight hours a day in a gym bench-pressing six hundred pounds of deadweights while simultaneously earning four PhDs was anyone's guess. He accepted the call and pressed the phone against his exquisitely chiseled jaw. "Hello, Princess."

He listened, closing his eyes, and shaking his head. "I warned them, I warned every one of them! They just wouldn't listen. You can't put eighty-seven billion dollars of skunk-ranching infrastructure in Tornado Alley and not expect disaster! Hang tight, I'm on my way!" He put on his favorite wife-beater, grabbed his keys, and headed for the garage. He slid behind the wheel of his mint-condition 1977 Pontiac Firebird, slipped the key in the ignition, and smiled as the engine rumbled to life. He stomped on the accelerator and tore out of the garage.

III.

Chet peeked through the window blinds of their refuge. "It's still out there. Who knew a Skunknado could be so patient? It's just pacing, back and forth, like it's waiting for us to come out."

"My dad's on his way."

Chet frowned. "What's your dad gonna do? Blow it up with dynamite?"

"Only a moron would come up with such a stupid idea, Chet." Bree shot him a scowl.

"Don't you know who her dad is?" Dr. Redmond wiped the lenses of his glasses with a handkerchief. "He's Jack Dammett, the legendary meteorologist."

"How come I've never heard of him?"

"He held some rather unpopular beliefs about the weather."

"What kind of beliefs?"

"That the weather isn't 100% predictable, and that no matter how hard we try to tame it, it'll never be controlled."

"That's absurd." Chet started to laugh but stopped when he saw Bree's face.

"He was right, you numbskull. That's what's happening now. Weather is resisting the dominion of man by destroying a huge component of the nation's economy."

Dr. Redmond looked up at the ceiling, listening to the repetitive thumping of skunks bouncing off the roof. "Jack was the lone voice calling in the wilderness, and he was driven from the profession, exiled from science. These days he spends his time in a third-world cesspit drinking away his pain."

"Where is he?"

"Detroit."

Chet winced. "My God, what the man has had to endure." He started counting on his fingers. "How far away is Detroit from Harmond? It'll take him hours and hours ..."

"He's here!" Bree jumped up and ran to the large, undamaged picture window and pointed outside. Jack Dammett stepped out of the car, taking a moment to look over his shoulder at the Skunknado before casually walking into the repair shop. Bree hurled herself at him, clutching him in a bear hug. "Daddy! I'm so glad you're here!"

"Hello, Princess. Love the uniquely rebellious hair."

"Thanks. Is that a new tattoo of Burt Reynolds?"

He pointed his shoulder to her. "Sure is."

Dr. Redmond stepped toward them, his hand extended. "Jack, it's good to see you."

Jack stared at Redmond's hand, but didn't shake it. "I warned you Jerry, I warned you all."

"I know. We just didn't understand. The skunk-ranching lobby was putting so much pressure on us, Congress was demanding action. We made a mistake. You were right; we were wrong. We scientists were so preoccupied with whether or not we *could*, we didn't stop to think if we *should*."

Chet scratched his head. "Why does that sound so familiar?"

"So, Daddy, what do we do now? The Skunknado is still out there, and it's up to us to deal with it."

Jack peered around the room. "What do we have to work with?"

"Just what's in this garage." Chet gestured around the room. "He pointed to the adjacent office. "There's a snack machine in there. Do you like Funyuns?"

Jack squinted at the device mounted on the top of the van. "Bree, is that my laser imager design?"

"Yeah, why?"

"Does it have a Mark IV interocitor?"

"No, I upgraded it to a Mark VI. How does that help us?"

A wide grin spread across his face. "I can reconfigure it to produce a high-power laser beam! Find me a screwdriver!"

IV.

Jack Dammett dashed from the safety of the auto repair shop carrying a modified version of his revolutionary laser imager on his shoulder. He climbed behind the wheel of his Firebird, and the engine snarled to life. He roared away, flashing his lights and honking his horn. The Skunknado rumbled along behind him, casually flinging skunks by the half-dozen in his direction.

The Firebird dodged overturned cars, random bales of straw, and a surprisingly intact Big Boy restaurant statue, complete with hamburger. Jack drove out of town with the Skunknado right behind him. He found a radio transmitter tower, and parked the Firebird just far enough from it to be noticeable. He snatched the laser imager and slung it over his shoulder. Jack leapt onto the ladder that led up the tower and started climbing, pausing only long enough to start up his AC/DC playlist on his cell phone. As *Back in Black* began playing, he dodged whirling skunks and other debris.

When he had made it about halfway up, the Skunknado picked up a fuel-delivery truck and crashed it at the base of the tower. It exploded, sending scorching flames roaring up toward Jack. The impact shook the tower and the laser slipped off his shoulder and fell. It caught on a protruding crossbeam that he'd not noticed before. It dangled precariously, potentially falling into the roaring inferno below at any moment.

"Dammit, Dammett." He loosened his grip and slid down the ladder. As he got closer to the imager, he could see the strap slipping off the crossbeam. He slipped his ankles between the rungs of the ladder and swung backwards, ending up hanging upside-down by his feet. He snatched the imager just as it was about to fall. Grunting, he effortlessly righted himself and started climbing the ladder again.

He made it to the top of the tower and knelt, pressing the laser to his shoulder. From his vantage point he could take in the immensity of the Skunknado, truly a monstrous manifestation of the malignant force of nature. For a moment he regarded the Skunknado, not with anger, but with pity. With compassion.

His cell phone rang, and he put down the laser to answer it. "Hello, Princess."

"Hi. So, are you gonna shoot the laser gun sometime soon? Chet says the snack machine is out of Funyuns."

"I was just contemplating the enormity of the moment."

"Oh. Well, I hate to ruin the moment, but we're about to resort to cannibalism here."

"Okay, okay. I'll talk to you later, Princess."

"Bye, Daddy."

He ended the call, restarted *Back in Black*, and picked up the laser. He aimed it carefully, sighting it through the fancy scope that he'd had the foresight to include in the imager's initial design.

"Smile, you son of a bitch!"

He pulled the trigger, and the more powerful laser beam blasted into the Skunknado. The laser wound itself around the whirlwind, each rotation wrapping it tighter in the powerful beam of light. The air within the Skunknado became superheated, evaporating the rain within it, initially becoming a writhing mass of steam, but as the scalding air mass expanded, the Skunknado's well-defined funnel began to lose coherence, shrinking as the laser cocooned it in a bright web of light. Skunks began to fall to the ground, where they scampered away, evidently tired of being flung through the air for hours on end. The Skunknado became a mere tornado again; then, choked to death by the unyielding laser assault, it roared once more in defiance and evaporated away to nothingness.

Jack Dammett stood, hoisting the laser onto his shoulder. He looked up just in time to see the sun emerge from behind the fleeting storm clouds. He descended the ladder, past the smoldering remains of the fuel truck, and found his still-pristine Firebird. Jack drove back to town, being careful to avoid the many skunks that the hardworking ranch hands of Harmond were already rustling into makeshift stockyards.

He found his daughter and her colleagues waiting for him outside the auto repair shop.

"Hello, Princess."

"Hi, Daddy. You know that's not how lasers work, right?"

Following the now-established trend, he replied, "It is now."

Dr. Redmond looked around the devastated town. "What do we do, Jack? Everything's gone."

"We rebuild, Jerry. We rebuild because we have to. We're down, but not out. We're never gonna be out unless we give up. This incident was a harsh lesson about man's hubris. We can't ignore nature and build a crucial and essential part of this fine nation's economy directly in the line of fire. We can do better. We need to do better. Man has no choice but to do better."

Chet stared wide-eyed at Jack. "I want to be just like you when I grow up."

"Of course you do."

Bree took the laser imager from her father. "At least our data is safe. Our Nobel Prize is assured." She opened the side panel of the imager and gasped. "The hard drive is fried! All our data is gone!" She dropped the laser to the ground and covered her face with her hands. "Now we'll never win a Nobel!"

"It's okay, Princess. You can have one of mine."

She sniffed, then smiled. "Thanks, Daddy."

"No problem, Princess."

Dr. Redmond shook his head sadly. "That's not how Nobels work."

Jack Dammett grinned. "It is now."

B. David Spicer graduated from Ohio University, earning a BA in English. His first name is Brian, but he thinks B. David sounds more artsy and pretentious. He's had short stories published in more than a dozen anthologies, including Gothic Fantasy: Cozy Crime *from Flame Tree Press,* Out of Phase *and* Wicked Deeds: Witches, Warlocks, Demons & Other Evil Doers *from Sirens Call Publications,* Strangely Funny II *and* III *from Mystery and Horror, LLC,* Pernicious Invaders *and* From the Corner of Your Eye *from Great Old Ones Publishing. He lives in Ohio and owns more books than ought to be legal.*

IN A SILENT WORLD

By Curtis A. Deeter

Putt, putt, putt went Doris as Humbert guided her around the trash-strewn, windy curves of Interstate 75. Here, he narrowly dodged a downed Sit-n-Play, and there, he squealed by some college kid's ejected mattress. There was just *so* much rubbage. Where was it all coming from?

"Slow down, dear," Miriam said, scrunched low in the passenger seat, teeth a-chattering.

Humbert, watching as their fellow travelers blurred by them on the left, applied pressure to the brake. Doris ground and howled, her pads years worn and rusted nearly through.

He'd had his truck—his baby—since the 1940s. She'd always been good to him, even when his wife wasn't. She always listened. Sure, Doris had lost her gleam over the years, and she sputtered smoke out her tailpipe like a French supermodel, but she got them where they needed to go. Most of the time ... sometimes.

"Watch out for that desk chair, dear."

"I see it, I see it," Humbert grumbled, swerving to avoid certain disaster. He studied the swivel chair in the rearview mirror as it disappeared as quickly as a turtle around the corner. "What are these South'ners doing with their lives down here? You'd think somebody just got sick of their house and dumped its contents out onto the highway."

The scattered U-Haul boxes, their contents carpeting all three lanes of the road, were a testament to the fact. Distracted by his distaste for the savagery of the Cincinnati natives, Humbert failed to notice the capsized microwave on time. He also failed to notice the red brake lights of the Mazda in front of them.

Luckily, Miriam was there to grab the wheel and whip them off the shoulder towards a closed off-ramp. Doris hopped the berm, tore through a strip of construction cones, rhythmically complaining *thwump, thwump, thwump* all the while, and finally plowed into the guardrail, bending it inward towards the ditch running alongside the road. Steam poured out of Doris's engine block. She gurgled and died.

"Ah sugar," Miriam cursed, as the truck rattled to stillness.

"Ah sugar? Ah *sugar*?! You 'bout killed us, woman."

"But we're still alive, aren't we?"

Humbert crossed his arms and harrumphed. If he harrumphed hard enough, maybe she'd feel sorry for him. It hadn't worked to this day, but he'd be damned if he stopped trying.

Gingerly, he opened the door and hobbled around to help Miriam out. Then they stood, watching traffic creep by, hoping someone saw them and stopped to help an elderly couple down on their luck.

An hour went by. Nobody stopped.

"Well, blast it," Humbert said. "Blast it right into Joo-ly."

Miriam shivered. "Is it just me, or is it cold all the sudden? A little old lady like me might catch her death out here."

"It's the middle a' June, Miriam. Did you bring your shawl?"

Before Miriam could answer, a little girl with a long, ethereal, flowery dress and pigtails came skipping towards them from the other side of the tree line. She stopped a few feet from the highway, bent over, and picked a wildflower, twirling it between her fingers before placing it over her ear.

"Be careful, little girl. This here road's dangerous as all get out."

"You shouldn't play here, dear," Miriam added.

The girl hummed an off-key version of "She'll be Coming 'Round the Mountain" as she sifted through a pile of garbage, completely ignoring Humbert and Miriam.

They repeated themselves, this time louder. Then, once again, but louder still and with their hands cupped around their mouths, with still no reaction from the girl.

"Did we die?" Miriam asked.

"That's stupid, woman. I feel as fit as a fiddle," Humbert said, approaching the girl. He went to put his arm on her shoulder, saying,

"Little girl, can you hear me? Are you …?"

But his arm went right through her body, and he tumbled forward into the ditch. His bones cracked and popped as he careened down to the pit's nadir.

"Dangit! Ope. Friggit'. Blast," he cursed.

Miriam ran to the edge of the ditch to see if he was okay. "Anything broken, dear?"

"You tell me."

"Seem fine to me. Get back up here."

At this point, they'd definitely gotten the girl's full attention. She giggled out of control, rolling back and forth on her back and kicking her legs with glee.

Humbert, struggling to pull himself out of the ditch, didn't share in the girl's joyful feelings. The morning wasn't going his way so far, and he was getting grumpier by the moment.

"What's so dang funny?" he said, brushing himself off and wiggling the kinks out of his back.

"Angry man fall down," she said in a loud, slightly monotonous voice. Miriam couldn't help but giggle, too.

Humbert, avoiding eye contact with both his tormentors, noticed the old, mission revival school up the hill. It was set back just off the highway, with a high brick facade, arched walkways around the entrances, and a beautiful red, slate roof. Above the front door, a sign told him what the building was and simultaneously answered all the questions he had.

"St. Rita's School for the Deaf," he said, nodding his head. "Huh."

A construction crane, wielding a wrecking ball, was skillfully removing layer after layer of brick from a large outbuilding. Debris from inside—bed frames, old picture frames, desks, you name it—was being tossed from the dwindling second story into the woods and, in some cases, onto the highway beyond.

So, this was why the highway had been covered with a variety of furniture and household items. It was also why the off-ramp they'd swerved into had been closed off, along with the road's shoulder.

Most importantly, the sign above the school itself explained why the little girl hadn't listened to them; she had been unable to in the first place, a condition Humbert was growing all too sympathetic to in his golden years.

"Huh?" he said again, missing what the girl was saying to him

151

and Miriam.

"Follow me," she repeated.

Without waiting for affirmation, she turned towards the school, skipping through the trees and up the hill. Her physical body phased in and out of reality as she drew away from the flabbergasted couple.

"Well," Miriam said. "You've always been after ghosts—*real* ghosts. Never thought we'd find any more, especially after all these years without one, but there ya' have it. Looks like I'm eating my words, after all."

"What are you on about, Miriam?"

"Can't you see? This is everything you've ever wanted. We've been across the entire Midwest looking for things like this. Now, all of a sudden, you want no part of it?"

"Things like what?" he asked, scratching a scab on his head.

"You're a blind old coot, Humbert. That little girl's dead. It's right in front of your face, and you can't even see it."

Humbert's face lit up. "I'll be darned ... ain't that somethin'. Should we follow her, then?"

They had retired. Well, Humbert's bad knees and Miriam's volatile colon had forced the issue, but after the young man—Ryan, Humbert thought his name might have been, and an upstanding young fellow at that, once you had gotten passed all his self-righteous, social justice warrior malarkey—had left their services, the ghosties and spooks just sort of ran dry. Maybe the kid had been a conduit. Maybe, without him, the washed-up old ghost hunters didn't deserve to see action. Maybe they were just too tired.

The girl beckoned from the parking lot, frantically urging them to get a move on. Behind her, the wrecking ball continued to swing: *whoosh, crash*, and a dozen old Macintosh monitors spilled out onto the lawn. *Krrrshplat*, an old steel refrigerator flattened them.

As far as journeys up small, low-grade hills go, theirs was an epic one, something to be told throughout the ages. By the apex, both Humbert and Miriam were on their hands and knees, panting and groaning. With a final burst of energy, Humbert grabbed his wife by her arms and hefted her back up to her feet, nearly throwing his whole back out.

Without giving them a chance to rest, the little girl motioned for them to follow, before running off towards the back of the building being demolished. The look of urgency in her wide green eyes was enough to reinvigorate their old limbs.

"What do you think she wants?"

"Donnu'," Humbert shrugged. "Whatever it is, she ain't taken' no for an answer. Come on, we're gonna' lose her."

In the clearing beyond the school itself, still quite some distance from the demolition site, a few things stood out. First, an empty playground, its swings rocking to the banshee call of the breeze, bigger gusts moving piles of wood chips from one side to another in little, invisible cyclones. Though no children were around for miles— other than the ghost girl—they could hear laughter and smell the sweat of kids hard at play.

Another startling sight was the sheer size of the school itself. Looking up to the eaves of the roof was dizzying, not to mention the overwhelming number of bricks that had gone into its original construction. Oh, the stories each brick could tell …

But, most of all, the flock of undead circling each other, arms outstretched and moaning gutturally, in the open field between the school and the crane stopped Humbert and Miriam dead in their tracks.

"Are those, are those … they … the …" Humbert stuttered, his dentures chittering.

The girl was back at their sides, tugging at the leg of his trousers and pointing towards the zombies.

"Come on, come on."

"Now wait one hootin' minute, "Humbert said. "I ain't following no little girl, 'specially some little no-name ghost girl, to an early grave with zombies suckin' on my brain stem."

"Oh, Humbert …"

"Don't 'oh, Humbert' me, Miriam. Seems a rational enough concern. I'm an old man. I ain't lived nine decades on God's green Earth to go out like that. Nuh uh."

Flies buzzed around them. The noon sun beat down on them, drawing beads of sweat from their foreheads—that is, from Humbert and Miriam's. Little known fact: ghosts don't perspire, they're just expired—and the heat had whipped up the stench of rot and decay from the zombies into a veritable frenzy.

"Erica," a timid voice said. "Her name's Erica."

"And that's supposed to make me want to get my legs gnawed on? Nope. No thanks." Humbert folded his arms, frowning so wide his chin flattened out, and looked away. Then, "What in the—where'd *you* come from?"

A nun, as transparent as a drop of rain, was standing next to Erica, protecting the girl in the frocks of her habit. She was stroking the girl's hair.

"Pardon us," she said. "Erica is a wandering spirit. She's always loved the wildflowers. Since the highway was built, I must keep reminding her not to stray down the hill. It's dangerous with all those automobiles zipping about. She'd never hear it coming if something, Heaven forbid, were to ever happen."

"Ah," Humbert said.

"Can I go play, Sister Catherine?"

"Yes. But stay away from the road. I mean it. I don't want to have to tell you again, young lady. Understand me?" The nun said, quickly signing each word with expertly executed flourishes in all the right places.

"Yes'm. Thank you, Sister Catherine."

At that, the little ghost girl named Erica frolicked towards the playground, humming "London Bridge is Falling Down" off-key the whole way there. As she crossed the threshold to the jungle gym, dozens of other children her age appeared, the sound of their innocent laughter both delightful and haunting. Sister Catherine watched, hands steepled at her heart, as Erica joined in their play.

"Erm," Humbert said, drooling.

"What my husband means to say is, what in the seven hecks is going on?"

Sister Catherine tittered.

"What's so funny, lady?"

Bowing her head, Sister Catherine said, "Apologies. I do not mean to offend. It's just that Erica has always been so shy. She never speaks to her classmates, yet alone strangers. She must have really seen something special in the two of you. Children never cease to surprise, do they?"

The end of her sentence was drowned out by another furious swing of the wrecking ball. Bricks cascaded down the side of the crumbling building, a claw-footed bathtub sliding down in their wake. A hairy, wolf-like creature was caught in the cascade, scrubbing his back with a loofa and whistling a tune. He disappeared into the rubble with a melancholy *ahhrooooow*.

"Never mind," Humbert said, trying to pretend he hadn't just seen that. "What's with this place?"

A deep sadness washed over Sister Catherine's countenance.

"The boy's dormitory has long been a staple for our humble school. When it was no longer suitable as living quarters, we used it as a haunted house to raise funds for the school. People all over Hamilton County came to us on Halloween, more than happy to donate to the cause at the risk of a fright. Last week, they announced it hazardous and began tearing it down. Now, all the spirits trapped within have nowhere to go."

"Urgh," one of the zombies said, half-heartedly.

"I think Erica brought you to us to help save them," Sister Catherine concluded.

Humbert wiped the drool from the side of his mouth. "But I thought you said the haunted house was just an attraction? A fundraiser …"

Miriam, wiping away her own tears, sniffled.

The wrecking ball continued to smack layer after layer of artisanally laid brick off the old dormitory, its operator half-asleep as he whirled it from side to side.

"Splatter some fake blood on everything, dim the lights, and set up a couple strobe lights and people will believe anything. Here at St. Rita's, we aren't known for turning anyone away: deaf, dead, or otherwise."

"It's true," groaned a zombie. "Er, I mean grrrhhh."

"Braaaaaaains," begged another.

"Well?" Humbert asked, looking to his wife.

"Well what, dear?"

A smirk crossed his wrinkled face. He stuffed his hand into his pocket, fumbled around, and pulled out a pin shaped like a ghost tossing a football. It glinted as the sun struck its polished surface. He hadn't worn it in a long time, but he always kept it handy. One never knew when duty might call.

"Ah, sugar," Miriam cursed. "I thought we were leaving all that behind us, Humbert. Aren't we getting too old for this sort of thing?"

"You said it yourself, we never felt younger than when we were chasin' ghoulies around with that kid. Greatest time of our lives."

"Greatest time of *your* life. I just want to get to this wine-tasting tour, kick my feet up and let my bunions air out, and take a well-deserved catnap. Since when was that too much to ask?"

"All the same, these fairy folks need our help. What are we going to do? Turn 'em down, just like that?"

Miriam sighed. "Yes, that's exactly what we're going to do."

Sister Catherine cleared her throat. "Please. John, Henry, Paul, and Gregory mean no harm. They're just lost. They have family down the road at the Landmark Memorial Gardens. If you could just take them there, drop them off, it'd mean the *world* to us. I think they'd be able to find their way home from there."

Humbert sneered. Even if he wanted to help, there was no way he could walk that far, yet alone while corralling four mushy brained, flesh-craving zombies. The thought alone was enough to do his heart in. Not to mention his broken-down truck sitting on the side of the highway. Sure, they could hop in the back and he could give them a ride in a jiffy, but that would require a running engine, something he fortunately lacked at the moment.

Miriam jabbed him in the ribs. She gave him The Look, sealing their fate.

"Ah heck," he said. "Lemme go see if I can't get the truck started. I can't say no, especially after you've convinced ole Miriam. She can be stubborner than me. I'll be the first to admit it."

"And the last," Miriam said, glaring.

Two hours later, with the help of one of the school's emeritus groundskeepers, mostly in the form of a series manly grunts and verbal reprimands, Doris was up and running. Any number of living mechanics couldn't have held a flame to old Willy Wumpets' level of moral support. Humbert drove her up the off-ramp, over some more cones, and through the grass, backing up as close to the zombies as he could without plowing over them.

Then, after everything had gotten off to such a strong start, they came to their first hurdle—and it was a doozy!

"Now what?"

Humbert tilted his head, scratching at his scab again. The four zombies were walking in circles, bumping into each other, tripping over their own feet, and doing other mindless, living dead type things. What they weren't doing was lining up to be driven back home.

"Should we get like a stick or somethin'? Or like a cattle prod?"

"That seems a bit … inhumane, doesn't it, dear?" Miriam said.

"Not as inhumane as these flesh-eaters. Seems like just the right amount of inhumane, if you ask me."

"Hmm."

"Uh …"

"Urrrgh, raaawr."

Then, an idea dawned. Scattered among the debris on the

highway, Humbert remembered seeing some roadkill. He didn't remember much anymore, but it was hard to forget the raccoon's face, frozen in rigor mortis, with its one eye dangling across the rumble strips. It had seemed fresh enough, but he couldn't be sure without closer investigation.

When he dismissed himself without an explanation, Miriam and Sister Catherine stood, hands clasped behind their backs, rocking back and forth on their heels, and avoiding eye contact. As far as ladies from the same generation were concerned, these were two that couldn't be more different. One had married Jesus, dedicated her life to helping impoverished children of one kind or another, and prayed every night. The other had married a slightly bigoted buffoon, who spent his entire life chasing after fairy tales. So, he had found some in the end; had it been worth all the time they'd lost together?

"Nice weather we're having," Miriam said. "Bit chilly."

"It's always chilly for me," Sister Catherine said.

"Er, sorry."

"Not to worry. There's no way you could have known."

"Is, uh, death a scary place? Aren't you supposed to be in Heaven? Sorry, where are my manners? I shouldn't ask such prying things."

"No, it's fine. Death isn't as scary as you'd think. Most of the time, it sort of sneaks up on you. For me, it happened in my sleep. I wasn't able to confess my sins and be absolved before passing. Maybe between that and there still being so much work to do, God kept me around for a bit longer. Girls like Erica, innocents unbaptized, need help too. They deserve love and guidance just as much as you and I. So, I'm grateful. It's hard sometimes, but humbling. Not many get the opportunity I've been given. The opportunity to …"

"Make a real difference. Yeah, I know what you mean," Miriam said. "Humbert and I have done things, helped people in ways that most people could never imagine, and I've always felt the same way. There was a young boy once, Eugene. He had so much love to give. I'll never forget his face when he recounted to us the horrors that he experienced, what those horrible kids done to him. Everything had been all fine and dandy until he opened himself up to them. Then …" she stopped, unable to relive their first ghost's final moments a second time. "Those are the moments, I guess, that we've lived for."

They shared a fleeting smile before Humbert reappeared, this time leaning on the support of his walker. The semi-rotted carcass of a raccoon was draped over the front bar. As he drew nearer, the zombies stopped circling each other, perked up, and sniffed the afternoon air. There was a sweet aroma they couldn't resist.

"Quick," Humbert said, freeing an arm to open the passenger door of his truck. "Get in."

Miriam acquiesced, nodding a curt goodbye to Sister Catherine. There was a mutual understanding between the two women—an understanding that, though you can always find common ground with someone no matter how many worlds' apart you might seem, they'd never have to see each other again, in this life or the next.

Humbert channeled his inner quarterback, bent his rattling knees, and lobbed the carcass into the bed of the truck as close to the cab as possible. Almost immediately, Doris lurched as John, Henry, Paul, and Gregory pawed and bumbled their way up into the bed for feeding time. When they were all up, huddled around the carrion, Humbert kicked the tailgate shut and sidled around to the driver's side.

Fumbling for the keys, he jumped as one of the zombies swiped down at him, but he was high-hanging fruit. It returned to masticating the roadkill in the back of the truck.

Humbert managed to get into the truck, started Doris up, and slammed on the gas. The banging and jostling from the back revved up his adrenaline. He laughed maniacally as Doris's back tires burned out in the grass, shooting chunks of dirt and turf behind them. Then, they were off.

Sister Catherine, once again coddling little Erica, waved as they disappeared down the street.

"Will they be okay?" Erica asked.

"Yes," Sister Catherine signed, raising and lowering her fist. To herself, she added, "So will we, darling. So will we."

Back in the cab of his truck, Humbert struggled to stay on the road while fending off one of the zombies, likely Henry or Gregory— due to the *obvious* complexity of their nature—who'd gotten bored with the raccoon and broke through the back windshield. It grabbed for Miriam, but Humbert barred it with his right arm.

"Back, ye foul beast," he yelled.

"My hair," Miriam said. "I just got it done!"

"You get your hair done once a week, woman. I think that's the least of our worries."

A second zombie squeezed the upper half of its body through

the window, wedging both of them in place. Though two snapping, oozing mouths trying to eat them were far worse than one, it was a Godsend of sorts. Neither could force their way in close enough to take a good bite.

And they were almost there. Landmark Memorial was right around the corner.

He accelerated faster, pushing the gas pedal down as hard as he could. The other two zombies, unsatisfied by their appetizer, were helping their friends break into the back of the cab. The metal around the window frame was bending inward, buckling under the weight of their bodies slamming into it.

"It's not going to hold," Miriam shouted.

"Yes, it is. Doris is built tough, unlike these vehicles nowadays. They don't build 'em like they used to. Imagine what these fellas woulda' done to one of them Pry-uses. Doris'll hold. She has to. Besides, we're here."

They drove right over the low iron fence surrounding the cemetery, sparks shooting out behind them.

"How do you plan on depositing them, then?"

"Like this," Humbert said, whipping the wheel to one side and slamming on the brakes. "Yeehaw!"

Doris spun out, the force of the sudden turn setting her on two wheels. As she spun, the zombies lost their balance and went flying out of the truck, banging loudly on the walls of the bed. They landed in the grass with a *splat*, one of them rolling into and crumbling an old headstone.

Humbert kept the gas down, leaving the zombies, the cemetery, St. Rita's School of the Deaf, the ghosts of little Erica, Sister Catherine, and all the other children who had once attended the school, and the bathing wolfman all in their dust. He white-knuckled the wheel, focused completely on the road, until they were well away. Then, he pulled over.

"Why are we stopped?" Miriam asked.

Without answering her, he leaned over and kissed his wife long and deep. She fought it at first, but then lost herself to her husband's sudden outburst of passion, her eyes slowly shutting in contentment.

"We're back, baby," he said, wiping his lips.

She felt light headed, but managed, "Oh my. I suppose we are."

He thumbed the pin in his pocket, feeling the words—really feeling them—for the first time in years. For a while, the words on that pin represented everything they stood for. It was their life, their livelihood, and the very fiber of their being.

Together, they were the ParaAbnormal ParaRelics, and they were indeed back, and with a vengeance. First, for the ninth time that day, he had to find a restroom. His bladder wouldn't hold much longer, and what sort of ghost hunter would he be wearing his pee-pants?

"Not the kind I want to be," he said with no explanation. "No, siree."

"That's nice, dear." Miriam forced a smile. "Whatever it is you're on about, can you pass the aspirin? My joints are simply *killing* me." She rubbed the bridge of her nose as Humbert fumbled through the driver side door pocket. "You know, I think I saw a porta-john back by the dormitory."

"Heh?"

"I SAID, I THINK I SAW ..."

"I'm just messin' with you, woman. I hear you just fine. Let's go, then."

Humbert had a sneaking suspicion, one he couldn't shake off. He didn't typically appreciate sneaking about, associating it with good-for-nothing teenie boppers and their "boom-boom" cubes, but this sort was okay, he supposed. Miriam wanted to go back to St. Rita's for the same reason he wanted to go back. It had just been so *exciting*.

Sister Catherine, and the children, were nowhere to be found, which was all the better because there were more pressing issues to attend.

The construction workers were all standing around, watching one guy move dirt from one pile to another—nothing unusual there—and even Humbert was able to get by them to use the porta-john without arousing suspicion.

Meanwhile, Miriam, whose blood sugar was rapidly dropping, tip-toed up to one of their trucks and snuck out a couple of sandwiches. She wasn't a thief, but the adrenaline had taken over.

Reunited and ready to rock, they stood around for a while, wondering what to do next. Then, they sat creakily on the grass. Chasing ghosts was easy when you just happened to stumble upon them; waiting around for them to show up was exhausting.

"Psst," a voice beckoned. "Over here."

Humbert and Miriam peered around the corner, looked at each other, and shrugged.

"I haven't got all day."

The stranger was out of luck. The simple act of standing up took Humbert and Miriam almost all day, but they were finally able to find the source of the summons. A cool, pale-skinned, Kat with a k, wearing a black tuxedo with extra-long coattails, was leaning up against the remnants of the building's brick facade. He was, in true "Kool Kat" fashion, chewing a broken toothpick and flipping a coin.

"Nice work you did with ze zombies. Impressive, even … for hoomans."

"Er, thanks?"

"Who are you, sonny?"

"Sonny? I'm nearly 1,000 years old, kid. And, until recently," he said, peeling his lip up to reveal fangs, "I didn't much care for ze sun."

The vampire stuffed his hands into his pockets, kicked off the wall, and swaggered towards them, his gait patient and smooth.

"Spare ze time to help me, too?"

Humbert knew how this ended. They'd talk until the sun went down and the construction crew headed home, Dracy-Q would spring too fast for them to save themselves, suck Humbert dry, and take Miriam as his eternal concubine.

Nuh-uh. No way. No how.

"I think we'll just be going now," Miriam said, sweetly. You almost expected a plate of chocolate chip cookies to come with her words.

"Not to worry, I won't bite. There's a lot of fake news going around about my kind, but we don't *need* hooman blood, just like you people don't *need* hooch. I've dedicated most of the last century trying to dispel these awful misconceptions. It's funny, people tend not to vant to listen to me. They see me, but don't hear my vords."

"They're probably too busy keepin' a close eye on those chompers of yours."

Miriam, the consummate sweetheart and forward-thinker, slapped Humbert's arm and shook a firm finger at him.

"All ze same," the vampire said, circling, "maybe you could help me. Just to make a tiny difference."

Humbert weighed the pros and cons.

Pro: it'd get them far away from having his neck incised and the life drained out of him.

Con: it sounded like an awful lot of work.

"We'll do it."

"Dammit, Miriam …"

The vampire, so pleased he hissed a little, excusing himself as if he'd just burped, threw his arms around them.

"Thank you, thank you. I just need you to help pass out some literature. Maybe to ze strapping young lads by the backhoe and in through ze mail slot of ze school. Teach them young, change ze world, no? I just can't get close enough without my skin tingling and my moostache singeing."

So, Humbert and Miriam passed out pamphlets like it was the 1930's all over again. The construction workers rolled them up, shoved them in their back pockets, and went about "supervising" each other for another hour or two. The mail slot at the school gobbled them up without as much as a "thank you".

Satisfied with another, much easier, job well-done, they returned to the vampire with a hop, or rather only a semi-hobble, to their step.

"Good. Wery, wery good."

"That's it?"

"For me, yes. Ze others, they von't be so easy."

As if they'd been there the whole time, an entire freakshow of spooks and baddies appeared behind the vampire. They kicked rubble around, genuinely wishing they were somewhere else, and occasionally bumped into one another.

There was an insidious looking clown, Finkelstein's monster (patent pending), three warty witches, an outrageously large family of ghosts, a lizardman with red fins jutting out of his veiny neck, a massive black wolf, and any number of other creepy creatures. Counting them alone was exhausting.

"Oh, sugar," Miriam said.

The wolf patted up to Miriam's side. Its face was vaguely man-shaped, and it was wearing a pink shower cap. The vampire leaned over to scratch it behind the ear, whispering something to the beast.

"Is that the …"

"Yes. Zis is Rover. He's agreed to accompany you, help you in any vay you need."

"Rover?" Miriam asked. "Not very original for a wolf-man, is it?"

"Ve're monsters, dear. Not poets."

She couldn't argue with that.

And Humbert couldn't cope with all that lay before them. The monsters had formed a queue, each expectantly awaiting some sort of assistance. Everyone wanted something. Everyone needed fulfillment of one sort or another, be it big or small, and they all expected it to come from someone else. Ghosts and goblins were no different in that regard.

Humbert sighed. "I'm going to need the strong stuff."

"I'll get the aspirin, dear."

At that, they pulled up their britches, buckled up for the long-haul, and called over the first individual in line. There was work to be done, and the ParaAbnormal ParaRelics were the only ones able, or willing, to do it, and by the looks of the beings standing before them, they'd do it straight into their graves.

"Ahem," Finkelstein's monster said, tilting her head from side to side. "I, er … I seem to have misplaced my bolts."

She looked forlorn and incomplete. Vast, empty holes where her bolts used to be graced her neck. She put her hands over one, pouting, but something about the "hoomans" made her feel like everything was going to be all right.

But that, my friends, is a story for another day.

Curtis A. Deeter is a writer of fantasy, science fiction, and horror, who typically weaves comedy into his stories. Storytelling has always been integral to maintaining his sanity. When he is not writing or reading, he can be found at the local brewery enjoying the tunes and sampling the brew.

He has several short stories published in various anthologies, including A Contract of Words, A Flash of Words, *and* Askew Horizons, *and he has three novels in the works. In April of 2019, his son came to meet everyone, and now he plans on writing a series of children's books about Theodore and his dragons.*

Author Website: https://CurtisADeeter.com/
Facebook: https://www.facebook.com/AuthorCurtisADeeter
Twitter Account: @CurtisADeeter

DIAL M FOR MARVIN

By Robert Allen Lupton

I stepped back from the railing on the old bridge, slipped on the ice, and fell on my ass. The little man, less than a foot tall, rolled his unlit cigar to one side of his mouth, and asked, "Did that hurt? It looked like it hurt."

"You scared me. What the devil are you?"

"I've been assigned to help you, watch over you, so to speak."

"I stood up in the moonlight and swirling snowfall and tried to keep my wet pants from sticking to my butt. "You mean like a guardian angel?"

"You should be so lucky. My name's not Clarence, and this ain't Bedford Falls. I'm more like a pixie on probation and you're my punishment."

I could barely see the lights from town, and there weren't any trains on the bridge this time of night. I slipped again—an evening of cheap scotch will do that—and grabbed the guardrail with both hands. "Well, 'not Clarence', I expect you're really nothing more than the aftermath of an evening of demolition drinking."

"Call me Marvin. I'm not a pink elephant or a rabbit named Harvey. I know who you are, I know what happened, and I know you're drunk. No one but a drunk would stand on a stupid railroad trestle in a snowstorm and talk to a pixie named Marvin."

"Are you calling me stupid?"

"I can call you George, Bill, or late for dinner, but it won't change the fact that it's past midnight, freezing cold, and snowing.

You're drunk on a railroad bridge, and your pants are wet. Stupid speaks for itself. Gentlemen of the jury, the prosecution rests."

My pants were freezing to my butt, and I'd lost my gloves and scarf. I wasn't drunk enough to not feel the cold. I squinted at Marvin. He was dressed in a three-piece suit, but he wore a leather WWI aviator helmet complete with earflaps. The goggles were pushed up above his brow and the straps hung loosely on the side of his unshaven face.

"I'm not stupid," I said, "I came out here to kill myself. My life is ruined."

"Sounds stupid to me. Do you think that you're the first man whose wife ran off with her boss? Life goes on. You can't die yet. There are a few things that you still need to do, not big things, mind you, but POOPHEADS, the Pixie Order Of Pixilated HElpfulness And Direct Succor, thinks that you're important enough to keep alive. Don't see it myself. If you'd just jump, I could go home right now."

I shivered and said, "Home? Can you take me home?"

"Sure, click your heels together three times and say, "There's no place like home."

I tried it and on the third click, I fell on my butt, again.

Marvin took his stogie out of his mouth and pointed it at me. "No place like home. What the hell are you thinking? Maybe you want me to sprinkle you with magic fairy dust so you can fly away home, my drunken ladybug."

"Can you do that?"

"Sure, I just have to get my little green suit and a wand. Oh, and I need you to say, "I do believe in fairies" a couple of hundred times. Wait, I think I heard a bell tinkle. That means an angel got his wings. Please, William, you're killing me. This ain't no fairy tale, and I'm not your fairy godmother. I don't make coaches out of pumpkins. You want to go home, start walking. You do know how to walk, don't you, just put one foot in front of the other. It's called taking steps. You know how to step, don't you? Stop when you get home."

"Is that a magic cigar?"

"Sure, that's why it went out in the snow. That's its secret power, it turns soggy when it's wet. I'm about as entertained by the weather and your foolishness as I care to be. I'll be at your house if you make it home."

"I'm not sure I can walk. Help me."

"I'm eight inches tall. I can't carry a cheeseburger. You're heavy, and you ain't my brother. I'm going to appeal to POOPHEADS for another assignment. I never should have turned that damn princess into a poodle. Who knew that she'd fall in love with a Shetland? Damn, it was a dog and pony show when they consummated that marriage. Destry rides again and again."

Marvin flicked the soggy ash off his cigar, grumbled, and disappeared. I looked over the guardrail, but I didn't see him in the blowing snow.

I stumbled home. When I got to my empty house, it wasn't empty. Marvin sat in front of the fireplace and he was using a bone china tea cup as an ashtray. I ignored him until I put on dry clothes and made a pot of coffee.

"I didn't expect to see you here, I was sure that you weren't real."

"Didn't expect to see you, either. You were too drunk to talk to on the bridge. I hope you sobered up on the way home. I tried to get reassigned, but POOPHEADS won't give me a break. I begged forgiveness, told them I was just horsing around when I pixied the princess. It was a doggone shame she signed on for the pony express, but I don't see why that's my fault. Turns out the princess is with foal, or puppy dog, or some such thing. No one wants a Shetdoodle running around the castle. So, William Robert James, I have to help you get your wife back or I'm exiled from the pixie world."

"What if I don't want my wife back?"

"Just kill me now. Either you get your wife back, or I'm your new roommate and I suck as a roommate. I'll probably keep a pet. I mentioned the potential of a Shetdoodle, didn't I? I hear some of the mixed breeds don't house train worth a crap."

I considered the alternative and decided that reconciling with Grace wasn't the worst thing that could happen. It wasn't like it was all her fault; there was plenty of blame to share. I told Marvin I'd take Grace back.

"Isn't that nice. Billy Boy, but the issue isn't whether you'll take Grace back. The challenge is convincing Grace to take *you* back. Apparently, POOPHEADS' Forward Looking And Preventive Prognosticating Entropy Restoration Society, FLAPPERS, projects that you and Grace will have a grandchild that will save the great grandchild of the pixie king. Not a descendent of the Shetdoodles, but the grandchild of Prince Brad."

"The pixie prince is named Brad?"

"Don't throw stones; you've got three first names, William

Robert James. What happened, Billy Bob Jim, was that already taken? Never mind, don't answer. The POOPHEADS' FLAPPERS say that I've got three days to help you get Grace back. We have to make Grace and her banker boss decide to break up. Get some sleep. I have to figure out how to make the banker view Grace as an underperforming asset and she needs to see him as a bad return on her investment."

I woke with the hangover I deserved. What a dream. I wished I had written it down. I rinsed out my mouth, which tasted vaguely like cheap cigars, grabbed four or five aspirin, and washed them down. The coffeemaker beeped, and I staggered to the kitchen. Heaven help me, Marvin was real. He was on the counter.

"It's about time, Rip Van Winkle. Pour me some coffee, I can't pick up the pot."

"How did you make coffee if you can't pick up the pot?"

"I put a spell on the broom, you moron. I'm small, not helpless. I filled the coffee machine with one cup of water at a time and I can lift a scoop of ground coffee. Damn, you're going to be a tough sell, I can't imagine how you got Grace the first time. Did she grow up in a cave? Were you the first man she met? Pour some coffee."

I poured us both a cup of coffee, sat, rubbed my bleary eyes, and said, "Hangover."

Marvin laughed, "I appreciate the offer, but no thanks. You earned it, you can keep it. I was a little hard on you last night, but I was never any good at mollycoddling drunks."

I was quiet; I wasn't good with hangovers. I wasn't good with drinking, either. I thought I'd been a good husband. I went to work, came home, and still loved Grace as much as I had ten years ago. We'd been happy until three days ago when she came home from work and announced that she was leaving me for her boss at the bank, Roger Wilco. I guess the world of account reconciliation and credit card balances was more exciting than I thought. "Marvin, I don't understand why she left me."

He took off his pilot hat and goggles and ran his stubby fingers through his thinning hair. "It's not your fault. I got in touch with POPSONG while you were passed out. That's Pixies On Patrol Searching Out Narcissistic Glamours. They checked out Grace's banker boss and it turns out he's a troll. That's not a surprise, most bankers are trolls."

I forced down some coffee and asked, "A troll like an under the bridge troll? What's a glamour?"

"A glamour is a spell that changes your appearance and a troll is a troll. They gravitate to banks, law firms, and insurance companies where they thrive by taking advantage of people like you. Pay attention: this is important. Roger Wilco was the account manager for a BARF, a Bad Ass Red Fairy, and when his mortgage went into default, he forced the fairy to put a love spell on Grace."

"That's a lot to take in. Grace left me for a glamourized troll because of a love spell cast by a red fairy? Why would the banker do that?"

"One question at a time. If you'd ever smelled a troll, male or female, you wouldn't ask why Roger wanted a human female. Second, fairies aren't really cute looking little butterfly-sized creatures who flit about in gardens and meadows. They have a dark side. Once a fairy has a pollen addiction, they'll do anything for a pansy. My last client was cursed by a red fairy with a twenty-honeysuckle-a-day habit."

"Anyway, Banker Boy bought his glamour years ago and things were fine until he became infatuated with your amazing Gracie. He sold the BARF a repossessed little bungalow with a great flower garden. All the fairy had to do was make payments, but Wilco knew that once the fairy started hanging out with the birds and bees in the marigolds, it was only a matter of time before he'd be in default."

I must have still been a little drunk because it made perfect sense to me. I wasn't completely convinced, but I wanted to be convinced. It was easier on my ego to believe that Grace had been led down the primrose path by some troll with the help of a pollen-addicted fairy, than it was to accept that maybe I hadn't been a perfect prince to live with. "I'm not sure that I believe any of this. I never thought that trolls, fairies, elves, leprechauns, sprites, or nymphs were real."

"Elf is a generic term, and sprites are only water nymphs. Doesn't matter what you believe." He puffed his cigar and used the lit end to set my napkin on fire. I almost fell out of my chair, and he poured coffee on the flames. "Well, Bucko, am I real enough for you? Do I need to burn your whole house down?"

"Okay, I believe you. How do I get Grace back?"

"We have to break the spell. POPSONG told me where Roger and Grace are staying. You asked me how I could help you, and the answer is simple. Fairies cast spells, and pixies can break fairy spells. I can cancel any spell, any glamour, and any curse. The bad news is that I have to be physically close to the victim."

169

"Why don't you just go to Grace and break the spell?"

"I'm less than a foot tall and I don't have wings. Everyone thinks pixies have wings, but we don't. People don't know the difference between a fairy and a pixie. They say we all look alike. Fairies come in all sizes and I can change sizes when I want. Roger and Grace have a room in a hotel by the river. Trolls like rivers. You drive me to the hotel by the water, and I'll dispel Grace before you can say Roger Wilco."

Marvin rubbed his nose on his shirtsleeve and I said, "When I think about it, the word pixie sounds a lot like pigsty."

"That's mean, and it would hurt my feelings if I had any. Clean up and get your car; we've got an appointment at the Riverview Inn."

I was only exceeding the speed limit by forty miles an hour when the police woman pulled me over. She was too pretty to be a cop. I handed her my license and registration.

She said, "Where's the fire?"

A butterfly flew through my open car window, hovered in front of my face, and flew away when I sneezed. The policewoman was prettier than I thought, and she smelled like a warm memory. I smiled and answered, "In your eyes, Officer."

She tapped my license and registration against her ticket book and smiled, "Well, Mr. James, maybe we can work something out. Perhaps, you'd like to come with me."

I was awestruck and couldn't speak. I just nodded my head, got out of my car, and followed her toward anywhere she wanted to go. Marvin jumped out of the car and chased after me. He pulled on my pants leg and screamed, "Pick me up. Pick me up." I put him on my shoulder and he slapped my ear with his leather helmet. "Moron, get back in the car."

I started to protest, and Marvin sneezed into his hand and smeared pixie snot all over the side of my face. Disgusting. He said, "Don't wipe it off, it'll break the spell. You have to leave it on your face until the troll lady is gone."

I said, "She's not a troll lady, she's beautiful and I'm pretty sure I love her." I put my arm around the policewoman and leaned to kiss her cheek, but her cheek and face were green and wrinkled. I lurched away from the stench of a cattle feedlot and the Wicked Witch of the West handed me my license and registration.

She shook her finger at me and said, "Get off my highway and take Marvin with you. I'll get you one day, you and your little pixie, too."

I hurried back to my car and drove away. I wiped the pixie snot off my face. Some of it had oozed onto my shirt, but I couldn't do anything about that. Marvin relit his cigar and giggled to himself.

"Slime? You slimed me. That's how you break a fairy enchantment, you blow your nose on someone's face? Really, that's the best you can do? It's not funny."

"No, it's snot. Pixies don't actually break spells. The disgust at being slimed or snotted overcomes the euphoric illusion of the fairy spell. There's nothing like a little mucus to make a person face reality. You're lucky I was here; that lady troll had you wrapped around her fat green finger. Now, you understand how glamours and love spells work."

I wanted to clean off my arm, but Marvin told me not to. "A little snot goes a long way. While you have some on your face and shirt, you'll be able to see through glamours and no one can cast a spell on you. Even a single dollop of pixie snot is enough. A little drop will do you."

"Just one drop. Will it work if it's diluted?"

"Certainly."

"Okay, then I've got an idea. I want to stop and buy some things." I parked at a super center and lifted Marvin onto my shoulder, hesitated, and asked, "Do I need to hide you? Won't people think something's wrong when I walk into the store with a little man on my shoulder?"

"I miss the good old days when I could pretend to be a monkey. No, other people can't see me, unless of course, they're not really human or have been pixie-snotted."

I had a vision of a crazed pixie dashing through the store slathering snot on everyone's ankles. I shook it away.

I bought a super-sized water gun with a half-gallon reservoir and a twelve-pack of bottled water. It was uncomfortable in the store. I could see people as they really were. Marvin whispered in my ear and pointed out some of the special people. "The lady with the blue hair, she's an ogre, and that family in the garden area, they're gnomes."

"They don't have red hats; how can they be gnomes?"

Marvin slapped me in the ear again and pointed out an orc at work in the produce department and a banshee at a checkout counter. I paid a blue-eyed kobold with a Germanic accent for my purchases and

171

held the door open for an ugly family of goblins.

I filled the water cannon with water, and Marvin sneezed into it repeatedly while I drove to the hotel. I strapped the cannon across my back. I was ready to disenchant an army of trolls. Marvin said, "POPSONG says that they're at the inside pool. Let's do this, Bucko."

Surprisingly, no one stopped me when I marched through the lobby. I hurried past humans and an assortment of other creatures. There were two women working in the lobby bar and they were gorgeous, even without their glamours. Marvin said, "They're dryads; once their forests are cut down, they follow the lumber and stay in the houses or buildings where the lumber was used. The little people working as maids and custodians are brownies. Brownies are harmless, but they'll steal anything that isn't nailed down. Remember the song about nailing your shoes to the kitchen floor? Brownies."

The pool area was crowded with men, women, children, selkies, water nymphs, and even a mermaid or two. Roger and Grace were sunbathing in lounge chairs across the pool. I asked Marvin, "Showtime?"

"Showtime. Fire at everyone. Rain snot and confusion on your enemies."

"My enemies?"

"Everyone, spray everyone. The people who are human will be able to see through glamours and the people who are Fae will be exposed."

People screamed when I sprayed them. Women didn't like their children swimming with selkies, and the mermaids had two levels of glamour. Once both levels were removed, they looked a lot more like Medusa than movie stars. Sharp teeth, too. People scrambled from the pool area. It looked like a fire drill. The other creatures ran and covered their faces with towels once their glamours were destroyed. I cornered two water demons, and locked them in the storage container the hotel used for pool supplies.

Marvin shouted, "Two in the box ready to go, because we be fast and they be slow."

I worked my way around the pool and trapped Grace and Roger behind the hot tub. Roger broke a soft drink bottle and held the jagged glass near Grace's throat. I pumped up the pressure, took aim, and my water cannon sputtered, dribbled out a thin stream, and stopped. It was still almost full.

Marvin said, "It's clogged up, I mean snotted up. It's useless."

Roger forced Grace around the hot tub and threatened us to stay back. I could see how he really looked. His unglamourous appearance was a pale bluish-grey. His pasty body was rotund with gangly legs and arms. His nose was long, and his teeth were yellow. I could smell him from where I stood.

Grace ignored the broken bottle, patted her troll lover and said, "Roger, stop it. I've got this."

Roger lowered the broken bottle and Grace put her hands on her hips and shouted at me. "William Robert, go away. I don't love you anymore. Leave me alone. I want to be with Roger. He makes me happy. For God's sake, a water cannon … Are you insane? Shame on you."

Marvin said, "Okay, time for plan B. Don't listen to her. Listen to me."

I took him off my shoulder and held him in both hands. "We have a plan B?"

"Snotball time," said Marvin and he fastened his aviator helmet straps for the first time since I'd met him and seated his goggles. He sneezed in his hands and rubbed them together. "Throw me. Throw me at them as hard as you can. We'll see how this troll stands up to a pixie snot rocket."

I wound up to throw Marvin and Grace snuggled close to Roger. I whispered to Marvin, 'You ready?"

"Roger Wilco. Throw me now. Flour in a bowl."

"Did you say flour in a bowl? Is that an enchantment?"

"No, you moron. It's not an enchantment. I said, fire in the hole. Can't you hear, did I get snot in your ears? Throw me before they get away."

Grace couldn't see Marvin, but Roger could. Grace must have thought I was pretending to throw a pitch, air baseball instead of air guitar. Roger dropped his broken bottle and used Grace as a human shield.

Marvin sped through the air like a little human cannonball. He held his hands out wide and screamed. "Incoming." Snot splattered when he hit them, and Roger's glamour and love spell were broken. Grace released the bumpy blue-grey troll and gagged at the smell. When the BARF-cast love spell dissolved, she threw up.

I pushed Roger, the troll, into the pool, picked up Marvin, reassured Grace that I still loved her, and we walked to the car. Once she was un-bespelled, Grace was shocked at what had happened. She said, "I'll file harassment charges against that creep first thing Monday morning. I'm so sorry."

Marvin made himself three feet tall and had dinner with us, said, "I'll be back", and left to report to POOPHEADS. Marvin left a supply of pixie boogers that I froze and kept in the freezer. Better safe than sorry.

We didn't see him again for five years.

When our first child was four years old, I opened the door to get the morning paper and there was a huge basket on the porch with a dog in it. It was a big dog with a mane and hooves instead of paws. Marvin sat on the stoop, smoking a cigar.

"Miss me? I brought you a present. She's a little princess. When she grows up, she'll be a good guard pony and will give the kids in the neighborhood doggy back rides. Turns out Shetdoodles see right through glamours. I figured you could use the help. I can't be everywhere, but I'll stop in and babysit your kid once in a while."

"It's good to see you, Marvin. Why a dog?"

"I can't take care of her. She's too big and she walks all over me."

"If you're firm with a dog, you can train them to obey you."

"You never understand," said Marvin. "It's a miracle that you lived to grow up. The dog obeys just fine, but I'm eight inches tall most of the time and she walks all over me. The pixie king sends me on lots of errands, and my friends won't dog sit for me anymore. Enjoy." He blew a smoke ring and vanished.

When our son, William James, saw the Shetdoodle, he ran and hugged her around the neck. "A doggie, you got me a big doggy. Love the doggy."

When William named the dog Frodo, I knew we were in the dog business for the long haul.

Our Shetdoodle barks and neighs at the people who come by the house. She doesn't bite anyone, but she sneezes and slobbers on folks when they pet her. She really hates the paperboy; I think he's an ogre. Seems like most solar salesmen and door-to-door missionaries are hobgoblins. Makes sense, if you think about it.

I took her to the vet because she drools all the time and her nose runs like a broken faucet. The vet was a druid priestess who could channel small animals. She was a great vet, but once the Shetdoodle slobbered on her, her real appearance frightened everyone. She told us not to come back.

Our friends, the ones who aren't brownies, dryads, or gnomes, ask us what kind of dog we have, and we tell them that she's a cross between a Marvin Terrier and a Snothound. They act like they understand and politely wipe the drool and mucus off their hands. Damn, I love that dog.

Robert Allen Lupton is retired and lives in New Mexico where he is a commercial hot air balloon pilot. Robert runs and writes every day, but not necessarily in that order. More than seventy of his short stories have been published in several anthologies and online at:

www.horrortree.com
www.crimsonstreets.com
www.aurorawolf.com
www.stupefyingstories.blogspot.com
www.fairytalemagazine.com

More than 200 drabbles based on the worlds of Edgar Rice Burroughs and several articles are available online at www.erbzine.com. His novel, Foxborn, *was published in April 2017 and the sequel,* Dragonborn, *in June 2018. His collection of running themed horror, science fiction, and adventure stories,* Running Into Trouble, *was published in October 2017. His annotated edition of John Monro's 1897 novel,* A Trip to Venus, *was released in September 2018.*

INTERVIEW WITH MR. RUFUS CRAIN: RORKSON COUNTY

By Cheryl Zaidan

The following is a transcript from a Rorkson County Police interview with Mr. Rufus Crain regarding the death of 13-year-old Sarah Bransford. The subject, Mr. Crain, aged 42, resides in Rorkson County. He has had two DUI arrests, the most recent taking place 3 years ago. The interview was conducted by Detective James Anderson of the Rorkson County Police Department one day after the incident. Mr. Crain is not a suspect, but it is believed that he may have information that can link a yet unknown suspect or possible witness to the murder.

1:00 p.m.

ANDERSON: Thank you for coming in, Mr. Crain. I understand you may have some information about last night's attack on Sarah Bransford?

CRAIN: Anything to help, you know. How're the kid's parents doing? Sorry. Stupid question I guess. I bet they're hurting real bad right now.

ANDERSON: It's all right, Mr. Crain. We need just to talk to you about last night.

CRAIN: Well, I'll tell you what I can, but I was a little out of it.

ANDERSON: We appreciate any information you can give us. You said previously that you were with a strange woman at the bar last night?

CRAIN: Yeah, I gave the description to that artist lady. Did she show it to you?

ANDERSON: Yes, she did, Mr. Crain. You described her as a young blonde woman. Is that correct?

CRAIN: Yeah, she was really pretty.

ANDERSON: And you had never seen her in this area before last night?

CRAIN: No, sir, I did not. You don't see many strangers round these parts, you know? I mean, Rorkson County ain't exactly what you'd call a tourist trap. I guess I should've known not to talk to strangers, but she seemed friendly. Do you think she had something to do with what happened to the kid?

ANDERSON: Truthfully Mr. Crain, we're not sure. That's why we need your help. Tell me, how old would you say this woman was?

CRAIN: About twenty-eight, twenty-nine. As I said she was real pretty. But when I mean 'pretty', you know, well she seemed pretty to me, but most girls don't talk to me too much, so I don't know. She might not have seemed pretty to you.

Anderson: Did she have any distinguishing characteristics? Like a tattoo, or a scar?

CRAIN: Well let's see … she was kinda short, not dwarfish, just the right height, you know? Oh, and she hadn't plucked her eyebrows in a long time. She had that Bert thing going.

ANDERSON: Bert?

CRAIN: Yeah, like Bert and Ernie. Unibrow. She was still good-looking, though.

ANDERSON: And you said you met her at 8:00 p.m. at Tony's Tavern?

CRAIN: Yeah, I saw her sitting there and I was thinking she had strange eyes. I forgot to tell you about the whole eye thing.

ANDERSON: Eye color? Blue?

CRAIN: Nope, they were brown, but kinda this golden brown, not dark just … golden.

ANDERSON: Noted. Anything else? Do you remember what she was wearing?

CRAIN: Nope. Might have been a t-shirt or a blouse or something. She had a skirt on. I didn't pay attention. Not much into "hot coacher" or what that high-falutin' fashion shit is.

ANDERSON: Okay, so what happened after you met the woman?

CRAIN: Well, me and her, we get to talking. Had a few drinks.

ANDERSON: So, you were drinking?

CRAIN: Well, yeah, I was.

ANDERSON: Was she?

CRAIN: Nope. Just drank glass after glass of water, like she was dying of thirst. I offered her a shot of rye whiskey 'cause that's what I was drinking. She about like to throw up when I said that. Said she couldn't stand the stuff. Made a face like this.

(Subject grimaced.)

ANDERSON: And she didn't tell you her name or where she came from?

CRAIN: No, she was kinda funny that way. Said she was traveling, and she was just stopping by here for the night. And I asked her name, and she said I could call her whatever I wanted to call her. So, I called her Melba cause, well, once I had a dog named Melba. Kind of stupid of me, huh? Called her my old dog's name. But I didn't particularly push her for what you'd call any personal information. Just liked talking to her, I guess. Enjoyed the company of a lady for a change.

ANDERSON: Tell me exactly what happened at the bar. How long were you there?

CRAIN: Well, we just sat around for a few hours. Just drinking ... well, I was. We weren't talking too much, just bullshitting, you know? Then, um, must have been about 11:00, that Bransford girl comes in.

ANDERSON: What happened next?

CRAIN: Little Sarah looked like she'd seen a ghost. She was rambling, in a right state. Said that she knew it was around and what killed all the chickens and why Ol' Morrison had come up missing. She was just talking, and her eyes were big as saucers.

ANDERSON: Did anyone try talking to her?

CRAIN: No sir. Except Tony, the barkeep, you know, the tavern's named after him. He still works there, going on twenty years now, that's the kinda guy he is, real hard worker. Anyways, he says to her, he says, "Hey, you're underage. Get outta my bar."

ANDERSON: What did Sarah Bransford do then?

CRAIN: She didn't move. Said she had to find some adults to listen to her and she couldn't get no one to take her seriously. Oh, and then she said "it" was after her.

ANDERSON: Did she say what "it" was?

CRAIN: No sir, she surely did not. What we thought, meaning the other people in the bar and me, we thought she was hopped up on goofballs or something. You know, these teens sniff that Lysol to get high now ... anyway, she got mad cause we all were laughing at her and walked out.

ANDERSON: Did you see her after that?

CRAIN: Nope. I did not. Course, now I wish I woulda listened to her. Poor thing ... I'm such a fucking idiot.

(Detective Anderson suggested a ten-minute break as the subject appeared visibly distraught.)

1:30 p.m.

ANDERSON: You okay?

CRAIN: No, don't think I'll ever be okay. But I guess I can go on.

ANDERSON: So, you're at Tony's Tavern and Sarah Bransford left. What did you do next?

CRAIN: Well, we all laughed our asses off at the poor kid. My lady friend, she was laughing at her too. Then Melba turns to me, she says, "Let's go for a walk in the woods."

ANDERSON: Where did you go?

CRAIN: Just the woods behind the tavern. And I'm thinking wow. Can't believe my luck. You know how you feel when you're about to get some? You know the feeling, right? You married?

ANDERSON: Yes, I am.

CRAIN: Well, maybe in your single days, you remember from then. Anyways, I knew what she meant. She wasn't looking for no walk in the woods neither. So, we go into the trees and we're by some of them old ash trees and she's like, "No, we can't be here," and she drags me deeper into the woods and starts kissing me …

ANDERSON: And?

CRAIN: Well, that's all that happened with that. I mean, she just kissed me. She was a real rough kisser too, all teeth and tongue. Oh yeah, you had been talking about them distinguishing characteristics? I forgot to mention one, she had a real strange smell to her.

ANDERSON: What did she smell like?

CRAIN: Like a farm, like hay. I didn't smell it on her in the bar, but when you're close to someone and they got their tongue in your mouth, 'scuse my French, you sort of notice that thing.

ANDERSON: Go on.

CRAIN: Ok, and so we were kissing, and she rubs my face with her hands, and they're rough, like calluses on them, you know? And I'm thinking, she's not all that hot now. Sort of cooling off on her. Must have had my beer goggles on in the bar. Oh yeah, I don't know if it's important, but there was something else about her hands.

ANDERSON: What was it?

CRAIN: Well, she had the longest finger, this one (Subject points to the ring finger on his left hand). You know, I never saw it before where someone had that finger that was longer than the others.

ANDERSON: Hmmm … that may be important. What did you do next?

CRAIN: Well, so we're kissing and I'm thinking she's not perfect, but it's been a long time since I got some so I'm going to soldier on. Pardon me, married man, but I am. And she touches me right here (Subject points to his belt buckle) and then she starts freaking out. Like totally starts screaming and backs away.

ANDERSON: Do you know what caused her to be afraid?

CRAIN: No, 'less of course she didn't like this. Maybe she was worried the 'Boss' thing meant I'd be too big for her or something.

(NOTE: Subject's belt buckle is silver with the word 'Boss' on it.)

ANDERSON: What happened after she backed away?

CRAIN: She ran outta the woods.

ANDERSON: And you followed her?

CRAIN: Sure, as hell did. I ain't been laid in a few years mind you, 'scuse me again. I wasn't about to give her up. But I couldn't find her nowheres. I did hear some strange noises out there though.

ANDERSON: In the woods.

CRAIN: Yeah, they didn't sound too far off. One of those sounds you always hear in spooky old horror movies. And I said to myself, that's it. Just decided to walk home.

ANDERSON: Did you walk home alone?

CRAIN: Yes sir, I did. And I was about halfway home, kind of still shook up you know, when I heard a girl scream.

ANDERSON: The Bransford girl.

CRAIN: Don't rightly know, but probably it was.

ANDERSON: Where were you when you heard the scream?

CRAIN: I was just outside of Hanson Street. Halfway home, like I said. I didn't see nothing though. It was dark on account of there's no streetlights there.

ANDERSON: And after you heard the girl scream, that's when you were attacked?

CRAIN: Yes, sir, I was. Didn't see it coming neither. I was walking down the street and I heard rustling. I was a little spooked out after the strange night I'd been having, so I started walking a little faster, like this (Subject puts his head downward), and I heard some sniffling behind me.

ANDERSON: Go on.

CRAIN: And that's when I got knocked down. I didn't see what it was that done it. Swear to God I didn't. Just knocked me down from behind, and I'm lying face down on the pavement with the wind knocked outta me. And then I felt a huge-ass pain in my shoulder, right here, and I blacked out. I don't know if it was because I was a coward, or in shock. Course, I'd been drinking, too. Do you think what got me was the same thing that got the Bransford kid?

ANDERSON: Possibly. Do you remember anything else about the attack?

CRAIN: No sir, I do not. That's all I remember what happened to me. Course I'm lucky, could have been torn apart like poor Sarah Bransford. But if that's so, and it was a wild animal or a dog or something, how come you want to know so much about my lady friend? She mixed up in this somehow?

ANDERSON: May I see your shoulder?

(Subject removes shirt. There is a large wound on his left shoulder. Trauma surrounded by several puncture marks.)

ANDERSON: Looks nasty. Did you have a doctor see that?

CRAIN: Nope, but I should. I don't know if what got me was human or animal. Could have been rabid either way though.

ANDERSON: Thank you for all the information, Mr. Crain. Is there anything else you can tell us about last night?

CRAIN: Yeah, one more thing. Don't seem important now, but

184

it sure was pretty up there ...

ANDERSON: What was it?

CRAIN: There was a full moon.

ANDERSON: Thank you again Mr. Crain. We'll be in touch.

END OF TRANSCRIPT

POST INTERVIEW NOTE: Repeated efforts to contact Mr. Crain since the initial interview have been unsuccessful. Local authorities believe that he has since left Rorkson County, and his whereabouts are currently unknown. He is not believed to be a suspect in the case, but authorities are interested in speaking with him again regarding the incident.

Cheryl Zaidan is a full-time marketer, part-time writer and hardcore dreamer who enjoys creating fictional characters just so she can do bad things to them. She currently resides in Michigan.

BASIL'S DREAM DATE

By Sarah E. Glenn

At the corner of Seventh and Magnolia, just past the convenience store, there's a little white house with a porch. And on that porch, if you happen to be walking by, is a reclining chair, vinyl cracked with age. More often than not during summer afternoons, you will see an older gentleman sleeping there. His name is Basil Hamilton, and he retired early from his city job last year. No wife, no children. House paid for. Pretty much all he does since he stopped working is sleep and grow tomatoes in his back yard. Most of his neighbors say that he's devoted to doing nothing. But that's because they don't know Bass.

Although Bass spends most of his time there on the porch, that's only his body. The real Bass is somewhere else, travelling, seeing places. He is an adventurer extraordinaire in his dreams—rescuer of maidens, fighter of dragons, you name it. From the time he was very small, he was a lucid dreamer; as he grew more practiced, he gained control of the dreams and where they took him. He began by visiting the lands in the books his mother read to him, then the places he saw in children's television shows. After Bass learned to read, he became a ravener of books, lifting freely from the worlds he read about to enhance his own fantasies. He visited Lilliput, Oz, Digitopolis, and Dictionopolis, among other realms.

By the time he was approaching middle age, Bass had gotten tired of wandering through other people's worlds and plotlines, so he began designing his own worlds. These satisfied his curiosity for a time, but there was no fun in always turning the dream in the directions he wanted to go—no surprises, and the other characters seemed flat when he had to tell them what to do. So, he decided to let the dreams go as they would. He would wander through them, allowing the dreams to take what shapes they did, reacting to them as seemed appropriate.

This proved to be the most satisfactory decision of all. Bass learned more about himself in one year than in the previous fifty. He resolved his feelings towards a father long dead and his mother, now vacant-eyed in a nursing home. His dreams would lead him down a path to an old conflict, and he would do and say what he should, secure in the knowledge that it was just a dream and not real life. If the results were unsatisfactory, he could back the dream up, like a video tape, and try again. The important part was to surrender control of his dream, so the ending was not one he had devised or forced.

Shortly after taking on this new direction, Bass knew this was what he wanted to do for the rest of his life. He worked overtime for a few years to finish paying off the house and learned gardening, so he could grow some of his own food. He also stocked up on canned goods during the weeks before he retired, so he would have extra supplies while he learned to live on the small pension the city provided to early retirees.

Bass had savings, of course; he had no social life to speak of, and since he had struck out on his own in the dreams, buying books had become less important. There had been no wife or children: why should he date, when beguiling women beckoned to him every night? In addition, he resolved that on the day the car couldn't be fixed anymore, he would walk wherever he needed to go. Bass told himself that if he ran out of cash, he was still young enough to do odd jobs or, God forbid, go back to work.

It was eighteen months after his retirement that he found the dream he couldn't change. He had been a young Prince in the dream, traveling through the woods. First, he crossed through the copper woods, then the silver woods, and then the gold. That wasn't the unusual part, though. It was what happened at the lake.

Basil had been sitting on a rock near the lake, polishing his enchanted sword and admiring the sunset, when a swan landed nearby, descending gracefully to the grass at the edge of the water. At least it had looked like a real swan, but then it shrugged, split its feathers open, and out stepped a beautiful girl, completely naked. She stepped into the water and proceeded to bathe not thirty feet from Basil, who was partially hidden from view by the rock. Afterwards, she scooped up the feathers and threw them on, changed back into a swan, and proceeded to fly away.

Basil, who had polished his sword so vigorously that he'd nearly cut himself, tried to back the dream up so he could see the girl again and speak to her. He discovered that he could not. He stood by the edge of the lake, wishing, willing the swan to reappear in the sky and descend again, but she wouldn't come. That had never happened to him before, and he didn't understand why.

For the next week, he spent most of his time in his dreams sitting by the lake, hoping that the girl would come back. He squinted into the clear sky and across the rippling lake, looking for a flash of white feathers or a figure gliding on the water. Each night, he tried to recreate the dream circumstances that had brought the lovely girl, but no amount of mental prodding seemed to help.

It was a frustrating three weeks later before she reappeared. Basil, who had become more familiar with metallic forests than he wanted to be, had begun adventuring in new territories, stopping by the lake at the end of the travels to see if anything had changed. When he got to the rock he'd been standing on so frequently, he saw a bird circling over the water. Crouching down, he waited. The swan he had seen before landed on the shore and split its feathers open again, revealing the same beautiful naked girl. She turned towards the water and Basil emerged from behind his rock, eager to talk with her.

"Pardon me for disturbing you, milady, but ..." This was as far as he got before she shrieked, rushed in a cloud of golden hair for her cloak, threw it on, and flew away in haste. Once again, Basil tried changing the dream—visualizing her changing her mind and flying back, trying to "find" a magic feather from her cloak to pursue her with, and finally trying to rewind the dream to before he made his stupid surprise move. None of these worked; there seemed to be some rules to this dream that he hadn't encountered in any other dream he'd had in his life.

This required research—a trip to the library. It had been so long since he'd been in one, the staff had all changed and no one recognized him any more. He headed directly for the section that held the folklore books, but discovered a shelf of personal investment guides there instead. Bass wound up in the kids' section, looking through the fairy tales. It didn't take him long to find stories of swan maidens; he murmured a silent thanks to Andrew Lang. Eagerly, he pored over the books to discover how swan maidens were captured. In each case, the young hero (for which he read himself) could not have the girl until he stole her cloak of feathers. If he hid it from her, he got to keep her; if she found it, he lost her.

Now that he knew what to do, it was merely a matter of being patient. The swan maiden would come back, and this time, she would stay.

Basil avoided the lake for a while, hoping that the maiden would note his absence and assume that he had been discouraged. If she were that afraid of strangers, she would certainly check out the area around the lake before bathing there again. In the meantime, he practiced cloak-grabbing at similar dream-sites, setting his own cloak at various lakeshores and making sudden rushes from different sorts of hiding-places to grab it. For maximum speed and stealth, Basil had to set his enchanted sword aside, along with his heavy boots and other confining garb. Two weeks later, he crouched by the lake again. He was ready.

He only had to wait three nights before she reappeared this time. The swan glided gracefully down by the water and landed on the shore. The swan-body opened and the girl emerged, naked and enticing as before. She hung the feathered cloak on a nearby bush and entered the lake. When Basil was sure she was entirely distracted by her bathing, he rushed from his hiding-place and seized her cloak.

The maiden must have immediately known what had happened, because she cried out and turned to look at him. "You! Put my clothes down!"

"No," Basil said, clutching the cloak closer. "You come here."

The maiden bit her full lower lip and returned to the shore. She was even more beautiful close-up than from a distance. "Please, give me my cloak back. My grandmother will be worried."

Basil had learned that to succeed at this dream, he needed to play by the rules. "We will go see her together. I am Prince Basil, and I want to ask for your hand in marriage."

"I can't marry you!" She looked up at him with large, dark-lashed eyes. They were so blue, they were almost purple. He was sinking into them when he realized that she had grabbed the corner of the cloak and was trying to take it back.

"No!" Basil and the girl both pulled on the cloak, trying to gain possession. Suddenly, there was a loud blaring noise and the girl vanished, leaving him holding the cloak. Bass cursed in a very unprincely manner and woke up. Who had made that noise when he was so close to getting the girl? He'd worked for weeks just to get to that point! He looked out his window but saw no source for the noise. It was dawn, around the time he used to get up for work. It had sounded like a clock alarm, but he hadn't used an alarm in years. That was part of why he had retired early—to stop having the screech of an alarm jar him out of the middle of an adventure. He had needed a really loud one to call him back, too.

Then, he realized the truth. The noise had not come from his environment, but from hers! She was another dreamer! Why hadn't it occurred to him before that he might not be the only one? Thinking back over the past few months, the dreams where the swan-girl appeared had only happened during the night hours—according to her schedule, not his. And if she were a dreamer, that meant she was a real person! It also meant that she existed in the real world, possibly in a place he could find while he was awake.

Bass changed his schedule so he spent more time sleeping during the late-night hours, the times she seemed to be asleep. He passed the daytime hours tending his garden and trying to devise ways of finding out where the girl lived and arranging to meet her. He had never, ever met anyone before in his dreams who was a real person, which meant that she must be special like him. After all, she had entered *his* dream, not the other way around.

It had never occurred to Bass to seek out other real-life people in his dreams because he'd thought no one else was like him; it was part of why he had always socially isolated himself from others. That would change, though, if he could meet the girl while awake. He decided, almost without any thought on the consequences, that if he found the swan-girl in real life he would marry her. He didn't care if she were seventeen or seventy, he would find a way. The possibility of sharing the most important part of his life with another person galvanized him into action during the daytime hours. He cleaned his house, a previously unimportant activity, and planted two new tomato plants in the back yard. For the first time in years, he went to the men's clothing store and bought a suit. He got his hair cut, too; he needed to look as good as possible when they met.

In the dreaming times, Basil sat by the lake, holding the cloak of feathers. Whenever he went there now, the cloak was there by his

191

stone. Perhaps he had taken possession of some part of her, because she returned to the lake after only one week.

"Give me my cloak back," she pleaded.

"Who are you?" Basil asked. "Where do you live?"

"I am the Princess Drusilla from the kingdom of the clouds. My grandmother will be very angry if I don't return. Please give me my cloak back."

Basil ignored the plea; there was no way he was giving her the cloak back if it meant she would permanently vanish. "No, not that name. Your real name. Who are you, and where do you live?"

"I am the Princess ..."

"No! Not your name here in the dream. Your real name, the one you use when you're awake."

"Awake? What do you mean?" She looked puzzled.

"You're dreaming. What's your real name?"

"A dream?" Comprehension crossed her features, then her face and body blurred around the edges and she vanished again.

It hadn't occurred to Bass till that moment that she wasn't as accomplished a dreamer as he was. This would take more time than he thought. It would require planning as well. Lucid dreaming had come quite naturally to him; how could he teach it to someone else?

The next evening, they met again. Basil tried drawing her away from the lake and further into the golden woods—deeper into his own dreams, he thought. He began by talking to her about the kingdom of the clouds, and found that she had six sisters (of course) and a controlling grandmother who was a witch. She must've read the same books he did. Again and again, he would steer the conversation around to her waking location and the details of her waking life; again and again, she would vanish at a critical moment and frustrate him greatly.

During his waking hours, Bass went over and over this problem, developing eye strain studying fairy tales, until he came up with a plan. In the dreams, he began to court the maiden. He didn't feel guilty about this ploy since his real-life goal was marrying her. He asked Drusilla if she were married, and she said that she was not. That was an encouraging sign; it might indicate that she was single in real life, too. "I would be proud to be your husband," Basil told her, drawing her deeper into the golden woods. "You are the most beautiful maiden I have ever seen." Drusilla seemed convinced that her grandmother would never consent to their marriage, but allowed herself to be drawn into the golden woods (and the silver, and eventually the copper) by

Basil nevertheless.

Once he thought she was ready, he made his request. Taking her to the copper wood, he lifted a great stone that would have given him a hernia in real life and showed her his own cloak of feathers. "I have been working on it," he said, "so we can fly together to the kingdom of the clouds and I can press my suit with your grandmother directly. If I give you your cloak back, will you take me there?"

She nodded. He tossed Drusilla's cloak back to her after donning his own; in the tales, swan-maidens couldn't always be trusted. She took on the shape of the swan and flew away, circling above the copper woods. Basil followed her closely, looking down on the woods and the glimmering lake where they had met. It all seemed small and flat as they left it, like one of the pictures in the fairy books.

They flew for a while until they approached a great bank of clouds that shifted back and forth into shapes resembling walls and buildings. One cloud shaped like a gate swelled open as Drusilla drew near, and granted them entry. They soared through and into a city of cloud-buildings, cloud-houses, and a cloud-courtyard. Something about the buildings seemed familiar to Basil, but he couldn't place it until he saw the roads leading to the cloud-castle, which appeared to be their destination. They ran in parallel pairs, with a silver thread between them that tickled his memory. Were those railroad tracks? More threads appeared, forming a cross within a diamond of roads. The cloud-town around them had to be Tebeauville, then. He couldn't believe she was so close to him!

They landed in front of the castle and took their cloaks off again. They began to cross the moat, but its walls began to lose form. Drusilla's shape began to blur and dissipate as well. With a sinking heart, Basil realized that she was waking up; she must be getting lucid again. "Drusilla!" he shouted, grabbing the nearly-intangible arm. "Drusilla, hear me! Meet me at the Haines Avenue Bridge tonight! Um—at nine!" Surely she would be off duty at whatever job she held by then. "Come there tonight at nine! In the real world! Please remember this, Drusilla, please remember—be at the bridge tonight!" The dream broke up entirely around Bass, and he found himself in his own bed again.

That evening, Bass drove his aging car to the Haines Avenue Bridge in Ware County—only an hour away! —and parked in the lot of a nearby fast-food restaurant. It was 8:45, after dusk. He was wearing the suit, which was itchy in the heat, and there were bugs trying to crawl under his collar. Brushing them off with a distracted hand, he walked towards the bridge. He had never been so nervous in his life. Here he was, waiting to meet a woman he had never really seen before, with every intention of asking her to marry him. He stopped near a streetlight, thinking of what a chance he was taking. What if she were very old? What if she were very ugly, or crabby like the ex-wives of his old coworkers? Bass decided that he didn't care what she looked or acted like; wouldn't it be worth it to have someone else to share the dream adventures with? To not be alone anymore?

At five to nine, an ancient Cutlass crossed the bridge and stopped at the edge of the ditch. The driver's side, which was turned slightly away from him, creaked as it opened, and someone got out in the dark. The princess? *His* princess.

"Drusilla?" Bass said, walking towards the car, the enchanted chariot bearing his princess. "Is that you, Drusilla?"

"Basil?" came the reply as the driver came closer and the streetlights fell on them both, illuminating the stocky form and bald head of Basil's princess.

Bald.

At the corner of Seventh and Magnolia, just past the convenience store, there's a little white house with a porch. And on that porch, if you happen to be walking by, are two chairs: one old reclining chair with cracked vinyl, and a La-Z-Boy, fresh from the store. More often than not during summer afternoons, you will see two older gentlemen sleeping there. The house is owned by Basil Hamilton, who retired early from his city job last year. Pretty much all he and his new friend do is sleep and grow tomatoes and cucumbers in the back yard. Most of his neighbors say that he's so devoted to doing nothing, he's had to hire somebody on to help. But that's because they don't know Bass.

Sarah E. Glenn is the editor of the Strangely Funny *series and a Jane-of-all-trades. She has a B.S. in Journalism, mostly because she'd rather write about stuff than do it. She also spent some time as a graduate student in classical languages, which helped her crossword skills greatly. Past occupations include: an art internship at a billboard company, helping doctors navigate a continuing education website, and updating listings in the telephone book. Her most interesting job, though, was working the reports desk for a police department, where she learned that criminals really are dumb.*

Sarah's great-great aunt served as a nurse in WWI. A hundred years later, this would inspire Sarah and her partner in crime, Gwen Mayo, to write the Three Snowbirds *mystery series, featuring two retired WWI nurses and an inventor slightly younger than Moses.*

Learn more about Sarah at: sarahglenn.com

THE LAST RESORT

By D.J. Tyrer

The Amoral Detective Agency had finally gone online, advertising itself across the World Wide Web, and business was booming. They had already gained a certain level of kudos in the occult underground, thanks to their willingness to consider cases that were not, in the strictest of senses, nice, and, indeed, a willingness to take on the cases at all, most investigators having the sense to stick to things as tracking down missing heirs and shadowing philandering husbands. In fact, they were doing so well that they could pick and choose which cases to take, as they lacked the time to investigate them all.

They, in case you were wondering, consisted of John D. Cohen-McDaid and his cynical sidekick, Bob.

John was a handsome chap of blurred but predominantly Jewish and Scottish ancestry, living in the Welsh town of Aberystwyth. John was a university student but was considering dropping out as detecting offered a better chance of future occupation than getting a degree. Still, he looked the part of a student with his longish black hair, black jeans and black t-shirt—his blazing green eyes being the only splash of color about him.

Bob, on the other hand, was an A-level student and dominated by a white jacket offset by black trousers and a black porkpie hat. Unlike John, Bob had blonde hair—once close-cropped, but now, shoulder-length—and, cautiously-alert brown eyes.

As well as sidekick and general dogsbody, Bob served as John's driver. Although he was older, John had just never got around to taking his driving test, always saying he didn't have the time.

Previously, the role of chauffeur had belonged to John's girlfriend, Mary M. Moorcock, with her Lexus, but they had broken up. There had been a series of precipitating factors—not least that their relationship was largely predicated upon a physical attraction—but things had really declined when Mary, taking to its logical conclusion her attractiveness to men, decided to become a stripogram. That had left her and John barely speaking and, when John had saved Bob first from a demonic entity, their relationship was officially over. John had been upset, especially over the loss of the Lexus—Bob's nondescript car rather lacking both gravitas and comfort.

Thus it was that the Amoral Detective Agency found itself reduced by one-third of its strength, just as business was booming ...

"Welcome! Welcome to Southend-on-Sea!"

Their latest case had brought them back to the famous Essex seaside resort with the world's longest repeatedly-mangled pier. They had been hired by Professor Outing of the British Museum to investigate strange occurrences at a dig site in his back garden. The gigantic, bearded bear of a man met them at his front door with a wide smile and a booming greeting of Brian Blessed-proportions.

"As you know," the professor helpfully explained, "not long ago, we discovered a wealthy royal burial in town. Well, I had long harbored suspicions that, beneath my patio, were the remains of a Roman villa, and the discovery at Priory Park was just what I needed to convince the Museum authorities to fund a dig here."

"But, you said something about a ghost?" John queried him.

"Indeed, I did! Indeed, I did!" the professor exclaimed. "We had barely pulled the patio up when the haunting began! A horrible skeletal figure would rise up from the ground as soon as night fell and cry, 'Doom! Doom!' All the workers refused to keep digging, believing the site to be cursed. I never believed in the supernatural, before, but now ... I'm convinced."

They weren't. People had a phenomenal ability to delude themselves into thinking the world was totally mundane, and the supernatural tended not to be so blatant—so, a ghost predicting disaster and sending everyone off in terror seemed just a little unlikely. In their experience, John and Bob knew such cases tended to have more prosaic explanations than a genuine haunting, whether pure fraud and fakery, or the work of a mage or an entity with an agenda.

"So, you want us to lay your ghost?" John asked.

"Well, um, get rid of it, certainly," the professor replied, not quite sure he understood, "and prevent whatever doom it portends from happening."

"Well," said John, "let's take a look at your former patio."

Professor Outing took them through the house to his back garden, where the concrete slabs that had formed a patio outside of his French windows had been torn up and replaced with a muddy pit.

"You didn't uncover the remains of any murder victims beneath your patio?" John asked, recalling that, statistically, 97% of all patios were laid solely to conceal corpses. "That would explain a lot."

"No, not a fragment."

"Baffling," said Bob.

But, John was closely examining the pit and had noticed something—the slightest hint of an angle beneath the soil. Clambering down, he began to scrape the dirt aside with his hands, revealing a flat wooden surface.

"What is it?" the professor demanded, loudly.

"It looks like a trapdoor of some kind," commented Bob, looking over John's shoulder.

"Yes." John nodded. "It would appear to be some sort of secret entrance. I suspect this is what your 'ghost' was protecting, trying to scare you off before you could uncover it."

"But, why?"

"To answer that," said John, "we must open the trapdoor. Stand back—I have no idea what we might discover."

Bob murmured the theme to a half-forgotten children's show.

Slowly, cautiously, with more than a little trepidation, John grasped the wooden cover and slowly lifted it up to reveal … a surprisingly small niche beneath it. All three of them let out a sigh of disappointment—they had all expected something like a hidden staircase leading to long-deserted and soggy smuggler tunnels, and found this rather uninspiring and anticlimactic.

"Is that it?" asked Bob.

"They—whoever 'they' are—must have already taken whatever was in it out, already," the professor observed, his sentence structure slipping from his control.

"Maybe not," exclaimed John, demonstrating the insightfulness that made him such a great, if amoral, detective. "Look—the trapdoor is double-hinged! You see, if we close it again, push it so … then open it the other way ... As I'm told the French say, *voila*!"

He opened it again, revealing, to their amazement, that the pit now contained a stairway leading down into stygian darkness.

"What?" exclaimed Professor Outing.

"How?" demanded Bob.

"Magic," explained John. "A simple dimensional hoodwink. It allows the door to exist in two quantum states until it is opened."

"So, I suppose we have to go down there?" asked Bob, dubiously, looking down into the inky blackness. "It smells bad."

"Yes, to both of those. Hmm, smells a bit like fish."

The professor offered them a cup of tea before they began their descent, but John declined. Bob would have liked a mug or three—anything to delay the moment—the pit looked pretty scary.

"Well, here we go," John said, boldly, after Bob had retrieved a couple of torches from the boot of the car.

"After you."

"Sure. Of course, devil take the hindmost, and all that," John retorted.

"Um, could we swap?" asked Bob, but John shook his head, before gesturing a farewell to Professor Outing, who was watching from the kitchen window, where he was busy making himself a pot of Earl Searle tea.

"You know," Bob said, "I really wish we were in there with him and not in the process of entering a smelly hole in the ground."

"Brave heart, Bob," said John, jauntily. "Brave heart."

The stairs were slabs of stone and the sides of the slanted shaft were constructed from similar slabs holding back the soil. They glistened wetly and were smeared with green-grey slime that made them slippery underfoot. There was a distinct smell of damp, a little fishy or salty, perhaps due to the nearby sea leaking its way into the hidden passageway.

John had heard there were rumors of numerous smuggler tunnels beneath Southend-on-Sea, but a magically-concealed entrance seemed unlikely for such a mundane use. However, he had also heard other rumors, of other tunnels beneath the town, tunnels that were anything but mundane—tunnels from which none returned, save the occasional lunatic, driven insane by whatever they had experienced down there. Was this one of those dark and mysterious tunnels?

He decided not to mention the likelihood of disaster and madness, lest it worry Bob.

The stairs seemed to descend forever, but that may have been an illusion due to the limited field of vision afforded by their torch-beams. Finally, however, they reached the bottom and discovered that it led to an entire labyrinth of subterranean passageways, ankle-deep in stinking, brackish water.

"I hope this doesn't have sewage in," sniffed Bob.

"Probably not, although we could be underneath a sewer, I guess. More likely it's just stagnant and vile. As long as you don't drink it, you should be fine. Still, best not to look up, just in case of drips."

"Do you think someone actually uses these?"

"Probably not, or not often," opined John, shining his torch around. "Although someone sure knows that they are here, or else they wouldn't bother trying to scare the professor off."

"Any idea what they hold?"

"I have a few suspicions," he replied, but refused to elaborate.

Suddenly, turning a corner, they discovered they had reached another set of stairs, disappearing upwards. At least, they assumed it was another stairway and not the ones that they had started from; the maze-like passageways offering a great likelihood of that being the fact.

"We should've brought chalk," Bob commented, "then we could've marked our way, and known if we were backtracking on ourselves."

John sniffed. "I have an unerring sense of direction."

Bob shrugged. "Oh, well—up we go."

The stairs going up were as steep, damp and slimy as the stairs they had come down. Indeed, it remained Bob's suspicion that they were the very same stairs. Still, there was a consolation that the smell decreased slightly, the further up they climbed.

Nearing the top of the stairs, they could see another trapdoor, like the one they had entered by.

"Um," said Bob, pausing, "what happens if this one is buried, too?"

"Well, if it opens upwards, like the other one, then, the answer is: not a lot. Otherwise, it is: get covered in an avalanche of mud. Shall we find out?"

He didn't wait for Bob to protest, but pushed it up.

The trapdoor swung open – to reveal an unexpectedly breezy open space. Clambering out, they recognized it as a place to which they had gone on a previous visit to the town—it was Southend-On-Sea's world famous, world's longest, and most-truncated pier.

Bob looked back down the open pit of the trapdoor; there was very clearly the stone-lined shaft of a stairway where logic dictated sea should have been visible.

"That is impossible," Bob concluded.

"Have you never heard the phrase 'A Wizard Did It'? You really ought to understand the concept, by now."

"Is this another quantum thingy?"

"Probably."

"Oh." You couldn't really argue with quantum physics, especially when it was wedded to magic. Especially when you could see a subterranean stairway where none could be.

John closed the trapdoor.

"Thank you." Bob sighed. "Seeing that open and the sea down there at the same time was doing my head in!"

"Now, I wonder if there is a reason why this trapdoor is here, or is it just coincidence? Shall we poke around?"

"Sure—but if they catch us here without having paid, we'll be in deep trouble."

"Huh, if they catch us, they'll wonder just how we got out here."

They looked around the area, but could see no obvious reason why there should be a supernatural trapdoor there.

"Maybe they haven't been used for years," Bob suggested. "That would explain why the one in the professor's garden was buried."

"Unlikely," John replied, as they headed back towards the trapdoor, "or, there would be no need to protect it."

"Unless it contains something …?"

"There is that," John conceded. "But, I do feel it more likely that the tunnels are still in use by—well, by whoever is using them— and, they don't want anyone else to know about them. I can't say I blame them; they must be jolly useful. But, surely, they must be used for more than just nipping quickly around town and saving on bus fare. No, there must be some more sinister reason for them. I think we shall have to try it again—come on."

He opened the trapdoor and they stepped through the impossible portal and climbed back down the stairs into the dank and wet tunnel system.

"You know," John said, not being the sort to keep an idea to himself, "if these tunnels exist in an extra-dimensional space—and, I think we can agree they do—then, all this water cannot be leaking in through the walls. No, I think it must have entered through one of the trapdoors. My theory is that one of them must open underwater, somewhere out in the estuary."

"I don't like the sound of that!" Bob gulped.

"Oh, we are quite safe. Safe as houses. Probably."

Bob tried not to think of all the houses that fell. Or, where they were going.

They plodded in silence through the twisting, turning tunnels until, finally, they reached another staircase.

"Right," said John, "let's look at where this one comes out."

"Just as long as it isn't under the sea."

"Oh, probably not—it's no more damp than the others. No anemones or anything. Come on."

They opened the trapdoor and received a shock even bigger than stepping out onto the pier. John and Bob found themselves in a sort of dressing room in which, amongst the dozen or so young women who had turned to stare at them in surprise, stood a half-dressed Mary M. Moorcock.

"John? Bob?" she exclaimed in shock. "What the hell are you doing here?"

"Well, commented John, observing the various women in various states of undress, "right now, I'm enjoying myself."

"Jerk!" exclaimed Mary in response.

"Actually," explained Bob, "we've been exploring a series of extra-dimensional corridors, one of which exits here."

"Oh," she said. "That actually sounds plausible."

"Yeah, what Bob said." John was still a bit distracted.

"Um, let me get my top on and let's go somewhere else, okay?"

"Take your time ...."

John's comment caused Bob's eyes to roll. John's eyes were almost out on stalks. Mary hurried and dragged them outside.

They were, it transpired, inside the Kursaal, where Mary had been attending the International Stripogram Conference being hosted there. Her career was going far. Now, they headed for a chip shop and, then, the sea wall, where they could eat and talk.

"So, who do you think are behind these passages?" Mary asked. Technically, she still wasn't speaking to John, but, in her surprise, wanted answers and so had to ask. Besides, Bob was to hand as an excuse.

"Well, my initial suspicion was that they belonged to the Ecumenical Church of St. Toad—rumor has it that they have a large local following. But I think that is a red herring. Or, squid. No, not them. It is my belief that the water in the tunnels is the clue to their ownership—if they open underwater, then, it is logical to assume that at least some of their owners are aquatic—and, that means the Cult of Coocoocachooloo. There is a rumor doing the rounds of the Occult Underground that they have a secret temple somewhere around here."

"But, what is their plan?" Bob asked.

"Mary."

"What?" she asked, confused.

"Well, not you alone, but the conference. I don't think it's a coincidence that you're here at the same time as all this is happening with a trapdoor in your changing area."

"But, what would the Cult of Coocoocachooloo want with stripograms like me?"

"Well, Coocoocachooloo's piscine servitors are well-known for fancying human women and producing hideous half-human hybrids. Remember Diddecombe? Maybe they are moving away from monogamy towards women of a cheap sort?"

"Cheap? Cheap! I'm not cheap!" Mary glared angrily at him. "I happen to charge a lot for a striptease."

"Whatever."

Bob nodded in agreement with John. "Cheap or expensive, it's demeaning."

"As if you'd know anything about it," Mary snapped at Bob. "I bet you're still a …"

"Okay! Okay!" John interjected. "Can we get back to the Coocoocachooloo conspiracy, please?"

"Huh, okay," sighed Mary, "but, I'm not convinced."

"Well, it's easy enough to prove. What is left of your conference, now?"

"Um, we have a seminar on 'Feminist Empowerment Through Stripping' and a lecture on 'Nudity and the Nation State' this afternoon. Then, tonight, we have the grand finale of the event—a mass strip before an adoring crowd."

"That's it!" John cried. "That's when the fishy-things will strike—during the finale. Grabbing you all when you're at your least clothed and carrying you for some impromptu impregnation."

"Urgh! Must you be so … so … clinical?"

"Hey, I'm only saying," he said. "it's not my fault they're not exactly sensitive lovers! Don't worry, though—Bob and I will be there to look after you."

"Oh, how reassuring."

The rest of the day passed without incident as Mary attended the lecture and seminar she had signed up for, whilst John and Bob prepared for the evening.

Finally, the finale arrived, and Mary took to the stage with her fellow delegates. John and Bob were in the audience. John was determined to keep a close eye on the strippers. It was a tough job and he was delighted to be doing it. Bob was utterly uninterested.

"Interesting …."

Just as John had predicted, just as the finale of the conference reached its finale, just as bras rained down on the audience, just as John was completely distracted, the fish-things struck! They had the general figure of men, but the specific details tended more towards herring and chub, and they were intent on having their very wicked way with the nearly naked delegates. Although their targets were clear, some of the inhuman cultists charged into the crowd of voyeurs who comprised the audience, driving them back and sending the auditorium into a whirl of chaos.

"Quick!" cried John to the stage assistants, who handled lighting and related things. He'd had the foresight to brief them beforehand and, although they had been doubtful, Mary had been able to convince them to co-operate.

With a crash, a strategically-placed pile of crates toppled onto the hyper-dimensional trapdoor that had been the humanoids' means of ingress, slamming it shut and sealing it beneath the resultant pile. Simultaneously, doors were sealed, lights went on, and the central heating shot up. John's cunning plan was to dehydrate the amphibious aberrations.

But, the humanoids were neither stupid nor apathetic and were not just going to stand there and be dried out—even with the distraction offered by the stripograms they were busy groping. No, they were determined to escape. Some rushed to the trapdoor and began trying to clear the crates; others ran over to the auditorium doors and attempted to wrench them open.

However, John's plan went beyond a passive drying-out. The stage assistants whipped nets out from the wings of the stage and began trawling for humanoids with vigor. Entangled in nets beneath the baking stage-lights with the temperature rising, they were doomed, becoming weak and sluggish.

"Help!" shrieked Bob.

The last of the fishy-things had grabbed Bob, who was now their hostage. All the others had been detained and the strippers on the stage were safe. Mary was busy demanding John's attention, post-trauma, but, as pleasant as she was to gaze at, he had heard Bob's anguished cry and turned to help.

The fish-person burbled something wet and phlegmy. It was probably a demand that they all be allowed to escape or else something would happen to Bob. There was now something of a Southend stand-off.

Bob struggled vainly. It looked rather as if a throat would shortly be slashed by monstrous claws.

They stood like that for about a minute, nobody moving and Bob moments away from death and/or dismemberment.

Then, John remembered that he was a Baal Shem. It was funny how it was possible to forget something so important—so plot altering—like that, but he had. Now, however, he intended to make up for the lapse.

Quickly chanting some words of power, he gestured at the haddock-faced humanoid and it flopped into a semi-senseless state. Without a full ritual behind them, John's powers were not that great, but they were enough to turn the tables on someone, *something*, not expecting them. Bob pulled away and left it to the stage assistants to capture the inhuman.

Bob ran over to John and embraced him. "Thank you! Thank you! Thank you!"

"Eww!" cried Mary, finger down her throat, as she watched Bob passionately kissing John in thanks for being rescued. There were also some "ahhs" from the incorrigible romantics in the nearly-naked crowd.

There was a SeaLife Center not more than a stone's throw away from the Kursaal and that was where the police took the aquatic villains. Some would be kept on display there, whilst others would be dispersed around the country to other SeaLife Centers, where they would prove a draw. A great result, it was generally agreed.

Of course, Mary was not terribly happy to discover that John and Bob had fallen in love, ending her chances of getting the man she considered hers back. Still she had her happy ending when a foreign billionaire, who had been in the audience, approached her, revealed he had fallen madly in lust with her body, and wanted to make her his richly-rewarded mistress. His happy ending followed soon after ...

The Kursaal and the International Stripogram Conference received plenty of free publicity and, as nobody had been killed or injured, nor had anyone successfully sued over it, they were very happy at the outcome.

The trans-dimensional tunnels were transformed into a tourist attraction to rival the pier, revitalizing Southend for several weeks before the Council managed to make a mess of things, and Professor Outing was able to proceed with his backyard dig, which uncovered evidence of an ancient Atlantean outpost, pleasing him no end and upsetting the archaeological apple-cart.

John and Bob sat on the sea wall watching the sun going down in the direction of London and, far beyond that, Aberystwyth. Each of them had an ice-cream with a flake in it and they were holding hands. Life suddenly seemed just right.

"You know, Roberta Jones," said John, "I really love you."

"And, I love you," Bob replied. She leaned over and kissed him. "I always have."

John wasn't quite sure what the future held—but, he had a feeling it would be bright.

Only, he just wished the tingle of foreboding in the back of his mind would cease. He leaned over and kissed Bob. Yes, that did it.

D.J. Tyrer is the person behind Atlantean Publishing, was short-listed for the 2015 Carillon 'Let's Be Absurd' Fiction Competition, and has been widely published in anthologies and magazines around the world, such as Strangely Funny II, III, IV and V *(all Mystery & Horror LLC),* Destroy All Robots *(Dynatox Ministries),* Mrs. Claus *(Worldweaver Press),* More Bizarro Than Bizarro *(Bizarro Pulp Press), and* Irrational Fears *(FTB Press), as well as on* Cease Cows, The Flash Fiction Press *and* The WiFiles, *and in issues of* Tigershark *ezine, and also has a novella available in paperback and on Kindle,* The Yellow House *(Dunhams Manor).*

Mystery and Horror, LLC
Somewhat Tongue in Cheek Present
The *STRANGELY FUNNY SERIES*

STRANGELY FUNNY I
STRANGELY FUNNY II
STRANGELY FUNNY 2 ½
STRANGELY FUNNY III
STRANGELY FUNNY IV
STRANGELY FUNNY V
AND
STRANGELY FUNNY VI

Only you can determine the fate of the series. Is your taste totally lacking refinement? Do you find humor in the twisted misadventures of monsters and men? If this kind of insanity makes your night, read them all and demand more.

Find us at www.mysteryandhorrorllc.com